"A playful and unique p_____ _____ _____ ____ ___
fast-and-furious dialogue all combine to make _Tangled
Up in Love_ the most entertaining romance read of the
year. Heidi Betts has a winning ability to mix comedy
and sensuality with a lively flair that puts her in the top
tier of contemporary romance writers."   —Lisa Kleypas

"Sexy, fun, and impossible to resist! I LOVED it."
—Lori Foster

"Heidi Betts gives romance a sexy, fresh twist!
Fantastic!"   —Carly Phillips

"Fresh, hot, and irresistible. Get _Tangled Up in Love_—
you'll love every page!"   —Leanne Banks

"A wonderfully witty work that will have you laughing
out loud.... The rivalry is wonderful and the sex is smoking hot."   —_Night Owl Romance_ (Top Pick)

"I absolutely adored this book. Usually not a fan of
comedic romances, I found myself laughing out loud
more than once. I loved it!"   —_Joyfully Reviewed_

"Heidi Betts has penned a humorous, entertaining tale
that will knock you off your feet... It's a purely enjoy-
able read that will keep you up late at night to finish."
—_Romance Reviews Today_

Knock Me for a Loop

Heidi Betts

St. Martin's Paperbacks

This is a work of fiction. All of the characters, organizations, and events portrayed in this novel are either products of the author's imagination or are used fictitiously.

KNOCK ME FOR A LOOP

Copyright © 2010 by Heidi Betts.

Cover photograph © Image Source/Corbis

All rights reserved.

For information address St. Martin's Press, 175 Fifth Avenue, New York, NY 10010.

ISBN: 978-0-312-94673-9

Printed in the United States of America

St. Martin's Paperbacks edition / February 2010

St. Martin's Paperbacks are published by St. Martin's Press, 175 Fifth Avenue, New York, NY 10010.

10 9 8 7 6 5 4 3 2 1

For my friends (past, present, and yet-to-come) at Herring Veterinary Services—Dr. Ronald K. Herring, Patti, Sally, Kendra, Jessica, Alisha, Janice, Lindsay, and anyone I might have missed. Thanks for always being there when I call—sometimes even at three in the morning (sorry about that!)—and for taking such great care of my kiddos!

With thanks (again) to Karen Alarie, who came up with the brilliant title for this one, and the hilarious way in which Zack and Grace first meet. And Darlene Gardner, for fact-checking me on the hockey stuff. Any mistakes are entirely my own, believe me.

Thank you also to my friend and neighbor, Shannon Maines-Bumbarger, who not only answered some questions I had about Saint Bernards, but whose own giant horse of a dog, Shelby, was my inspiration for Bruiser. Sadly, we lost Shelby recently, but for the record, she never had to wear a hand-knit sweater, hat, or booties. She did, however, get her toenails painted on a regular basis. (The yellow, orange, and white "candy corn" nails for Halloween were my favorite.) We love and miss you, Shelby!

And last but not least, in loving memory of my own sweet kitty, Angel, who passed away just as I was finishing this book. It sure isn't easy writing without you sleeping at my feet, baby.

Cast On

Charlotte Langan's late-model station wagon, complete with faux wooden panels running the full length of both sides, rumbled beneath her, sending pleasant little ripples into her feet, up her short legs, and along the narrow line of her vertebrae. The heat was turned up full blast in an attempt to counteract the brittle cold of Cleveland, Ohio, in mid-December.

Holiday decorations were up already—and had been since just after Thanksgiving—lining the damp streets and filling lighted storefronts. Christmas was one of her favorite times of year. The colors and raised spirits and festivities. Not to mention presents! Whether she was giving or receiving them, oh, how she loved the presents. What other time of year did a woman have such a bona fide excuse to shop until she dropped?

Flipping on her right turn signal, Charlotte maneuvered her car—which she imagined handled much like a refrigerator on wheels—into the lot of a local strip mall, then began to drive slowly up and down the rows of cars already parked there. Using the steering wheel for leverage, she hoisted herself up and forward for a better view as she peered through the windshield searching for an empty spot.

When she finally found one near a brightly lit over-head lamp, she pulled in—it only took six or eight tries—cut the engine, and set the parking brake. Because a woman could never be too careful, and the parking lot *was* on a slight, probably fifteen-degree incline. Then she grabbed her knitting tote from the passenger side of the seat beside her and climbed out of the station wagon.

Frigid air swamped her, and she tugged the hood of her thick, fluffy fleece coat up and over her head, tightening the strings until she was sure she looked like the Jolly Green Eskimo . . . or maybe a giant lime Popsicle.

Her bright purple faux Ugg boots splotted against the slick asphalt as she goose-stepped her way across the lot and pulled open the door to The Yarn Barn. A wall of blessed heat smacked her full in the face as soon as she stepped inside, and she sighed with warm-ing pleasure. Loosening her fuzzy hood and tugging at her thick, hand-knit alpaca mittens, she made a beeline for the back of the store, where the rest of her Wednesday-night knitting group would be waiting.

Because the Yarn Barn hosted a number of craft groups and craft-related classes throughout the week, a large meeting nook had been set up in the rear. Sev-eral mismatched chairs were arranged around a low coffee table, and there was a refreshment area off to the side, complete with snacks and both hot and cold beverages.

At the moment, there was nothing Charlotte wanted more than a steaming cup of cocoa clutched between her ice-cold hands, but she would settle for the famil-iar comfort of her size-eight needles and the warm caress of the alpaca-fiber yarn she was using to knit a long, variegated cardigan as it ran through and around her fingers with every stitch.

Already, she could hear the staccato clack of needles clicking together beneath the voices of the women who were already gathered and busily working on their respective knitting projects. A sweater here, a scarf there, and several pairs of slipper socks to keep toes toasty over the long, cold winter or be stuffed into stockings for Christmas.

"Aunt Charlotte!" Jenna cried, catching sight of her over the top of one of the backward-facing chairs.

Sitting in that chair was the strikingly beautiful Grace Fisher, who turned along with everyone else to watch Charlotte's approach. "I swear, Charlotte, you look more like a troll doll every time I see you," she quipped.

Charlotte chuckled with amusement. Some people might have taken Grace's remark as an insult, but Charlotte was delighted with the description. From the moment Grace had first tossed out the comparison and then gifted Charlotte with one of the little plastic figurines to show her what she was talking about, Charlotte had been hooked.

That doll had been the first of what was turning out to be quite the Troll collection. She had one with yellow hair on her mantel, one with blue hair on the dresser in her bedroom, one with green hair on the back of the toilet in her bathroom, and the one with flame-orange hair that Grace had originally given her hung from the rearview mirror of her station wagon, where she could admire it on a regular basis.

She just loved the little buggers. Like Cabbage

Patch dolls, they were so ugly, they were cute, and she'd made it one of her goals in life to get her own bright orange, beehived hair to stand as tall as theirs. She was close, too; only a few inches to go.

"We were beginning to wonder when you'd show up," her niece said as Charlotte struggled out of her oversized coat and let it drop to the floor beside an empty chair. Patting the well-shellacked dome of her hair to make sure the hood hadn't done irreparable damage, she took a seat and pulled her craft tote onto her lap.

"Sorry. I got busy with my babies and lost track of the time," Charlotte told them, referring to her beloved pack of alpacas.

That wasn't entirely true, of course. She'd finished feeding and bedding down everyone in plenty of time, but when she'd returned to the house to collect her things before leaving for the weekly knitting meeting, she realized she didn't have the skein of pink yarn she'd made for Grace.

Special yarn.

Very special yarn.

A year ago—give or take a few excitement-filled months—Charlotte had almost by accident stumbled across a delightful secret. The solid oak spinning wheel that had been handed down through the women in her family for generations was *magic*. Not run-of-the-mill magic, either, but the very best kind—the kind that brought true love.

Charlotte had grown up with her mother and grandmother telling her stories about the enchanted, true-love spinning wheel, but she'd thought they were just that—stories. It wasn't until recently that she'd remembered the old wheel, hidden and collecting dust in a corner of her attic. She'd dragged it downstairs (no easy feat for a woman of her somewhat advanced age and limited height), cleaned it up, and used dyed fiber from her own alpacas to spin a skein of soft black yarn that she'd then given to Ronnie, one of the young women in her knitting group.

At the time, Ronnie had been head over heels in hate with a man who wrote for a competing local newspaper, and Charlotte thought they would make the perfect guinea pigs for her enchanted-spinning-wheel test run.

When that had turned out better than great—Ronnie and her beau were now living together, and Charlotte expected a wedding announcement any day—she'd used the wheel to spin another skein of enchanted yarn.

Fluffy and purple this time, for her own dear niece, Jenna, who had been divorced and miserable. Charlotte hadn't actually expected Jenna to reconcile with her ex-husband; she'd thought the yarn would bring some other young man into her niece's life instead. But since the two now seemed deliriously happy together, and were planning to tie the knot a second time just before Christmas, she certainly wasn't going to complain. As far as she was concerned, that simply proved that the spinning wheel *did* bring true love to those who used the yarn it created.

Now there was one more person in need of the wheel's very special powers.

Poor Grace. Another of Charlotte's favorite knitting group members, she was such a lovely, vibrant woman. And she'd been even more lovely and vibrant in her happiness over being engaged to Zackary "Hot Legs" Hoolihan, the star goalie for the Cleveland Rockets and one of the city's homegrown heroes.

Happy, that was, until she'd walked into Zack's hotel room one day last summer while he was on the road with the team and found another woman in his bed.

Though Charlotte had been out of town at the time, she'd heard the whole sordid story when she got home. Zack denied any wrongdoing, but Grace was adamant that she wasn't blind and knew what she'd walked in on.

According to Jenna and Ronnie, Grace had gone a bit crazy after discovering her fiancé's infidelity. Charlotte had seen her mini-meltdown firsthand when Grace went on the air of her self-titled local cable television show, *Amazing Grace,* and spent the entire half hour ranting and raving about the perfidy of men in general and Zack in particular. But apparently she had also taken a baseball bat to Zack's cherry-red Hummer, and gleefully tossed his clothes and assorted other belongings out his sixth-story window.

Although Charlotte couldn't blame Grace for being upset, she thought such blatant destruction of property was a little over the top. Especially since Zack just as publicly and vehemently proclaimed his innocence.

Though she tended to side with Grace on the matter—after all, they were both women who knit, and yarn sistahs needed to stick together—Charlotte wasn't sure exactly what to believe. As with most disagreements, she suspected the truth lay somewhere in the middle.

What *was* clear, however, was that Grace's life was

in desperate need of some divine intervention. A little sprinkle of fairy dust to help her get over the pain of her *dis*-engagement . . . and hopefully find love again.

That's where Charlotte came in.

Just call her "Matchmakin' Mama," she thought with a private giggle.

She'd dyed more of her babies' soft, beautiful fiber a bright, bold pink, and then used her family's secret enchanted spinning wheel to weave a wonderful skein of yarn just for Grace.

Which was why she couldn't possibly have left the house this evening without it.

But she'd found it, thank goodness. Right where she'd left it, too—in a wicker basket beside the sofa in her living room, along with several other homemade balls of yarn.

Now she simply had to find a way to slip it to Grace sometime during their Knit Wits meeting and ensure that she put it to good use. Otherwise, the magic that the spinning wheel infused into the yarn would never get a chance to create a true love match.

And it *would* work. Of that, Charlotte had no doubt. The wheel's yarn had worked twice before, and she was certain it would work again for Grace. After all, the third time was, as they said, the charm.

Around her, the gals chitted and chatted, discussing their weeks and their latest knitting projects, and men. Men always seemed to be a popular topic of conversation, whether the group was admiring a specific physique or bemoaning their fickle, infuriating hides.

Being the eldest member of the group—and, sadly, the one most removed from a romantic relationship of any kind, unless she counted her enormous love for her alpaca babies and barn cats—Charlotte tended to sit back and enjoy the animated conversations rather than offer her own opinions about the opposite sex.

Girls these days . . . Charlotte was far from being a prude, but some of the stories her knitting buddies told could strip the Garnier Summer Wildfire #968 right off her hair and send it blooming in her cheeks. Not that she would ever let them know their banter teetered on the far side of her moral alphabet. (As in Triple X-Y-Z.)

In her day, young women didn't make time with as many young men as they apparently did today. They also didn't share the intimate details of their relationships with anyone who would listen.

But Charlotte considered herself a modern, sophisticated woman, so she took it all in, and even made a few mental notes for herself. Not many—she was too afraid her eyes would go blind and her fingers would burn down to the bone if she tried to write them out. And granted, she hadn't had the opportunity to put her womanly wiles to the test in quite a long time, but one never knew when Prince Charming might come galloping—or in her case, shuffling—into one's life.

Luckily, not everybody was as miserable in her love life as Grace and Charlotte.

A few were married and raising families, including Melanie, who tried her best to get away from her two small children long enough to attend the weekly knitting meetings.

A few were college-age girls who were enjoying their youth too much to tie themselves to any one boy yet.

Then there was Jenna, who was jump-out-of-her-skin, the-hills-are-alive-with-the-sound-of-music in love with her ex- and soon to be re-husband, Gage. Always had been, and the whole world knew it. It had just taken a few years of misery, a premature divorce decree, a couple pints of tequila, and some magic yarn to get them both back on the same page.

And Ronnie was right there twirling around on the hillside with Jenna, glowing so brightly over her happiness with Dylan Stone that she practically burst into flames every time someone mentioned his name.

Charlotte's gaze slid to Grace. Ronnie was telling them about the past weekend, when she'd gone away with Dylan to a remote mountain cabin. Apparently the temperature had been too low and there had been too much snow on the ground to do much more than stay inside in front of a blazing fire. Charlotte rather suspected that had been the point to begin with. Why else would anyone leave the frosty temperatures of Cleveland in the middle of winter to vacation in an even more glacial location?

Charlotte also suspected she was the only one who noticed how uncomfortable Ronnie's story was making Grace. Though a smile was firmly painted on her lips, it was strained and the attempt at outward amusement didn't reach her eyes.

If Ronnie had known that her animated account was causing her friend even a modicum of discomfort, she would have clammed up in a nanosecond, but Grace was so good at hiding her emotions and playing the part of a perfectly coiffed, perfectly content public figure that she had everyone around her fooled. Even her best friends.

They didn't call her "Amazing Grace" for nothing, after all.

But Charlotte saw. And she knew that no matter how hard Grace pretended to be over the devastation of her broken engagement, in reality it was still tearing her up inside.

Not for long, though. God and true-love magic willing, Grace's shattered heart would soon be mended.

Almost before she knew it, the hour drew to a close, and everyone started tightening stitches and rolling up loose yarn, putting away their works in progress. Butterflies fluttered in Charlotte's stomach as she saw her opportunity.

Jumping to her feet, she hurried to shrug into her coat and sidle up to Grace before anyone else could join them.

"I have a surprise for you, dear," she said quietly, reaching into her bag for the carefully woven skein of silky-soft pink yarn.

Grace's gaze lowered as she reached to accept Charlotte's gift, and Charlotte noticed that the polish on Grace's perfectly manicured nails matched the tint of the yarn.

Oooh, this was wonderful! She'd known pink was one of the young woman's favorite colors, but having it match her nails had to be a sign. A sign that this particular skein of magic yarn was, indeed, meant for Grace.

"That's so sweet. Thank you, Charlotte."

The words were sincere enough, but they didn't carry Grace's usual flare of enthusiasm. Everything about her these days was muted, as though a bubble of unhappiness surrounded her.

"Make yourself something special with it," Charlotte suggested, wanting to press and make sure Grace started using the yarn as soon as possible. "Maybe after you finish that pretty sweater you're working on now." Which only had one more sleeve and some trim work to go.

Lips curving in a halfhearted smile, Grace leaned down to buss Charlotte's cheek. "I will. Thank you again."

Well, it wasn't exactly a blood oath to begin knitting with the new yarn before the clock struck midnight, Charlotte thought with a mental sigh, but it would have to do. Now all she could do was cross her fingers and her toes and hope to heaven the enchantment of the ancient spinning wheel held true and worked its wonderful magic once again.

Row 1

The spray of hot water from the hotel's fixed-mount shower head hit Zack Hoolihan between the shoulder blades, soothing stiff muscles as it rolled the rest of the way down his body.

He shouldn't be this damn sore after a couple hours on the ice for charity. It wasn't like he'd been out there giving it his all in a grudge match. But that hadn't made their opponents launch the puck in his direction with any less force or hit the ice any less hard when he'd smacked into it time and again.

This wasn't a good sign, though. He was only thirty-six . . . too damn young to be feeling this damn old, and nowhere near ready to be skating toward retirement. If his body didn't cut out the stiff-and-sore bullshit and get with the program, though, pretty soon he'd be out there trying to block goals with a walker.

With a sigh, he turned around and let the water pelt his face and chest, then reached for the soap and started lathering up.

The guys had mentioned going out for pizza and beer later, but Zack knew from past experience that plans for a simple dinner with the rest of the team often turned into an all-night tour of every bar and strip club in whatever city they happened to be visiting. He wasn't much up for that tonight.

Instead he figured he'd stay in, maybe order some room service or see if his friend Dylan, who was currently traveling with the Rockets as a team reporter, wanted to grab a bite at one of the hotel's on-site restaurants.

Rinsing off, Zack turned off the water and pulled back the shower curtain, reaching for a towel from the rack on the wall as he stepped out of the tub. He dried off quickly, then used the towel to wipe the steam from the wide mirror above the sink and countertop before wrapping the strip of terry cloth around his waist and knotting it over his right hipbone.

With a sigh, he rested his palms on either side of the sink basin and leaned forward to study his reflection. Yeah, he was a good-lookin' guy. It was no surprise women swarmed all over him.

Of course, ninety percent of those women were puck bunnies, which meant he could have had three eyes and an ass where his mouth was supposed to be, and they still would have thrown themselves at him.

Too bad he felt like shit. It wasn't the aches from exerting himself on the ice or the bruises that would cover him like graffiti by morning from stopping three-inch disks of vulcanized rubber flying at eighty miles per hour with his body.

No, the lack of sparkle in his eyes and enthusiasm in his spirit came from the fact that he hated being on the road. What used to be the best part of his job as star goalie for the Cleveland Rockets, he now considered nothing more than a hassle. Whether playing an away game or doing the off-season practice and goodwill charity stuff like now, he would have much preferred to be back home and closer to Grace.

Going on the road. Hanging out with the guys. Partying until all hours and getting more tail than any man had a right to. Reasons one, two, and three—aside from a genuine love of the game—that he'd decided to play hockey professionally in the first place.

Then he'd met Grace, and "the road" turned into nothing more than a long, lonely highway dotted with indistinguishable hotel rooms and games he barely remembered by the time he got home. Hanging out with the guys paled in comparison to spending a quiet night on the couch, watching old movies with Grace wrapped in his arms.

And forget about other women—blond, brunette, redhead; tall or short; built like a supermodel or the girl next door . . . not a one of them had the power to turn his head anymore. Not when he was engaged to the funniest, smartest, sassiest, most beautiful woman in the world.

He wished she were here now. He'd walk into the other room, drop the towel, and show her how appreciative he was of her willingness to follow him from city to city. Or maybe he'd simply crawl under the covers with her and hold her close while they flipped channels looking for one old movie or another.

The black-and-whites were her favorites. Maybe because Grace herself looked so much like a fifties starlet. She was a Marilyn Monroe of the twenty-first century, all platinum curls, pouty lips, and a figure that made him want to fall to his knees and thank God for creating womanly curves.

Or maybe Grace had somehow taken on the characteristics of a fifties starlet because she spent so many hours admiring them.

Pushing away from the bathroom counter, Zack ran his fingers through his still-damp blond hair. He'd be back in Cleveland by the end of next week. He could survive that long moving from hotel to hotel, putting on the rough-and-tumble playboy act for fans, and playing his heart out on the ice.

But when he did get home, he was heading straight to Grace's apartment, and he didn't intend to let her out of bed for a week.

He was just reaching for the knob when a knock sounded on the outside door. Couldn't be room service, he thought, since he hadn't called in an order yet. Maybe it was someone from hotel maintenance to work on the faulty heating and air system he'd reported earlier. Or better yet, Dylan, which would save him having to call his buddy's room about getting together for dinner.

Since he didn't think a maintenance guy or even Dylan would appreciate a half-naked greeting, he yanked open the bathroom door with the intention of grabbing a pair of jeans and a T-shirt before answering. Lord knew there were enough discarded clothes scattered around the floor to dress a third-world country. Grace got on his case all the time about his abysmal housekeeping skills. But then, that's why he'd hired a *housekeeper*.

On the way out of the bathroom, he stubbed his toe on the heavy metal door and cracked his shoulder into the jamb. Muttering a low oath and cursing minuscule hotel rooms that weren't designed to accommodate professional athletes who topped six feet and pushed the scales at two hundred fifty pounds—most of it muscle—he changed his mind about scrounging around for something to wear and went straight to the hallway door instead, where whoever was on the other side continued to rap.

Bad mood etched clearly on his face, he yanked the door open . . . and froze when he found Grace staring up at him. He blinked in surprise, wondering if his earlier fantasy about having her on the road with him had conjured her out of thin air. Or maybe he'd slipped on the slick tile of the bathroom floor, cracked his skull on the edge of the tub, and was hallucinating.

Nice hallucination, though. She looked amazing, her hair a mass of sexy curls and her lips a glossy rose bow on her heart-shaped face.

"Hey," he said, running his fingers through his wet hair as he tried to absorb the fact that she was actually standing in front of him. "What are you doing here?"

"What do you think I'm doing here?" she replied saucily. Her grin widened as she stepped into the room and pressed herself against his tall frame. "I came to rock your world, big boy."

At that declaration, his lips curled and the fog cleared from his brain. He didn't know how she'd gotten here or why she'd decided to drop in on him, but at the moment, he didn't particularly care.

"Well, okay, then," he said, wrapping an arm around her waist. "Come on in. Don't mind the mess." Shifting them both out of the way, he let the door swing closed.

"I never do," she shot back with a chuckle.

Pulling away slightly, she leaned back against the wall running between the bathroom and the rest of the suite. She raked him from head to toe with a hot gaze, using two manicured nails to tug at the towel he was still holding low on his hips.

"I think I'm overdressed," she murmured, a wicked glimmer shining in her ice-blue eyes.

As far as he was concerned, if she was wearing anything more than him and a smile, she was over-dressed.

"I should say so." He let his gaze wander over her curvaceous figure and felt his temperature spike. "You need any help remedying that fact?"

"Oh, I think I can handle it," she teased.

Slipping away from the wall, she continued to face him as she walked backward into the main area of the room. Step by slow step, while her fingers worked to free the buttons running down the front of her blouse.

Her heel caught on something and she stumbled. They both glanced down to find her standing in the leg hole of a pair of discarded BVDs.

"Nice," she said, shaking her foot and kicking the briefs aside.

Zack expected her to return to her little striptease. Was salivating for it, actually. The small terry-cloth towel at his waist didn't act as much of a cover to begin with, but with the front taking on a telltale tent-ing with his growing hard-on, he might as well have been naked.

Instead, Grace slowly turned her head to the side, focusing on the king-size bed. He had no doubt that's where they'd end up, but he was in no rush. He was fine with watching her undress, then maybe taking her up against the dresser, on top of the round table in the corner, in the chair currently tucked under the small desk . . .

When Grace returned her attention to him, her eyes no longer glittered with smoldering desire. Her mouth was no longer tipped up seductively at the corners. In fact, she looked downright angry.

"Is there something you'd like to tell me?" she asked, her previously sultry tone replaced with icicles sharp enough to maim.

His brows knit. "Huh?"

Zack was used to his fiancée's rapid-fire changes in mood. Women in general were mercurial, he'd found, able to go from laughing to yelling to crying in two seconds flat. And Grace, he knew, could be more emotional than most.

Having her launch into an hour-long tirade because of some injustice she read about in the newspaper or tear up over a Hallmark commercial had taken some getting used to. His favorite, though, was when she started laughing over the silliest things, like a joke she'd heard at the studio or a remembered scene from a movie she'd seen months before.

He'd never known her to go from hot-for-his-bod to rip-his-face-off in the blink of an eye, though. And damned if he knew what he'd done to piss her off.

She cocked her head to the right, and he followed her gaze. Shock like a blast of cold air hit him full in the chest and had his heart plummeting to his gut.

The blonde in his bed climbed to her knees and let the sheet drop, revealing a skimpy pink bra-and-panty set.

"Hi," she chirped with a too-sweet smile. "I didn't want to interrupt."

Zack couldn't have been more surprised if a band of rodeo clowns had jumped up and started dancing around the room.

"What the hell are you doing here?" he snapped.

"You know, I was just asking myself the same question."

Unfortunately, this response came from Grace, not the puck bunny who'd somehow sneaked into his room while he was in the shower.

Fingers flying, Grace rebuttoned her blouse, then charged for the door, pushing past a still-stunned Zack before he had a chance to stop her.

"Grace, wait."

This was unbelievable. How the hell had this woman gotten in? And how the hell could Grace believe he'd *invited* her?

Hand on the knob, not bothering to turn around, she shot back, "Fuck you. Or better yet, let your bimbo do it."

"Grace!"

Heedless of his near-naked state, Zack caught the door before it closed and raced after her. The towel flapped around his legs as his bare feet pounded down the carpeted hallway. She was already several yards ahead of him, ignoring his repeated calls for her to stop, to listen.

"Shit," he muttered as she slammed through the stairwell door.

Tucking his chin into his chest, he put on an extra burst of speed, determined to catch her . . . then came to a screeching halt as the elevator to his right whispered open and an elderly couple stepped out. The woman's eyes went round as golf balls and she gasped, turning seven shades of red.

Glancing down, Zack's own face flared with heat as he realized he'd lost his towel and was now standing bare-ass naked in the middle of a Marriott hallway, scaring the bejeezus out of two people who looked old enough to be his grandparents.

In his estimation, he had three choices: keep running after Grace in the buff and risk blowing out pacemakers or shocking mothers and small children—not to mention having his picture wind up on the front page of every tabloid in the country; go back for his towel, *then* take off after Grace again, pretty much risking the same three results—albeit on a slightly smaller scale; or return to his room, put on some clothes, and hope Grace hadn't disappeared from the hotel completely before he could catch up with her.

He didn't think any of those options would work out a hundred percent in his favor, and Grace had likely hit the lobby already at the rate she was going.

Releasing a sigh of defeat and pent-up frustration, Zack offered a wave of apology to the couple still standing frozen in shock a few feet in front of him and spun around to head back the way he'd come. He grabbed up the fallen towel as he passed, but didn't bother using it to cover up again. Instead, he let it dangle from his tightly clenched fist as he stalked to his room and punched the door open so hard, it crashed into the wall behind.

The woman—the scheming little tramp who had

started all this—was still perched on his mattress, batting overly mascaraed lashes at him in what he supposed was meant to be a look of innocence.

Letting the damp towel fall to the floor, he found the nearest pair of earlier-discarded jeans and yanked them on.

"I don't know who you are or how you got into my room," he bit out, not bothering to glance in her direction as he grabbed a wrinkled T-shirt from the top of the bureau and pulled it over his head, "but if you aren't out of here in three seconds, I'm calling the cops."

"But—"

This time, he did look at her. Hands on hips, nostrils flaring, and teeth grinding so hard he expected to shatter a molar, he began to count.

"Three."

Her eyes went wide and she twisted her head, searching desperately for her clothes. Zack almost hoped she wouldn't find them. He would relish calling both hotel security and the local police and having her hauled away in handcuffs.

Aside from breaking and entering, he didn't know what the hell he could have her charged with, but he'd come up with something. Attempted robbery. Sexual harassment. And just plain fucking up his life.

"Two."

She slipped a short, low-cut black dress over her head and tugged until it covered her ass. Or most of it, anyway. Grabbing up a small clutch purse, she stepped into a pair of heels tall enough to give her a nosebleed, and rushed toward the door.

With her hand on the knob, she turned to cast a

glance at him over her shoulder, moisture beading on her lashes.

Normally, a woman on the verge of tears would have had his throat going dry and his stomach twisting in knots. But if this particular woman didn't disappear at the speed of light, he was very much afraid he'd *give* her something to cry about.

He'd never in his life laid his hands on a woman in anger, and he wasn't about to start now. If she were a man, though, she'd have been eating his fist by now. Or maybe dangling by an ankle outside the hotel room window.

"I just—"

"One."

The single word must have carried enough threat, enough menace, to let her know he meant business, because in the next second, she was gone, the door whooshing closed behind her.

Zack stood in the empty, silent room for long minutes, not moving, barely breathing. He was so pissed, he was shaking. And damned if he wasn't scared, too.

Scared Grace would be gone by the time he managed to get downstairs.

Scared Grace wasn't going to believe he hadn't invited that woman to his room, even though he'd been as shocked as anyone at her sudden appearance.

Scared that no matter what he said or did, his ass was in a sling and he was going to lose her.

Scrubbing his hands over his face, he took a deep breath, then moved to the nightstand and picked up the phone. He dialed Dylan's room and waited for his friend to answer.

"Yeah?"

"Hey, it's me," Zack said without preamble. "I've got a problem."

"Boy, do you ever."

Zack tensed, his fingers tightening on the handset. "She's there?"

"She was. Dragged Ronnie out of here like her feet were on fire. Just when things were starting to get good, too," he mumbled only half under his breath. Then, in a near-accusatory tone, he asked, "Did you really have another woman in your room?"

"No!" Zack snapped. "I mean, yes." He shook his head, confusion warring with his rising temper. "I'll explain later. Do you think I can catch her?"

"Hell if I know. Want me to meet you at the front of the hotel and we can search the parking lot for Grace's car?"

"Yeah, thanks."

Zack hung up, searching for his cell phone and a pair of shoes before leaving the room. On the way down in the elevator, he dialed Grace's number, praying for her to answer, but not surprised when voice mail picked up instead.

"Grace, it's Zack. I know what you think, but you're wrong. Call me back so we can talk about it, okay?"

Disconnecting, he stared at the lighted elevator panel as it slowly counted down the levels to the lobby.

With a curse, he flipped his phone open again and hit the button to redial Grace's cell. "Come on, Grace, don't be like this. It's not what you think, babe, I swear. Call me."

The elevator doors swept open and he pocketed his phone as he stepped out. Dylan was waiting for him at the front entrance. Without a word, they walked outside and headed in opposite directions to scour the parking lot. Ten minutes later, they met up back where they'd started.

"No luck on my end," Dylan said. "You?"

Zack shook his head, not trusting his voice. The sinking sensation in his gut was getting worse, and he had a feeling it wasn't going to get better anytime soon.

He almost wished he hadn't run that woman off, after all. If she'd stuck around, he could have asked how she'd gotten into his room in the first place, what the *hell* she'd thought she was doing, and forced her back to Cleveland with him so she could tell Grace in person that he hadn't invited her up and *definitely* hadn't slept with her.

"You wanna talk about it?" Dylan asked quietly.

Zack thought about shaking his head again. At the moment, there was only one thing he wanted—to find Grace and make her listen, make her *believe* him. Barring that, going back to his room and getting blind, stinking drunk sounded like a pretty good idea.

But Dylan was one of his best friends, so maybe he'd understand. Besides, it would be nice if at least one person he knew believed he wasn't a two-timer.

"Some groupie got into my room while I was in the shower. I didn't even know she was there till Grace spotted her, but now Grace thinks I cheated on her."

His lips flattened as he gritted his teeth, and he shoved his hands deep in his front pockets.

"Well, don't worry too much," Dylan offered, slapping him on the back. "Ronnie's with her, and will probably be able to talk some sense into her by the time they get back to Cleveland. Come on, let's go get a drink or something."

Rolling his shoulders, he did his best to resist the urge to leave his team high and dry and head back to Cleveland himself, even if it cost him a year's pay in cab fare.

"No, thanks," he told his friend as they started walking slowly back toward the bank of elevators. "I don't think I'd be very good company right now. I'm just going to head up to the room and try giving Grace a call." Another one or two or a million, if that's what it took. "Maybe she's calmed down a bit by now and will let me explain."

They stepped onto an elevator behind a couple of giggling teenage girls. They were staring at Zack and whispering behind their hands, but he ignored them. He was in no mood for fans right now, not even the young, fairly innocent ones.

When the elevator stopped at Dylan's floor, he stepped off, then turned back and held the doors open, his gaze locking on Zack. "Let me know if you need anything, okay? I'll be in my room all night."

Zack heard the concern in his friend's voice, saw the hint of worry bracketing the thin set of his mouth. Later, he knew he'd appreciate it. But for now, he just wanted to get away, be alone . . . and maybe put his fist through a wall.

He nodded, and Dylan dropped his hand, letting the doors slide closed. The teenagers got off on the next floor, leaving Zack to ride the rest of the way up by himself.

His feet felt like lead weights as he walked slowly down the hall to his room, opened the door, and stepped inside. Taking a seat at the end of the bed, he studied his reflection on the blank surface of the television for long minutes before flipping open his phone one more time and hitting the button to speed-dial Grace—her apartment this time rather than her cell.

For a second or two after her voice-mail system picked up, he remained silent. What was there to say that he hadn't already told her in his last two messages? So he settled for the most important thing.

"I love you, Grace," he said in a rough whisper. "I didn't cheat on you with that woman. I've never cheated on you, and I never will."

But somehow, even as he flipped his phone closed and continued to watch the hollow-eyed man looking back at him from the flat gray panel of the TV screen, he knew the words wouldn't make a difference. He knew, deep down in his soul, that he'd already lost her.

Zack sat bolt upright in bed, chest heaving, perspiration dotting his forehead.

Shit, he hated that dream.

Probably because it wasn't really a dream, but a nightmare that forced him to relive the worst day of his life over and over and over again.

Scrubbing his hands over his face in an effort to wash away the feelings of panic and impotence brought on by the dream, he threw back the covers and climbed out of bed. Leaving the lights off, he padded naked to the bathroom, then grabbed a pair of boxer briefs from the arm of a chair on his way to the living room.

His housekeeper, Magda, had been there only a couple days before, but already the place was a pigsty. Most nights, after he got home from practice, games, or going out with the boys, he was just too damn tired to pick up after himself. Too tired to do more than dump his equipment inside the door, grab a beer or a slice of cold pizza from the fridge, and crash on the couch until he could work up the energy to drag his sorry ass to bed.

And the sad part was that he did it on purpose. He pushed himself extra hard on the ice and used any excuse he could come up with to stay out late, all so that on those rare occasions when he was alone, he would be too exhausted to think about Grace.

It had been six months since the breakup. Since she'd overreacted to something that hadn't even been his fault and refused to let him explain.

Six months, and still everything reminded him of her.

He drove a brand-new blue Hummer only because she'd destroyed his red one.

His empty apartment was only empty because she'd stolen his dog.

Even the ice, which used to feel like a second home to him, was cold and uncomfortable now because it brought back memories of how he and Grace had met.

With a sigh, he bypassed the hole in the wall where she'd planted one of his hockey trophies during her post-supposed infidelity tantrum and dropped down on the sofa across from the TV. Flipping it on to ESPN, he sat back and reached for the pile of yarn in the center of the glass-topped coffee table.

This was something else he'd taken up only after Grace had left him—under the misguided notion, he supposed, that if he shared more of her personal interests, she'd be more likely to come back to him.

His two closest male friends—Dylan and Gage—

had recently learned to knit for their women, who were also members of Grace's weekly Knit Wits knitting group. One on a dare, and the other because yarn and needles apparently acted as an aphrodisiac with ex-wives who didn't really want to be exes.

But if *they* could do it without having their Man Cards revoked, then he'd figured he could, too. And maybe once Grace heard he'd taught himself to knit— *for her*—she'd be impressed enough to at least be willing to hear him out on the whole bimbo-in-his-bed issue.

That had been in the beginning, when he'd believed she had a modicum of mercy in her soul and that there was still a chance of getting her back.

Her refusal to speak to him for months on end, either on the phone or in person—hell, he'd even tried e-mail, texting, flower delivery, and Candygrams— had finally made him realize nothing he did was going to make a difference. She was never going to forgive him for what she *thought* he'd done, and he was damn tired of jumping through hoops in an effort to get her to see reason.

So he'd given up. No more phone calls, no more flowers, no more parking outside the craft store or Penalty Box waiting for her to come out. His stalking— and groveling—days were over.

He'd thought he was over the worst of the nightmares, too. The more he'd come to terms with the fact that Grace was truly gone and not coming back, the less they'd plagued him.

And the only reason he could think of for why they'd suddenly come back, why he'd felt extra antsy and tense the past week or so, was tomorrow.

Tomorrow, he would see Grace for the first time since last summer. Tomorrow, he would be expected to stand beside her, share air space with her, paste a smile on his face, and pretend his nerve endings weren't jumping beneath his skin like live wires.

Concentrating more on the soft feel of the chocolate-brown wool yarn slipping through his hands than the Penguins/Oilers recap on the television screen, Zack wondered if he should just call Gage and beg off. His friend would understand. He wouldn't like it and would probably be hurt—even if he didn't admit as much—but if anyone understood the push and pull of being in the same room with an ex, it was Gage.

Fingers going white around the size-eight needles he was using for this particular pair of slipper socks, Zack did his best to school his breathing and tamp down on the sour, squirming sensation snaking up from his gut.

If he didn't show up tomorrow, everyone—including Grace—would know why.

Call it pride, call it male ego, call it plain old-fashioned stubbornness, but damned if he was going to let the world think he was too chicken to face his ex-fiancée half a year after she'd kicked his butt to the curb. And he would eat broken glass before he'd let *her* think he was afraid to face her.

He'd done nothing wrong, dammit. Grace might have judged him and found him guilty without a shred of real evidence. And the press may have labeled him a womanizer, skewering him in every newspaper and magazine in the country. But *he* knew the truth and had nothing to be ashamed of.

Finishing the row he was working on, he tossed his

knitting aside and pushed up from the sofa, padding back toward the bedroom and the master bath. It wasn't yet four A.M., but he was used to being up early and putting in a full day. So he'd grab a shower, fix himself a nice, big breakfast, then jump into his tux and head down to the courthouse.

He had a wedding to get through.

Row 2

The first time Jenna Langan married Gage Marshall, she had been a June bride, wearing a white, full-length gown with lace and pearls, a veil covering her short, dark hair, and a billowing train sweeping behind her. The wedding had taken place in a church decorated with ribbons and bows and live flower arrangements, the ceremony witnessed by more than two hundred and fifty guests.

The second time Jenna and Gage tied the knot, it would be in front of a judge and only a handful of their closest friends and relatives. Instead of a long white gown, the bride was wearing a cream-colored tea-length dress a little more suitable to the scaled-down ceremony, but no less beautiful. Her bouquet was a bunch of bright red poinsettias suitable to the holiday season, and the bridesmaids had been asked simply to wear something classically festive in the red and/or green of the bridal/Christmas color scheme.

Grace, who had opted for a red satin dress that fell just above her knees and was decorated with a string of sparkling rhinestones along the scoop neckline, thought her friends had the right idea. No fuss, no muss, just get hitched and move on with your life.

Of course, this was Jenna and Gage's second marriage—to each other, no less—so they'd already experienced the bells and whistles and fairy-tale excitement. This time around, they just wanted to make things legal again and get down to the business of starting a family.

Ironic, considering that the reason for their divorcing in the first place had been Jenna's desire for children and Gage's equally strong insistence that they avoid procreation at all costs. Somewhere along the line, though, they'd patched up their differences.

It must be nice, Grace thought wryly. Not only to have had the big, beautiful wedding, but to have rediscovered the love of your life.

Her own wedding would have been amazing, she knew. She could picture it all in her head, down to the smallest detail, and she'd hired some of the city's best wedding planners to ensure that everything was perfect. Sponsors of her show, *Amazing Grace,* had been tripping over themselves to offer her gowns, makeup, limousines, flowers, and gifts for her guests—all in hopes of getting their company and product names into the public eye or having her thank them personally on the air afterward.

As tempting as it was to imagine walking down the aisle in a ten- or twenty-thousand-dollar designer dress, though, Grace had been determined to handknit her own wedding gown. From the moment Zack had proposed, she'd begun mentally working on the pattern and sharing updates of its progress with her viewers on the air.

It had almost killed her to unravel every delicate

stitch, to undo what had taken her months upon months of painstaking work to accomplish.

But while Jenna had been lucky enough to reunite with the love of her life, Grace's Prince Charming had morphed into a lying, cheating ball of slime. She would never get her fairy-tale wedding or her happily ever after. She'd never get to wear her homemade wedding dress or spend her honeymoon in Paris.

Taking a deep breath, she pasted a smile on her face and continued the job of touching up Jenna's makeup while Ronnie dug into a fabric tote for a pair of cream satin pumps to replace the heavy, fleece-lined winter boots Jenna had worn to the courthouse.

The three of them were standing in one corner of the judge's chambers, fluffing and fussing, while Gage and Dylan stood in another. The ceremony was officially scheduled for one o'clock, so they had a few minutes yet—not to mention that they were still missing the judge and a couple of guests, Zack included.

Zack.

Grace's stomach went tight and her teeth clenched just thinking of him. Even though everything about this day—especially having to be in the same room with Zack—cut like a knife, Grace would walk naked down Superior Avenue at rush hour, in the middle of an ice storm, before she would do or say anything to put a damper on Jenna's happiness.

So she would smile, and she would make sure it reached her eyes. If anyone could convince the world she was brimming with enthusiasm, it was Grace. Her job required it.

Never mind if she was tired and not feeling much

like pretending she cared about the stay-at-home-mom versus moms-who-work debate.

Never mind if she had the flu and was running a temperature of a hundred and three.

Never mind if she'd just walked in on her fiancé *in flagrante delicto* with some peroxide-blond whore of Babylon and had her heart broken into pieces.

No matter the circumstances, no matter what her true emotions might be, she was expected to bat her eyes, flash a grin, and put on the Ritz in front of the camera. And the more popular she and her show became, the less often she was able to let her hair down and breathe a sigh of relief outside of her own apartment.

Part of her didn't mind; she'd worked hard to reach this point in her career, and she'd chosen the public-celebrity path knowing exactly what she was getting into. But another part of her wanted to scrub the makeup off her face, climb into a pair of ratty old sweats, and refuse to wash her hair for a week.

Today, though, she'd been more than happy to get all dolled up and make sure she looked not just decent, but freaking fantastic. She wanted to make sure Zack knew what he was missing and what he'd given up for a quick roll in the hay with Miss Black Roots and Plastic Boobs.

The judge and his clerk walked in just as Grace finished adding a dab of glitter to Jenna's lashes, and just behind them was the devil himself.

Most people probably thought Lucifer had red skin and black hair, horns and cloven feet. But Grace knew the truth. He was tall and blond, with pearly white teeth and a smile that could charm the panties off a nun.

Steeling her spine and making sure no trace of emotion other than pleasure for the bride and groom was visible on her face, she turned and followed Jenna as she moved to take her place beside Gage.

At six foot three, Gage Marshall was a handsome, extremely well-built man. The rippling muscles that filled out his arms, chest, and abdomen could put professional wrestlers to shame. And anyone with eyes could see he was head over heels in love with his wife. Soon-to-be-wife. Soon-to-be-wife *again*.

Geez, this remarriage stuff was complicated.

But where other guys might be sweating, wringing their hands, or shifting from cold foot to cold foot with a case of prenuptial nerves, Gage was steady as a rock. His mouth was quirked up on one side and he hadn't taken his gaze from Jenna since they'd entered the room.

Grace's heart squeezed with renewed regret. She'd almost had this—a wedding day, bridal jitters, true love.

And then Zack had gone and fucked it all up.

She cast an angry, sidelong glance in his direction before regaining control of her features.

Okay, so he was handsome, too. Slightly taller than Gage, but leaner and more athletic, his sleek musculature was due more to hours spent on the ice than lifting weights at the gym. He also had a head of full, wavy blond hair that had prompted the press to compare them to Barbie and Ken more than once while they'd been together.

He looked exactly like what he was—a playboy. And she'd been well aware when they met of his reputation with women, that he went through them faster than a box of Kleenex. Or condoms.

So why the hell had she let herself believe *she* would be any different than the dozens of women he'd seduced, slept with, and discarded over the years?

Oh, yes, things would be different with them. He'd grown, matured, was ready to settle down. She was The One, so of course he would never stray, never look at another woman, never cheat on her.

Ha! She hadn't been The One, she'd just been *another one* in a long string of women who had fallen for his blue-eyed, wavy-haired, crooked-grinned spiel.

And she'd been an idiot. For a smart, highly educated woman, she'd apparently been walking around with a giant dunce cap on her head for the past couple of years.

Well, no more of that. The blinders were off, and she could read Zack's number loud and clear. It flashed across his forehead like a neon sign: 666.

In truth, though, she was still hurt *and* pissed, and suspected she always would be.

She should probably also be relieved. It would have been worse, she thought, if she'd discovered his faithlessness after they were already married. If he'd lied to her for years on end, run around behind her back, made a fool of her. If they'd had children together who would have been affected by his betrayal and an ugly divorce.

Yes, it was better this way. At least she'd only lost a couple years of her life, her trust in men, and for a short while, a modicum of her sanity. All things she could bounce back from.

Had bounced back from.

Well, okay, was working to bounce back from.

She'd been doing really well the past few months, too—right up until she realized she would have to see, be in the same room with, and possibly even *speak* to Zack at her best friend's second wedding.

Nightmares, *not* sweet dreams, were made of these.

Right before the holidays, too. Merry-freaking-Christmas to her.

Gage and Jenna moved to stand before the judge, and the rest of them fell in line behind them, Grace and Ronnie at Jenna's side, acting as bridesmaids, and Zack and Dylan at Gage's, acting as best men.

"Wait!" Jenna cried out suddenly, making everyone jump.

Gage paled visibly, his Adam's apple bobbing as he swallowed hard. "Oh, God," he muttered, "please tell me you haven't changed your mind."

Jenna chuckled, shaking her head and patting his cheek with the hand not still wrapped around her bouquet of poinsettias.

"Of course not. But Aunt Charlotte isn't here yet, and she'd never forgive me if we did this without her."

Before the words were even out of her mouth, they heard a shuffling from the hallway and turned to find short, round, mop-headed Charlotte bustling into the room. Her cheeks were pink with cold, despite the fact that she was bundled like an Inuit from head to toe.

"I'm here, I'm here," she called out between panting breaths.

Tossing aside her giant macramé handbag, she shrugged out of the ghastly, lime-green coat that made her look like a linebacker . . . or Shrek . . . or the Jolly Green Giant's half-sister from the vertically challenged side of the family.

Beneath the coat, she'd dressed appropriately—if hideously—for the occasion in a long, nearly shapeless white dress covered in holly leaves and berries. It looked as though she'd run out of time and grabbed the nearest holiday tablecloth to wrap around herself.

Grace inhaled deeply and bit her tongue to keep from laughing out loud. Poor Charlotte. She loved the woman dearly, but had never met anyone with worse taste in clothes. And hair. And makeup.

One of these days, she, Jenna, and Ronnie would have to invite Charlotte out for a Girls' Day Out makeover at the mall.

Makeover, ha! Try major fashion overhaul. They would try, ever so gently, to explain that carrot orange wasn't necessarily an appropriate hair color. Nor was Hubba Bubba pink for lipstick. And never, ever, under any circumstances did lime green and grape purple—the color of Charlotte's god-awful fuzzy Ugg knockoff boots—go together.

Then again, Charlotte was an entity unto herself. A funny, quirky character who kept them in stitches, both intentionally and unintentionally.

Maybe attempting to change the outside wrapping wasn't the smartest idea if it risked changing the inside package. Because inside, Charlotte's heart was solid platinum and bigger than all seven continents put together.

Rushing to Jenna on her short, stubby legs, Charlotte stood on tiptoe and pressed a big, pink-tinted kiss to her niece's cheek. "Sorry I'm late, dear. You know I wouldn't miss this for anything."

"We wouldn't dream of starting without you," Jenna replied, even though that's exactly what they'd been about to do.

Tablecloth dress, Ugg boots, foot-high Lucille Ball

beehive and all, Charlotte tromped to the end of the bridesmaid line and took a place beside Ronnie.

With everyone who was supposed to be there finally in attendance, Gage and Jenna joined hands, the judge cleared his throat, and the ceremony began.

Zack knew that at a wedding, the most beautiful woman in the room was supposed to be the bride. And Jenna looked great, no doubt about that. But she wasn't Grace.

If she were standing in a crowd of supermodels, Playboy Bunnies, and *People* magazine's most beautiful women from the past ten years combined, Grace still would have put them all to shame.

Not that he should care, or even notice. Not anymore.

But while the judge went about putting a legal stamp on Gage and Jenna's relationship in a bit of a monotone—no great surprise, considering how many times he probably said the words in a week, a month, or a year—Zack's attention seemed compulsively fixated on Grace's full, red-tinged lips; the wavy, perfectly styled fall of her hair; the fire-engine-red dress that hugged her curves, framed her breasts, and made her legs look incredible.

He should have been able to tell her as much. To whisper hot, seductive words in her ear, and promise to strip her bare the minute they got home.

Instead, he was forced to stand here and act like everything was fine while inside his stomach clenched and the blood curdled in his veins. He no longer had the right to touch her or even think about her in those terms. If he did and she found out, she'd probably try to scratch his eyes out.

Or maybe knee him in the groin, if the narrow,

blistering glares she'd been aiming in his direction on and off were anything to go by.

Shit, he shouldn't have come. He knew it would be a miserable afternoon. And why in God's name did he feel compelled to walk over to her and *apologize,* to ask her forgiveness, to beg her to give him a second chance, when he'd done nothing wrong?

He knew now why so many guys on the team stuck to casual, short-term relationships and had personal policies against ever getting serious with a woman. Zack had always thought their blustering about bad mojo and women messing up a guy's game was all just superstitious garbage, but now he wasn't so sure.

As much as it pained him to admit it, he'd been crap on ice—literally—since Grace had stormed out of his life and refused to speak to him. He knew the rest of the team was talking behind his back, knew they were speculating that his best days were behind him, and that he should turn in his stick and jersey before he ruined the Rockets' chances for getting to the playoffs and bringing home the Cup.

And maybe they had a point. If he couldn't give the game and his fellow players one hundred percent of his attention and a hundred and ten percent of his effort, then he didn't deserve to be out there.

The sound of clapping cut into his dismal thoughts, and he realized the judge had apparently done the whole "man and wife" thing, moving on to "you may now kiss the bride." Gage and Jenna were locked at the lips, exchanging a fairly chaste kiss—at least considering how hot he knew the two were for each other—then broke apart, turning to their friends with wide, joyous smiles on their faces.

Zack joined in the cheers and well wishes, all the while keeping Grace in his sights as she hugged her friend, then retreated to a far corner of the room to collect their things.

Knowing he was asking for trouble, but somehow unable to stop himself, he followed.

"Grace."

He said her name softly, not wanting to startle her or draw the others' attention, but still she stiffened and her fingers turned white where they curled around the strap of her purse.

Movements as regal as a queen, she straightened, then looked him square in the eyes, her lips pulled into a tight, flat line.

"I have nothing to say to you, Zack."

"Good," he replied, shoving his shoulders back and stuffing his hands into the pockets of his black wool pants. "Then maybe you can listen for a change."

Her brow rose in both annoyance and warning. During their time together, he'd learned her body language and facial expressions well, and the raised brow typically served as a flashing yellow caution light, like the rattle of a snake's tail.

He hadn't meant to snap or lace his words with accusation, but he was damn tired of feeling like the bad guy in this situation. And though there were moments—especially late at night, when he was alone in his apartment and regret swamped him—that he'd have gladly fallen on his knees and begged her to come back, now wasn't one of those times.

He finally had her cornered, able to speak with her face to face instead of trying to reach her through electronic voice-mail boxes, ignored e-mails, or messages via friends that got no response, and he intended to take advantage of it.

"I know what you think," he told her in a low voice, taking a quick step to the left to block her from leaving, even as he was careful not to crowd her too much. "I know why you're angry. But you're also wrong. I didn't invite that woman into my hotel room. I have no idea who she was, I never touched her, and I kicked her out as soon as you left. I didn't cheat on you, Grace, and it would have been nice if you'd trusted me enough to at least give me the benefit of the doubt before kicking me to the curb."

He straightened and stepped back. Grace's face remained stoically impassive, but he didn't care. The lead weight of resentment and unspoken clarifications that had been spoiling inside of him for months suddenly lifted and he felt a thousand times better.

He didn't have her back. He hadn't cleared his name with her, or her friends, or the press, or anyone else in the free world who thought he was a scum-sucking dog. But he'd said his piece, he'd gotten to look Grace in the eyes and tell her in no uncertain terms that he *had not slept with another woman, dammit.*

And now it was over. What was that term shrinks liked to use? Oh, yeah—*closure.* He had closure, which hopefully meant those freaking nightmares would go away, and he'd be able to pull his head out of his ass long enough to help the Rockets actually win a game for a change.

Raising her other brow, Grace crossed her arms over her chest, pushing her breasts together to create even more impressive cleavage.

Zack's blood heated and started a slow trek toward

the South Pole, but only, he thought, because he'd have had to be dead and in the ground a good two months not to feel at least a modicum of arousal at something like that. When it came to a nice set of tits swelling out of a dress like that, his dick wasn't particular about who they were attached to.

"Are you finished?" she asked in a tone cold enough to freeze mercury.

If the question was meant to intimidate him or lure him into starting a fight, it missed its mark.

"Yeah, I think I am," he responded. Then he turned on his heel and walked across the room to rejoin the rest of the wedding party, feeling better than he had in a very long time.

Row 3

"This is very weird," Ronnie said, crossing her legs tailor-style and dropping onto the pillow she was using to cushion a spot on the floor. *Moonstruck* played on the television screen along the far wall as Grace finished pouring two glasses of rich, red wine before following suit.

"What is?"

"Having Girls' Night Out without all the girls."

"What?" Grace asked. "Did you want Jenna to cut her honeymoon short just to join us for take-out Italian and rented movies?"

Ronnie's mouth twisted, and she reached for her glass. "Yeah, I think I did," she replied before taking a small sip.

For a second, they merely looked at each other, then they both threw their heads back and laughed.

"All right, so maybe not," Ronnie admitted. "I'm sure she's having a better time getting all sexed up in St. Thomas—"

"For a second time, no less, when I've never even been there once," Grace interjected, an unspoken *hmph* lacing her tone.

"—but it's still weird."

"And what am I, chopped liver?"

"Definitely not chopped liver," Ronnie assured her. "You are the filet mignon of girlfriends."

Grace rolled her eyes. "Thanks. I think."

Grabbing her half of the takeout from the pile in the center of the table, she flipped the plastic lid off the aluminum container of spaghetti and meatballs— and was immediately accosted by a big, wet nose snuffling under her arm in an attempt to nudge its way closer and closer to her supper.

"Stop it, you big pig," she chastised, pushing back against the giant, scruffy Saint Bernard at the same time she tried to use her body to protect her food.

Not that she didn't love the overgrown mutt. He'd helped to save her sanity and mend her broken heart after her breakup with Zack in ways she never could have expected. Considering the noxious breath and mutant salivary glands that came as part and parcel of the furry monster, it was a minor miracle she hadn't dropped him at the nearest animal shelter within minutes of leading him out of Zack's apartment.

She'd hated the mangy beast for years while she and Zack dated. Deemed him nothing more than a stinky, overgrown nuisance, and had often hinted that Zack should get rid of him so they could get a smaller pet—like an elephant or a humpback whale. Or at the very least, one that could be considered "theirs" instead of "his." She'd sort of had her heart set on a cute little shih tzu or Pomeranian.

But what had started out as an act of revenge— stealing Zack's dog, just like she'd stolen his favorite hockey stick—had ended up being one of the best decisions she'd ever made.

The newly named Muffin might outweigh her by a good fifty pounds and cause her to send her sofa cushions out to be steam-cleaned on a weekly basis, but she loved the stupid canine and couldn't imagine not having him around.

Even if it meant having a snotty dog snout poking at her dinner.

"You'll get some," she promised the still-searching pest, "just wait your turn."

Grabbing the extra plate she'd brought from the kitchen for just this purpose, she scooped a good share of spaghetti—and one of the two meatballs—out of her own dish, and set it on the coffee table in front of the dog.

Well aware of the routine that had to be followed before anyone else could enjoy their meal, Ronnie waited until Muffin's face was buried contentedly in his Italian cuisine before lifting the lid from her own four-cheese lasagna. Before the night was through, there was a good chance she'd end up sharing, too, and she knew it.

"What happened to weaning him off of human food?" she asked without a hint of censure in her voice.

"I thought about it," Grace replied blandly. "It didn't work out."

"What happened?"

Grace shrugged. "He only needs a couple bites to get it out of his system, and it's easier to let him have a taste than to listen to him whine."

For a second, Ronnie didn't respond. Then she said, "He kicked your butt, didn't he?"

"You have no idea," Grace admitted, rolling her eyes. "It was like trying to tame a rabid wolverine. I spent three days scraping food off the ceiling."

Ronnie laughed, reaching for a slice of garlic bread.

Carbs might be the enemy, but South Beach, Weight Watchers, Jenny Craig, and every other diet promising amazing results went the way of the wind on Girls' Night. Girls' Night Out was the perfect excuse to fulfill their fat, carbohydrate, sugar, and alcohol cravings without guilt. After all, the number-one rule of Girls' Night was *No Guilt Allowed*. No Guilt, No Diets, and What Happens on Girls' Night, Stays on Girls' Night.

"So you want to tell me what you and Zack talked about at the wedding?"

The question came out of left field, making her suck in a breath, which caused her to choke slightly on a bite of pasta. She'd been hoping no one noticed that little incident—or at the very least wouldn't ask her about it. Mainly because seeing Zack again had disturbed her more than she wanted to let on.

Except for an awkward confrontation soon after she'd walked out of that hotel room and not looked back, she hadn't seen him in person since. And even though she'd braced herself for running into him at the wedding, it hadn't gone at all as she'd anticipated.

Being near him again had hurt just as much as she'd expected. A mix of longing for the way things had once been and anger at his betrayal had caused her stomach to roil and her palms to go damp.

Given the number of times he'd called, e-mailed, and attempted to visit her both at her apartment and the television studio over the past six months, she'd expected him to accost her much sooner and with much more irritation. What she hadn't expected was his quiet approach, his calm declaration of innocence. It had caught her off guard and struck her nearly speechless.

"We didn't talk so much as he spoke and I listened."

"What did he say?" Ronnie wanted to know.

Grace twirled her fork in her spaghetti, watching the strands of pasta go around and around while she thought about Zack's words and the sincerity in his eyes while he said them.

"The same thing he's been saying all along—that I mistook the situation, and he didn't cheat on me with that woman."

She kept her attention on her meal and her voice light, as though it didn't matter to her one way or the other.

"You know," Ronnie said, slowly and carefully, as though she were afraid of saying the wrong thing, "Dylan believes him. Apparently, when Zack couldn't catch up with you before you left the hotel, the two of them met up and searched the parking lot. Dylan didn't see a woman with him, or any signs of one, and I guess Zack was pretty upset."

"I was upset," Grace reminded her.

"I know, but . . . What if, because you were so upset, you jumped to the wrong conclusion?"

Grace's head snapped up and a single blond brow quickly followed. "You're taking his side now?"

"I'm on your side, you know that," Ronnie replied. "If you said the sky was green, I'd agree with you. I guess I just can't stop thinking what a shame it would be for you two not to be together if this is one giant misunderstanding. You made such a terrific couple, and if you're wrong, if he really didn't cheat on you . . . then you'll be losing out on something truly special."

"So why is this the first time you're telling me this?" Grace wanted to know, only slightly annoyed.

"Because my knee-jerk reaction was the same as

yours—that Zack was guilty as sin. But seeing as how he hasn't backed down about being innocent after all these months—even with his very closest friends—I just have to wonder, that's all." Then Ronnie sighed. "All I'm saying is that I'd hate to see you lose something so important on principle alone. Especially if it turns out you're wrong."

It took Grace a moment to get past her initial impulse to argue, to defend herself. And as the urge to fight and defend slowly passed, she let herself absorb and contemplate Ronnie's words.

Okay, so what if Zack were innocent?

Her immediate response was to give a harsh mental scoff and don an invisible suit of armor to protect herself.

But then she thought, *Well, damn, there's the knee-jerk reaction Ronnie had been talking about.*

Had she been doing this all along? Had she fallen back on pointing fingers and heated accusations because they felt safe to her? Because it was easier than opening herself to more pain, more disappointment?

Letting her arms drop to her sides, she moved slowly back to the table and curled up once again on the cushion she was using to sit on so her butt wouldn't go numb. Her hand shook as she reached for her wine and downed the entire glass.

The rich liquid filled her mouth and warmed its way down to her stomach. Nice. Exactly what she needed. Now if she could just mainline another gallon or two, she thought she might be able to get her emotions under control.

Muffin, who had practically licked the etchings right off his plate in an effort to consume every speck of spaghetti sauce, sat up, gave a low, odious belch, and padded behind Grace to climb onto the couch. Three roomy cushions wide, and he took up nearly all of them.

"I'm sorry," Ronnie murmured quietly from the other side of the table. "I didn't mean to upset you so much. I shouldn't have said anything."

"Yes, you should have," Grace said, surprising even herself.

Leaning forward, she grabbed Ronnie's hand and gave it a squeeze. "You're being honest, and even if it's not something I want to hear, maybe it's something I *need* to hear."

Her throat grew tight, and she paused a moment to swallow and blink back tears. Ronnie's eyes, too, were glistening with moisture, she noticed.

"And who better to slap you upside the head when you're being an idiot than your very best friend?"

Ronnie gave a watery chuckle, and Grace joined in, relieved when the heaviness in her chest began to ease.

Grace set her glass on the table and said to herself as much as to Ronnie, "I've replayed that scene in the hotel room in my mind a thousand times. And seeing that other woman in his bed . . . I don't know, Ronnie, it just seems so painfully obvious. You see women all the time whose men are running around on them, and they're the only one with blinders on so thick they can't see it—or aren't willing to see. Or wives of politicians whose husbands get caught red-handed, with their pants around their ankles, and the women just stand by and take it. To each her own, I guess, but that is *soooo* not me. I expect more from a relationship, and I sure as hell expect more from the man I'm supposed to marry and spend the rest of my life with."

As though sensing her distress and wanting to offer his sympathy, Muffin stood up and put his head in her lap. Grace leaned down to kiss the top of his head and pet him absently as she said, "I mean, I caught him with a half-naked woman *in his bed*. It's kind of hard to deny undeniable proof—and something I saw with my very own eyes."

Ronnie shrugged. "I know, I'd feel the same way if I were you. But can I ask you something? What is your heart telling you?"

Grace considered that for a long, drawn-out moment, and then she murmured, "That I made the right choice."

A few hours later, after they'd finished their take-out Italian cuisine, polished off the bottle of merlot, and half watched, half snoozed through *Under the Tuscan Sun,* Grace yawned and stretched out full-length from her position on the floor. Muffin's loud, staccato snoring echoed just above her head from his carefree drape along the entire length of the sofa.

White was perhaps not the smartest decorating choice for someone who owned a giant, slobbering Saint Bernard, but then, she hadn't *had* a giant, slobbering Saint Bernard when she'd chosen the color scheme. Next time around, she would definitely go for darker shades, like Drool Pool Brown and Fur-covered Chestnut.

She was even considering covering all the furniture in plastic like some 1950s hausfrau whose main goal in life was to keep her god-awful yellow and green floral living room set perfectly pristine for all eternity. Of course, in Grace's case, it wasn't a matter of keeping things pristine, but simply avoiding the need to replace her furniture every couple of months due to doggie wear and tear.

Though it was barely ten o'clock, she and Ronnie had both had a long week, and their starchy dinner was beginning to take its toll. Add to that a fair amount of alcohol and a conversation that had put her emotions on the mother of all roller coasters, and she thought she could easily crawl into a cave and hibernate until spring.

"You don't have to go, you know," she sleepily told Ronnie, who was pushing herself vertical, looking not much more alert than Grace felt.

"I do," her friend replied reluctantly. "Dylan's all excited about spending our first Christmas together, and I promised I'd be home tonight so we can drag ourselves out of bed at the crack of dawn to go tree hunting."

Grace made a sound in her throat that was half snort, half groan, pushing up on her elbows and climbing reluctantly to her feet, as well.

"I know," Ronnie agreed. "He wants a giant Douglas fir. I want something we can blow up with a tire pump, then squeeze flat and store away after the holidays."

Grace chuckled, moving to the entertainment center and hitting the button to eject the rented DVD. As soon as that was done, she switched to TV mode and automatically—all right, maybe not entirely automatically—switched to Cleveland's main sports channel.

"Make him haul the thing in by himself, then out again after Christmas, and clean up all the dead needles in between, and he'll never bug you about getting a real tree again," she said, punching down the volume on the television and hoping her voice covered enough of the noise from the screen to keep her friend from getting suspicious.

"No kidding," Ronnie said, moving across the room to gather her things. Once she was bundled from head to toe, and ready to brave the wind and frigid temperatures of Cleveland in December, she raised her head to meet Grace's gaze. "He's taking me home to spend Christmas Eve with his parents," she said softly.

"Oooh, holidays with the folks. He must really like you," Grace teased, shoving a couple of take-out containers under her arm to be taken to the kitchen, washed, and added to the recycle bin.

"Yeah," Ronnie agreed with a smile bordering on weak. "I don't know why I'm so nervous about that. I've met his parents. We've done lunch and a couple of dinners. But Christmas . . ." She gave an indelicate shudder.

Grace sympathized with Ronnie's bout of nerves, but she couldn't claim to know anything about spending holidays with the S.O.'s parents. At least not from personal experience.

She'd never realized before how odd that was. But then, neither she nor Zack had exactly grown up like the Brady Bunch. Or the Cleavers or Ozzie and Harriet.

More like Ozzie and Sharon.

Her own mother had been a B-movie Hollywood starlet . . . but an A-list wannabe. She'd harbored dreams of fame and fortune and a star on the Walk of Fame, but had never gotten close to any of them. Instead, she'd gotten involved with too many untrustworthy men—managers, talent agents, and assorted lovers—who promised her the world, but delivered only lies, disappointment, and misery.

Drugs, alcohol, bad choices, and bad judgment had all driven Lola Fisher into an early grave. Much like Marilyn Monroe, she'd been found dead one morning in her own bed, booze on the nightstand and an assortment of pills spilled across the pink satin sheets.

Grace had been only twelve years old at the time, and to this day, she still wasn't sure if her mother had accidentally overdosed or taken her own life. The medical examiner's report had revealed exactly nothing; the media had run rampant with outrageous versions of both possibilities; and the gossip mills had speculated on everything in between.

It was an accident.

It was suicide.

It was murder.

It was tragic and senseless and left a little girl who'd had only one parent to begin with—and not a terribly doting parent, at that—an orphan.

Blinking rapidly and swallowing hard to dislodge the sudden lump in her throat, Grace hurried into the kitchen to dump her armload of trash into the sink. For a second, she stood there, hands curled around the edge of the counter, head down, breathing carefully in and out, in and out.

It had been years, *years* since her mother's death. Since she'd been heartlessly packed up and sent halfway across the country to be dumped on the doorstep of a grandmother she'd never met. How could it possibly still have the power to catch her off guard and shake her up like this?

Ridiculous. It must be the late night. The movies. The evening's topic of conversation. The holiday season. Anything other than actual sentimentality, when Grace prided herself on her distinct lack of sentimentality.

Pushing the precarious thoughts and emotions to the back of her mind, she returned to the living area, where Muffin was still snoozing and Ronnie was still bundled up like the Abominable Snow Monster.

"You'll be fine," Grace assured her, picking up where they'd left off so her friend wouldn't suspect she'd dashed into the kitchen in an attempt to actually run away. "Take a nice bottle of wine for them—and a couple more for yourself"—she added with a sly wink—"and act like it's any other, nondenominational visit."

Ronnie inhaled deeply and nodded as best she could with only her eyes, nose, and mouth visible. "I suppose you're right. And he's going with me to my parents' for New Year's, so I suppose it's only fair."

"There you go," Grace said, turning back to the coffee table to collect more leftovers.

As she leaned down, reaching for the empty glasses and bottle of merlot, a movement on the television screen caught her attention. She raised her head, expecting to see the usual for a hockey game— well-padded and suited-up players skating their hearts out, zipping up and down the ice, cracking their sticks into that little black puck like their lives depended on it.

Instead, the action was in slow motion for an instant replay, and what she saw made her heart tumble down to her toes, hitting every rib and internal organ along the way.

"Oh, my God." The words slid past her lips on a hiss of air as the oxygen left her lungs. The bottle she'd just picked up slipped from her numb fingers, cracking into the edge of the table on its way to the carpeted floor, and she slowly followed it down, her knees turning to jelly.

"Oh, my God," she said again. Gaze riveted, she sank to her knees, only peripherally aware that Ronnie was moving toward her, shifting her attention to the TV, as well.

"Oh, my God." This time, it was Ronnie who breathed the words in disbelief. And then she was yanking off her hat and gloves, unwinding the scarf from her neck, and digging into her purse. Cell phone in hand, she punched frantically at the tiny buttons.

Somewhere in the back of her brain, Grace registered her friend's actions, and even some of what the play-by-play announcer was saying to describe the events taking place at Quicken Loans Arena, but she couldn't seem to make sense of it.

She didn't know who the Rockets were playing, and didn't particularly care. All she knew was that—thanks to yet another instant replay—a player from the opposing team, suited in white and black, was racing down the center of the ice, shifting his stick from right to left, right to left as he steered the small disk of vulcanized rubber toward the Rockets' net.

In front of the net, weaving slightly in his typical defensive stance, was Zack. And then the puck was launched, went flying. Zack deflected, kept the black-and-white team from scoring a goal, and sent the puck back in the opposite direction.

A second later, that first player hit Zack square in the chest. His back hit the metal frame of the net with what looked to be brute force before both men lurched sideways and began to fall . . . and were quickly covered by half a dozen other players from both teams.

That in itself wouldn't have been so bad. Hockey was a rough sport. Zack had garnered his share of cuts and bruises. He'd suffered bone fractures and breaks, concussions, muscle pulls. It was a minor miracle that he'd managed to retain all of his own teeth—for which Grace had always been unaccountably grateful.

But as they went down, Zack's helmet flew off and his left leg caught on the edge of the net.

The leg held, but his body didn't, twisting him like a Twizzler beneath the weight of a dozen players.

Grace knew it wasn't possible to actually hear the rending of bones and tendons, or the smack of his head hitting the ice, but she could have sworn she did. Could have sworn that above the clamor of the crowd, of razor-sharp skate blades cutting over the ice, of the grunts and sounds of impact from the dog pile itself, she heard Zack's injuries taking place one by one.

Even so, she might not have been concerned if the part of the incident they replayed most often wasn't the part where everyone got up and skated away to resume play.

Everyone except Zack, who remained unnaturally still, his blue and red Rockets jersey a stark contrast to the crystalline ice beneath him.

"What's going on?"

Ronnie's voice, harsh and demanding, broke through Grace's stupor. It took a moment for her to realize, though, that her friend wasn't talking to her.

"We're watching it," she said into her cell phone. "How badly is he hurt?"

Dylan. She must be talking to Dylan. He was at the arena, covering the game for *Sports Weekly,* and he would be able to give them better updates than the commentators, who even now were merely speculating about Zack's condition.

Where the hell was the team doctor?

Why wasn't anyone calling 911 or doing something to help Zack?

Or had they already, and she just wasn't seeing it?

Because she wasn't there! Dammit, she wasn't there!

While they'd been dating, she'd attended all of his home games. And if it hadn't been for these last six, hellish months, she would have been there right now. And if she was . . .

If she was, she might have altered something, made some small difference in their lives so that Zack wouldn't be lying on the ice, unmoving and . . .

No, she wouldn't think it, not even for a second.

"Okay. Keep us informed."

After clicking her phone closed, Ronnie sank to the floor beside Grace and wrapped an arm around her shoulder, hugging her close.

Just as she did, the picture on the screen changed, this time showing medical personnel surrounding Zack. The team physician lifting Zack's eyelids to check his pupils, taking his pulse. Paramedics with a stretcher, waiting for the signal to load him up and transport him to the hospital. They were all moving too damn slow for Grace's peace of mind.

"Honey." Ronnie whispered the endearment slowly, softly, in the tone of voice people used when they had to break bad news and they didn't want the other person to have a complete and total nervous breakdown.

Grace started to shake her head. She didn't care what her friend told her, she wouldn't accept it. Zack was fine. She might not love him anymore, but she didn't want him to be hurt or . . . worse. He was fine, and she wasn't going to let herself believe differently.

"Honey," Ronnie said again, "Dylan says it's bad. Zack is unconscious, and the doctor can't get him to respond. His head cracked the ice pretty hard. His leg is messed up, too. They're taking him to the hospital, and Dylan is going to follow. We can meet him there, if you want."

Still numb and reeling, Grace sat where she was until all of the television coverage was over. Until she'd seen Zack loaded up on the stretcher and wheeled off the ice. Until the rest of the Rockets, who had surrounded their fallen teammate as closely as they could, broke away.

As soon as there was no camera trained on Zack and she knew there was no chance of catching another glimpse of him, she turned to her friend. There was nothing but concern and compassion in Ronnie's eyes, and she knew that if she said the word, they'd be in the car, headed for the hospital in a flash.

But was that what she wanted? Did she want to sit

in a crowded emergency room waiting area, pacing and worrying about a man she wasn't supposed to care for anymore?

All of her friends—save the two who were currently honeymooning in St. Thomas and didn't even know about Zack's accident—would be there. All of Zack's teammates, the Rockets coach, the team doctor, and other assorted team associates would be there.

The press would be there. Reporters from all of the media outlets, both large and small. Newspaper, magazine, television . . . Cameras everywhere, snapping her picture, speculating on whether she and Zack were back together. Whether she was grief-stricken over his accident or secretly pleased that the man who'd two-timed her was finally getting his just deserts.

Could she deal with that? And when Zack woke up—because he *would* wake up—did she want him to know she'd been there the entire time, waiting for a report on his condition?

The former lover, fiancée, and almost-wife in her screamed *Yes!*, wanting to jump up and race to the hospital in her pajamas and bare feet.

But the woman-done-wrong and public personality behind that persona definitely didn't want the attention or the gossip that would follow. Or for Zack to think he meant more to her than he should after what he'd done to her.

Ronnie's gaze bored into her, waiting for her to make a decision. But even though it felt as though her insides were being sliced to bits by a thousand tiny razor blades, she didn't have an answer.

Stay or go?

Remain strong or admit her vulnerability to Zack and to the world?

She didn't know what to do.

She just didn't know . . .

Row 4

Zack—formerly "Hot Legs"—Hoolihan sat in his wheelchair, left leg propped straight out in front of him, staring at the fifty-two-inch screen of the state-of-the-art plasma television taking up nearly every square inch of the far living room wall.

His friends had been so damn impressed when he'd bought the thing and invited them over to christen it with a weekend of chips, beer, pizza, and the NBA finals. Little did they know his main reason for replacing his perfectly good thirty-two-inch flat screen was because he'd needed something to hide the hole Grace had left when she'd rammed one of his hockey trophies straight through the drywall. He'd come home to find the ass end hanging in the air like the minuscule hockey player had gotten stuck during some botched escape attempt.

The trophy he could live without.

The hole he couldn't live with. Not staring at him every day, reminding him of the woman who'd put it there and what had driven her to such violence in the first place.

Not that she had a reason to be so pissed off. He should have slapped her with a lawsuit to get his apartment repaired, his belongings replaced, and his dog returned. It was no less than she deserved.

And he missed Bruiser, dammit!

The apartment was too quiet without his heavy, padded footsteps. His rattling snores. And Zack hadn't sat down in a puddle of drool in months.

Who knew a man could come to miss having a wet ass?

Zack stabbed the tip of one needle through a stitch on the other, looped his yarn, and kept knitting. The past month while he'd been "recovering," he'd gone through enough yarn to cover all of Cleveland and made just about everything he could think of that he could actually put to use. A scarf, a hat, a couple pairs of slipper socks. He'd thought about trying his hand at a sweater, but though he had the time, he wasn't sure he had the talent or patience.

So instead, he'd begun knitting thick, warm squares that could then be stitched together into blankets and donated to the local VA hospital. He'd heard about the need for that sort of thing through a teammate whose wife volunteered around the city, and it had sounded like as good a way as any to pass the hours that had turned into days that had turned into weeks. After all, it wasn't like he'd be back at practice or back on the ice anytime soon.

He made another vicious stab at the yarn, then forced himself to take a breath and relax before he either broke the damn stuff or screwed up the consistency of his stitches.

A knock at the door made him jerk, but only slightly.

He didn't get a lot of visitors these days, mostly because he was such a bear to be around, no one could stand him for very long.

Even Magda, who got paid to come in once a week and clean up after him, kept a wide berth. She would make him a sandwich or something for lunch when she was around because she disapproved of his living off potato chips and delivery, but that was about it.

Since Magda was in the kitchen running a load of dishes through the dishwasher and getting ready to take his dirty clothes down to his apartment building's laundry room, he let her answer the door while he shoved his needles and the afghan square he was working on deep between the arm of his black leather sofa and its first overstuffed cushion.

Knitting was a private hobby, and something he would prefer no one else—not even his closest friends—know about.

If the media found out, it would be a public relations nightmare. His fellow Rockets would rib him endlessly, call him a pussy, a pansy, a eunuch, and worse. His fans would probably do the same, as well as losing respect for him and going as far as booing him when he skated onto the ice.

If he ever skated onto the ice again.

And if his friends—specifically Gage and Dylan—discovered his secret, then it would be even worse. Not that they'd tease him—at least not much—since they had both taken up a bit of knitting in one form or another over the past year and wouldn't have a lot of room to talk.

No, the worst part was that they would know *why* he'd taught himself to knit. They might not verbalize

their thoughts, but they would *know* it was something
he'd done after Grace left him in hopes of possibly
winning her back . . . and they would pity him.

Well, he didn't need their pity.

God, he was so sick of the sentiment, he wanted to
vomit. First, Grace had left him and he'd been pitied
for either being a cheating ass whose ex-girlfriend
didn't believe in pulling her punches . . . or because
he'd moped around like some homeless, flea-ridden
pup who had been kicked around too much and just
wanted to go off somewhere to die.

Yeah, he'd been that pathetic.

Then he'd gone and made a bonehead move on the
ice. He still wasn't sure exactly how it had happened,
but he was man enough to admit that his head hadn't
been in the game properly for months before the accident. He'd been distracted, hurt, annoyed, and phon-
ing it in.

The irony was that he'd just started to drag himself
up, dust himself off, and get back to work, putting
the entire mess with Grace behind him in an effort to
help his team win game after game and once again
make it to the playoffs.

He'd been all over that game, blocking shot after
shot to keep the other guys from scoring. And then
something had just gone . . . wrong.

Maybe he'd pushed himself too hard too fast.
Maybe he'd overestimated his skills. Or maybe it was
just one of those times when life threw a curveball,
and there was nothing to do about it except look back
and wish you'd done things differently.

Whatever the case, he'd launched himself one way
to keep the puck from making the net, his left leg had

remained extended, and the player who had shot the puck to begin with had barreled into him full force.

It hadn't been pretty, according to witnesses. Luckily, he'd lost consciousness the minute his head hit the ice and didn't remember much of anything before waking up in the hospital with his cracked skull wrapped like a mummy, his leg covered in a hip-to-toe cast and elevated by wires, and tubes pumping some truly amazing painkillers into his veins.

Sinking down in his chair, he slouched his shoulders and linked his hands low on his stomach— which, okay, had gone a little soft over the past month, thanks to his lack of mobility and dietary choices— pretending to be involved in the action taking place on the TV screen.

Shit! he realized belatedly. Leaning forward, he grabbed the remote from the glass-topped coffee table, grimacing when the movement pulled at his knee and sent pain shooting up the full length of his leg.

Punching buttons, he quickly changed the channel in case whoever was at the door ended up coming in. All he needed was for someone—close friend, mild acquaintance, or complete stranger—to discover that in addition to taking up knitting, blowing off rehab, and letting himself go to fat, he spent his days watching soap operas.

They were surprisingly interesting. He started with *The Young and the Restless* when he rolled out of bed around noon, then tried to catch *One Life to Live* and *General Hospital*. He liked *Guiding Light* and *Days of Our Lives*, too, so sometimes he would TiVo those to watch later.

And God bless SoapNet. If he missed a show, he

could catch the recaps there, as well as all-day marathons of older episodes and even serials that were no longer on the air.

He wasn't proud of his new hobby, but he wasn't ashamed enough to give it up, either.

The voices at the door grew louder, and he returned to his apathetic slump. He heard Magda complaining in rapid Spanglish, followed by lower, hushed tones.

Zack sighed and closed his eyes, rubbing two fingers over the spot between his eyes where a headache was brewing. He got them a lot these days, thanks to the concussion he'd suffered when his helmet had flown off and the back of his skull had smacked the ice.

They seemed somehow worse, though, when his friends showed up unannounced and tried to bully him into getting better and giving up his life of leisure.

Well, the joke was on them. He liked his life of leisure, and suspected they'd be only too happy to join him if they got a gander at some of the chicks heating up the sheets on daytime television.

Thirty seconds later, slow footsteps sounded behind him. When they came to a halt, he felt both their breaths on the back of his neck and their censure over the fact that he was still in his wheelchair, in the exact same spot as the last time they'd stopped by to check on him three days before.

"Don't you ever get out of this damn thing?" Gage asked, voice soured with annoyance. He punctuated the question by kicking one of the wide wheels of the chair with the toe of his boot.

"Where am I supposed to go?" he returned, not

bothering to turn his head in their direction. "It's not like I can do much with this bum leg."

Dylan came around, skirting his chair and the low coffee table, and took a seat on the sofa . . . dangerously close to the spot where Zack had hidden his needles and yarn. Zack watched his friend's progress, careful to keep his eyes front and center rather than letting them stray to something he'd prefer not to have to explain.

As Gage moved around and took a seat at the opposite end of the couch, Zack shifted the chair to face them better, getting situated just in time to have Dylan start in on the lecture du jour.

"You wouldn't still have a bum leg if you'd go to physical therapy like you're supposed to."

"The doctors say you'd have almost full use of it by now, be up and around and that much closer to getting back on the ice, if you weren't being such a stubborn ass."

This from Gage, whose tolerance levels were significantly lower than Dylan's. Both had been fully sympathetic while he was in the hospital and soon after his release. They'd helped him get home, stocked the cupboards and fridge with easy-to-reach and easy-to-prepare foods, and gotten the apartment set up for someone with limited mobility.

But their sympathies had grown short and their tempers long when he'd blown off his first appointment at the rehabilitation center. And then the second and the third and the . . .

They'd tried finagling, browbeating, even bribery. But what was the point?

He'd seen the X-rays. He'd heard the doctor explaining his injuries to the others even before he'd been fully conscious. It was bad.

In a word, his knee was fucked up.

He could be early to every physical therapy appointment, do every exercise they recommended and then some, and there were still no guarantees he'd ever play hockey again. In fact, chances were good—better than good—that he would never return to the ice. He'd be lucky if he ever walked again, and even that would most likely be with a limp.

So why the hell should he bother?

All he knew was hockey. He'd never done anything else, wasn't *qualified* for anything else. And even if he had been, who wanted to go from being the star goalie for a professional hockey team that had been to the playoffs seven times and brought home the Stanley Cup four of those years, to selling insurance or asking, "Would you like fries with that?"

It wasn't like he needed the money—he had enough socked away to last him three lifetimes—so he would just as soon be left alone.

His friends thought he was wallowing, giving up. He preferred to think of it as cutting his losses. Why waste time or energy on getting his knee to function at fifty or seventy-five percent when it still wouldn't put him back in his Rockets jersey?

"I like being a stubborn ass," he tossed back in response to Gage's charge. "It suits me." Just like his ribald T-shirt collection—the one he was wearing now said THEY CALL IT PMS BECAUSE "MAD COW DISEASE" WAS ALREADY TAKEN—and the basketball hoop fastened to the wall above his laundry hamper suited him.

Before they'd broken up, Grace used to tease that he was a little kid at heart. When she was in a good mood, at least. When she was angry with him, she'd complained that he had a Peter Pan complex and needed to grow the hell up.

The first time she'd accused him of such a thing, he'd had to look it up. He'd thought being called Peter Pan meant he liked to wear green tights and was light in the loafers. Instead, it simply meant there was a part of him that didn't want to grow up.

And what was so wrong with that, anyway? What was wrong with having a sense of humor, being young at heart, not taking life too seriously? As far as he was concerned, there were a lot of people in the world who could stand to loosen up a little and let the sticks fall out of their asses. Maybe a corny T-shirt or two would do them some good.

"You're not just being stubborn," Dylan tried again, his tone more soothing and cajoling than Gage's, "you're being stupid."

Well, so much for soothing, Zack thought with a mental eye-roll.

"You're only hurting yourself, Zack. No one else is keeping you in that wheelchair. No one else is turning you into a pathetic, housebound invalid. That's all on you."

"Gee, thanks for the news flash," he responded with heavy sarcasm.

"That's it," Gage bit out, pushing back to his feet. "I'm done with this shit. Sit there and mope. Feel sorry for yourself. Crawl into a hole and hide from life. Whatever."

The last was delivered with a healthy dose of disgust

and frustration while Gage towered over him, face angry and muscled torso bulging with barely restrained violence.

"But don't expect me to hold your hand or coddle you any more than we already have. I'm out of here."

Leaning down, he grabbed an open bag of Cheez Doodles from the table and pitched them in Zack's direction, hitting him square in the chest and sending air-puffed snack pieces and artificial-cheese-flavored dust flying.

"You're on your own, buddy."

With that, he turned a scornful glance to Dylan and added, "If you know what's good for you, you'll walk away, too. Leave him to wallow in his own misery."

And then he stomped off, his heavy, booted steps echoing across the wide-plank hardwood floors, followed by the hard slam of the front door.

All was silent from in the kitchen, Zack noticed. No doubt Magda had her head cocked and her ears primed, hanging on every word of the rather one-sided conversation taking place not twenty feet away.

Not that Gage's raised voice could be missed. A couple decibels higher and he could probably be heard all the way down at the waterfront.

Moving more slowly and with less agitation than Gage, Dylan put his hands to his knees and stood to look down at Zack.

"I wish I could say he's wrong or overreacting, but . . ." He shook his head. "What's going on with you, man? What happened to the fun-loving guy who would do anything for a laugh, anything on a dare? The friend we used to like hanging out with because he never took anything too seriously and reminded us that no matter how tough things got, there was always some stupid story or joke he could pull out of his hat that could crack us up. And what about the star goalie who was always there for his teammates, always insisted on partying after a game, even if they'd taken a loss?"

Though Zack tried not to make eye contact with his friend, it would take a blind man not to see the confusion, the concern, and yes, the *pity* in Dylan's expression. He locked his jaw and let his back teeth grind for a while.

It felt good. Took his mind off the throb in his knee and helped him block out the tune his friend was playing on the world's smallest violin.

"We miss you," Dylan said, finally bringing his speech to a close. "And I think Gage may be right—until you get your head on straight, figure out whether you want your life back or want to sit here feeling sorry for yourself . . . I don't think we can come around anymore. You really are on your own."

Skirting the glass-topped table with slow, deliberate steps, Dylan crossed the room and let himself out of the apartment. The click of the door, much softer and less emphatic than Gage's angry slam, still managed to ring in Zack's ears like the gong of a bell.

A low ache pulsed in his chest. Guilt? Regret?

Eh, they'd get over it. Give them a week and they'd be back, ready to watch the next big game on his fifty-two-inch plasma, peace offerings of pizza and beer in tow.

Maybe he'd even play hard-ass and insist on a few strange, hard-to-get toppings like papaya or crawfish.

Mmmm, sounded good. Maybe that pang in his gut wasn't guilt or regret, after all. Maybe it was plain old hunger.

Glancing down at the front of his cheese-dusted T-shirt, he picked up a doodle and popped it in his mouth, savoring the sharp flavor and massive, ongoing crunch as he chewed.

Hiding away from the world. Feeling sorry for himself. Couldn't take care of himself. Ha! He couldn't wait for his friends to figure out just how wrong they were.

In the meantime, he'd be just fine by himself.

He always was.

Row 5

One week later . . .

If ever there was something Grace *did not* want to do, this would be it.

She stood outside the door to Zack's apartment, trying to school her breathing, slow her pulse, and *not* either throw up or run away.

But she wouldn't—throw up *or* run away, that was.

The first because it was messy and undignified, and there was nowhere to do it properly in the otherwise empty hallway.

The second because it would be proof that she was nervous about what she was about to do—which she would admit to only under threat of death . . . or having the fat sucked out of her ass with a bendy straw and no anesthesia—and because she suspected her presence was truly needed.

Not *deserved*, but needed.

Her friends had been bugging her for weeks to check in on Zack. To talk to him. To do *something* in an attempt to draw him out of his apparent funk.

Oh, they'd been subtle and even creative about it,

but the pressure—and hints the size of cruise liners—had been there nonetheless.

Grace had done a pretty good job of ignoring them, too . . . until last Wednesday's Knit Wits meeting, when she'd discovered through Jenna and Ronnie that things had apparently gotten so bad with Zack that even his very best friends, Dylan and Gage, had given up on him. They'd recapped the guys' last visit, and each detail they'd shared had only made her stomach tighten and her heart sink lower than it had been before.

What they were saying, the man they were talking about, didn't sound like her Zack. Or the Zack formerly known as hers, at any rate.

The man she had been engaged to had always been the life of the party, with a zest for life sometimes hard to keep up with. An injury on the ice—no matter how serious—would barely have made a dent in that level of gusto. He would have followed doctors' instructions to the letter, plus some, and done whatever was necessary to heal, recover, and bounce back like a jai alai ball.

Hearing that he *wasn't* bouncing back, was sitting around like a slug, *stagnating* in his own desolation, was just enough to push her feelings about Zack and his post-accident condition from apathetic to concerned. She suspected that was her friends' goal in being so specific and dogged in their recounting of Dylan and Gage's confrontation with Zack the week before.

So here she was. Palms sweating, stomach churning, reluctance pouring through her veins like toxic waste.

She raised her hand to knock, determined to get in, check on him—maybe kick his butt to get him moving in the right direction, if need be—and get the hell out. But before her knuckles connected with the thick wooden panel, she realized that Zack might still be in bed.

It was only eight in the morning, and he'd never been much of a morning person to begin with. Plus, if Zack really was as depressed and withdrawn as everyone implied, there was a chance he spent most of his time in bed or asleep.

Even if he wasn't, he still had a badly damaged leg—one he *hadn't* been going to physical therapy for, the idiot—and was in no shape to rush around answering doors.

Letting her purse strap fall from her shoulder, she balanced the overstuffed bag on her knee and started digging. She *shouldn't* still have a key to Zack's apartment, but knew she did.

She'd used it to get in the night she'd discovered his infidelity and wanted to destroy him by destroying everything he owned. After recovering from the initial shock and feeling moderately regretful of her actions, she'd told her friends she flushed the key the same as she'd flushed the engagement ring he'd given her.

She hadn't, though. She'd kept it—just in case. After all, one never knew when their ex-fiancé might once again do something stupid or the "woman scorned" rage might rear its ugly head and need to be vented by throwing more of his clothes off the balcony.

The loose key was, of course, floating around at the very bottom of the oversized bag, beneath her own ring of keys, a pack of gum, container of Tic Tacs, and a couple of wadded-up tissues. And she, of course, located it only after rummaging around for fifteen minutes, searching through every inside and outside pocket, and removing just about every large item first.

Finally, though, she had it in hand and slipped it into the lock. As she turned it, and simultaneously turned the knob, she caught herself murmuring a short prayer beneath her breath that he hadn't also flipped the dead bolt or hooked the chain; otherwise she would end up banging on the door to wake him—and possibly a few of his neighbors—after all.

But just like the Zack she used to know, the current Zack hadn't bothered to secure his apartment past the automatic lock installed within the doorknob mechanism.

Stepping inside, she closed the door behind her on a soft click, then turned to take in the silent, shadowed space surrounding her. Large windows lined the far wall, letting muted, early morning light spill halfway across the oaken floorboards, but the rest of the apartment was empty and as dark as it could get at this hour of the day.

The coffee maker in the kitchen wasn't gurgling with fresh brew. There was no bread in the toaster, crisping to a golden brown. The TV wasn't on in the living room, and the water wasn't running in the bathroom.

It was eerily quiet when she was used to Zack's place always humming, always being filled with noise. A television or radio playing almost twenty-four hours a day. Friends sprawled on the sofa, eating, drinking, laughing, and more often than not playing armchair referee to one sporting event or another. A foosball battle taking place in one corner of the room, a video game in the other.

Setting her purse on the credenza just inside the door, she tiptoed through the house, inspecting things as she went along. He'd put a giant, flat-screen television—even bigger than his old one, which had been mammoth—on the wall where she'd stabbed one of his beloved hockey trophies through the plaster. She wondered if he'd bothered to patch the hole first, or just slapped up the expensive new toy and forgotten about it.

In general, the apartment was clean, which meant Magda was still coming in once or twice a week to pick up after him. But there were still clothes strewn about, still open bags of chips, empty snack wrappers, and dirty dishes littering the place. Enough to let her know he probably hadn't eaten a fruit or vegetable or anything outside of the junk food family in a good, long while.

Grace made her way to the bedroom, ignoring the wave of reluctance that swamped her, the tug of regret that pulled at her heart, and the hoard of memories her brain offered to let her relive.

No, thank you. Memories of other times she'd been in his room, in his bed, were something she definitely did not need. She didn't even want to think about the last time she'd been there, bawling her eyes out and cursing Zack for being a cheating, lying prick while systematically cutting all of the keepsakes in his professional scrapbooks into teeny, tiny pieces.

Not her finest moment, but it had felt damn good at the time.

The bedroom door was slightly ajar, but she didn't hear any signs of movement, so she pushed it open a little farther. Once again, darkness greeted her.

The blinds had been pulled to keep out even a hint of daylight, but she could still make out Zack's tall, broad frame lying diagonally across the bed.

He was on his stomach, naked but for a pair of plaid flannel boxer shorts, his hair a long, straggling blond mess. The sheets were twisted and bunched around him, but not covering much more than his feet.

A trickle of attraction, of desire, snaked through her bloodstream, warming her from the inside out and causing a familiar ache to settle low in her belly and between her legs.

She wasn't proud of it, but she'd missed him. God, the way they used to heat up those sheets together . . . It had made atomic bombs and spontaneous combustion look like the fizzling little sparks that came from a cheap plastic lighter when the flint wouldn't catch.

Or maybe, she thought, narrowing her eyes and re- minding herself of his infidelity, she missed men in general. She hadn't slept with anyone since breaking up with Zack, so it wasn't a stretch to realize she prob- ably just needed to get laid. She should find herself some hot, willing stud and ride him like a Kawasaki KX450F at Motorcross. (So some of Zack's sports fanat- icism had sunk in—sue her.)

Lord knew she'd had opportunities. There were guys at work who flirted with her, dropped hints that they wouldn't mind going home with her now that she was no longer attached to a professional hockey player who outweighed them by fifty pounds of pure muscle and would gleefully pummel them into human pan- cakes if they so much as looked at her cross-eyed. Maybe she should take one of them up on the offer.

And those weren't the only men sending out signals.

With a face as high-profile as hers—and frankly, a body that rocked, thank you very much—she was the recipient of long, lusty looks just about everywhere she went. She could crook a finger in the middle of Ninth Street and lead a string of drooling males straight into Lake Erie in the dead of winter, if she liked.

Whether she wanted straight-up, no-strings sex or another ring on her finger with the promise of forever, it wouldn't take much on her part to get them.

The problem was that ever since she'd kicked Zack to the curb, she couldn't seem to work up an interest in either of those things. Indiscriminate, anonymous sex didn't appeal—as fun as that might be, and as much as it would serve Zack right for cheating on her with God knew how many puck-bunny bimbos.

And she was in no hurry to jump into another serious relationship, either. As gun-shy as she was from Zack's betrayal, she might never again trust a man enough to get within six football fields of walking down the aisle.

But she wasn't here to rehash her relationship with Zack or bemoan her nonexistent relationships with other males of the species. She was here to kick a little sense into her jackass ex-fiancé so her friends would get off her back and stop trying to guilt her into caring how he spent his days or whether his knee was healing properly.

Flipping the wall switch just inside the bedroom door, she stalked across the plush eggshell carpeting and threw open the thick drapes hiding a set of French doors that led to the balcony. Sunlight that was growing brighter with each passing minute streamed through the floor-to-ceiling windowpanes and across the unmoving figure taking up three-fourths of the king-size mattress.

Okay, that didn't work quite as well as she'd expected. Used to be the merest hint of daylight would rouse Zack even from the deepest of sleeps. He might wake up growling like a lion, but he always woke up.

Moving closer to the bed and scanning the area around Zack, Grace noticed for the first time the open prescription bottle on the nightstand. A couple of stray pills rested on the oak tabletop beside a glass with about half an inch of amber liquid at the bottom.

She lifted the glass to her nose and sniffed, at the same time picking up the pill bottle to read the pharmacy label.

Nice. Mixing Vicodin with Jack Daniel's. Things were even worse than she'd thought.

Returning the loose pills to their bottle, she did a quick search of both nightstands and their drawers, the area surrounding the bed, and the bathroom medicine cabinet to see if she could find any more drugs—prescription or otherwise. Then she took the glass of whiskey and the pill bottle and headed back to the kitchen.

She pulled her cell phone from her purse, replacing it with the Vicodin, and hit the button to speed-dial Ronnie. Her friend answered on the third ring.

"I'm here, and you're right," Grace said without preamble. "He's a mess."

"What are you going to do?" Ronnie wanted to know. Given the background noises, she was obviously at work.

"I need the name and number of his orthopedic

surgeon so I can call and make an appointment. Do you think Dylan would have that information?"

Her friend hesitated for a second, but then answered, "I think so. At the very least, he'll probably remember who was in charge of Zack's case at the hospital. He could probably even call the team's coach and find out who Zack is supposed to be seeing about his knee."

"Good. Can you take care of that and call me right back? I think he should get in to see somebody today, if I can swing it."

"All right."

Again, the words were hesitant, and Grace rolled her eyes, tempted to slap her phone closed before Ronnie could start on the concerned friend/Twenty Questions routine.

"What?" she bit out instead. "Go ahead, whatever it is, just spit it out."

"Are you okay? Being there, I mean? How did Zack react when you showed up?"

"I'm fine. The sooner I can deal with this and be done with it, the better," she added flatly, "but I'm not going to have a nervous breakdown or throw any more of his belongings off the balcony, if that's what you're worried about."

At least not yet, and unless Zack really pissed her off.

"And he's still passed out in bed, so he doesn't even know I'm here."

A couple of seconds passed while her friend seemed to absorb that, then Ronnie said, "If you need anything, promise you'll let me know. I can be there in ten minutes, tops. Jenna, too . . . I'm sure she'd be happy to drop by and help you out if you needed it."

"If I need backup, you mean?" Grace asked, a hint of humor slipping into her tone and making her smile. "You guys should have thought of that before you started laying on the guilt-trip shit so thick. But I promise to send up smoke signals if I get into trouble, Cagney."

Ronnie chuckled. "Roger that, Lacey."

Who that left Jenna to be, Grace had no idea, but she hung up with her friend and moved on to the kitchen, where she dumped the last swallow of whiskey down the sink and stuck the glass in the otherwise empty dishwasher. She did a little search-and-destroy mission while she was in there, seeking out other sources of alcohol.

The open bottle of whiskey she emptied, then tossed in the recycle bin. The beer in the fridge she removed and stuffed to the back of a high cupboard shelf where Zack wouldn't be able to reach it with his injured leg, even if he tried. First chance she got, she'd pass it off to one of their friends who could put it to good use.

That taken care of, she headed back to the bedroom. No tiptoeing this time. This time, she wanted him to hear her.

But apparently it was going to take more than her heavy footsteps to wake him from whatever drug- and booze-induced stupor he was in. A marching band and foghorn blast, maybe.

"Hey," she said, leaning over and poking him in the bare shoulder.

God, he had a nice back. All smooth and broad,

with skin just begging to be stroked and occasionally scratched.

Her brows knit and her mouth turned down in a frown. Down, girl! she chastised herself. No thinking sexy thoughts about the bad man. She was here to whip him into shape, not whip herself into a frenzy of unrequited lust.

"Hey! Sleeping Beauty!" she called, more loudly this time.

Good Lord, was he even alive? she wondered crossly. He was clearly breathing, even letting out a snuffled snore from time to time.

Hmm. All right, time for the Nurse Betty routine.

Canting herself sideways over the bed again, she lifted one of his eyelids to study his pupil.

"Hey, Zack!" she tried in a near-shout.

Seriously, how he couldn't be plugging his ears or pulling a pillow over his head by now, she'd never know.

He gave a sudden short snort, startling her into dropping his eyelid and jumping back.

"Whata hellif gona?"

Which she took to mean, *What the hell is going on?*

"Don't wake up on my account," she told him blithely. "This is the first time you've ever brought me true pleasure in the bedroom."

He quirked a light blond brow—or tried to, at least. "Grace?"

It sounded like he had a mouthful of sawdust, but she understood him well enough to make out her own name.

"The one and only," she replied brightly.

"Grace," he breathed on a sigh. "You came back."

Row 6

Whoa. Note to self, Zack thought, while his brain pounded out a reggae beat inside his skull, *no more mixing pain pills with alcohol.*

It was the first time he'd ever done that, and only after spending the better part of the night praying for sleep to come.

His knee had hurt like a bitch all day, the Vicodin the doctor had prescribed not making a dent in the steady ache and sharp stabs of pain. He'd taken twice the recommended dose in half the recommended time period, but even that hadn't helped. So he'd resorted to a couple swallows from an old bottle of Jack he had left over from a long-ago bachelor party.

It had apparently done the trick, but now he was thinking it had done it a little too well. His knee still hurt—but then, didn't it always?—and he was suffering the mother of all hangovers for his trouble.

Oh, but that wasn't the best part.

No-ho, of course not. Because fate or karma or Jesus Christ Superstar—whatever the hell was out there fucking with his life like a Tinkertoy—couldn't be happy with making him feel like just ordinary crap. He had to pass through the Seven Levels of

Crap-related Crap first. So far, he felt as though he'd waded through about twenty feet of sewer water, a football field of knee-high cow patties, and a landfill full of dirty baby diapers.

But that still left four more delightful levels of abject misery, one of which apparently included saying something truly humiliating in front of the woman who'd kicked him into the shit pool to begin with.

God in heaven, he hoped he hadn't said it aloud. Please, God, Jesus, Buddha, Allah, and Bob's Big Boy, let that sad, pathetic, embarrassing *You came back* have been only in his head. A bad dream wrapping up what had started as a half-decent fantasy, and *not* something that had actually passed his lips to be heard by the one person who would take great joy in holding it over his head and rubbing his nose in it for the rest of his natural life.

There was a chance—prosciutto thin though it might be—that the unintentional utterance *had* only been in his head.

You came back. What the fuck could he have been thinking?

Dropping his head until his chin touched his chest, he let the pulsing heat of the shower drum the nape of his neck and slide down his back.

A noise from the other side of the closed bathroom door jarred him from his lingering lethargy, and he sat up straighter, reaching for the soap. He hadn't bathed in a while, and was sure he smelled none too fresh, so he spent a little extra time sudsing up.

Truth was, his knee was thoroughly fucked up, which made getting in and out of the tub nearly impossible. On top of that, when he did make it inside to shower, he had to sit on a plastic stool like some ninety-year-old invalid. He'd rather stand out on the balcony buck naked during a thunderstorm than use the freaking thing, but the current temperatures didn't exactly make that an appealing prospect, and no rain was expected for at least another month or two.

If Grace hadn't prodded him with her damn bony fingertips and elbow, he wouldn't have bothered getting out of bed, let alone climbing into the shower. But she'd insisted, promising him a cup of hot coffee as soon as he was finished, and using her body as a crutch to help him hobble to the bathroom.

A body that was wrapped almost head to toe in some soft, pink velourish stuff. No one could pull off pink quite the way she did, even if it was of the track-suit variety.

The fact that she had JUICY stamped across her ass didn't help matters, either.

Having her see him like this . . . not just injured and more under the influence of booze and meds than he'd have liked, but *helpless* and *needy* and *pitiable* . . . made him feel even worse than the throbbing in his head and queasiness in his stomach. It made him feel like less of a man.

And given how much less of a man he'd felt the past several weeks, that was really saying something. He was surprised someone from the Man Club hadn't come by to revoke his dick and balls.

A tap on the door made him jerk in surprise, and he dug in even harder with the bar of soap.

"You okay in there?" Grace called through the closed wooden panel.

Yeah, hunky-freakin'-dory. Just a grown man, in

the prime of life, sitting on an invalid stool to wash his ass crack.

In answer to her question, he couldn't work up much more than an annoyed grunt, but he knew she heard him because she responded brightly, "All right, let me know if you need anything. Your coffee is ready when you are."

The promise of caffeine—and possibly a bottle or two of aspirin—spurred him to speed up his motions. He finished lathering up, then pushed himself none too easily to his feet to grab the handheld shower head. He had to sit back down to rinse, but got the job done in record time before he leaned forward to shut off the water.

Grabbing the fluffy white towel from the toilet lid where Grace had set it for easy access, he rubbed it over his hair, then started to dry the rest of his body. Before he got past his chest, another knock sounded, and the bathroom door swung open.

"I heard the water stop, and figured you could use a hand," Grace informed him, moving closer.

To her credit, she kept her attention locked on his face. If their positions had been reversed, he didn't think he'd have the same self-control. If she'd been sitting in the tub, naked but for a bunched towel covering her sweet spot, he'd have been looking everywhere *but* at her face—and imagining what was under the towel, to boot.

Of course, he knew what was under that hypothetical towel, the same as she knew what was under the one he was currently holding over his crotch.

Not a good direction for his thoughts to be traveling right now. Imagining her naked, remembering the things they used to do together both with and without clothes on, was a one-way ticket to a woody he definitely didn't need at the moment.

Bad enough that getting turned on when he had nothing more than a bath towel to hide it would make the condition kind of hard to miss, but getting turned on in front of his ex-fiancée was akin to smearing honey on his junk and walking into grizzly territory.

No, thank you. That kind of ridicule and degradation he could do without.

"Swing around, and I'll help you out," she said, stepping forward.

And speaking of humiliating experiences, his inner Bob Barker announced in the same booming voice he might use to invite someone to "Come on down!"

All the same, Zack swiveled around on the stool, carefully lifting his injured leg up and over the edge of the tub, putting weight only on his good leg as Grace gripped his elbows and helped hoist him upright.

The towel fell to the floor, and she bent to retrieve it, wrapping it around his waist herself, then tucking in the ends while he kept his hands firmly on her shoulders. She didn't seem the least uncomfortable with his brief nudity or the need to assist him with basic activities he should have been able to manage on his own.

Unfortunately, he couldn't say the same. This whole bloody mess made him uncomfortable. From needing help to get around his own apartment, to having his name and photo splashed across the front pages of newspapers and magazines, along with headlines speculating on whether he'd be back in his position as goalie for the Rockets by next season or was becoming Cleveland's version of Howard Hughes.

The Howard Hughes thing hadn't actually sounded like such a bad deal until about . . . oh, eight thirty-five this morning. Something about having his ex carry him to the bathroom and help him wash his balls just took all the fun out of becoming an eccentric recluse.

"You could use a shave, too," Grace decided suddenly. She pointed to the closed toilet lid and gestured for him to have a seat.

He followed the direction of her finger, but stayed where he was, balanced none too steadily on his right leg.

When he didn't move, she cocked her head, a question clear in her eyes. "What?"

"I don't think so," he replied tightly. "It's winter. A beard will keep me warm."

Her lips pursed a moment before one corner turned up in a grin. "What's the matter—don't you trust me so close to your throat with a razor blade?"

His own mouth twisted. "I don't trust you anywhere near me with anything sharper than a ball of yarn."

As soon as the words were out, he muttered a silent curse. Knitting references probably weren't the smartest for him to be making. Not if he wanted to keep his little hobby a secret. And he *especially* wanted to keep it a secret from *her.*

One blond brow quirked up over her robin's-egg-blue eyes. "You'd be surprised how much damage I can do with an innocent ball of yarn."

Of that, he had no doubt. He was also intimately familiar with her talents with a Louisville Slugger, a pair of scissors, a lit match, and the most dangerous weapon of all—her dagger-sharp tongue.

"But I promise not to use your razor for evil, only for good. After all, if I'd come over here to hurt you, do you really think I'd have helped you get cleaned up first?" Her right brow lowered only to have the left rise in equal mockery. "If that had been my intention, I'd have done it while you were still unconscious."

Pressing against his arm and chest, she maneuvered him exactly where she wanted him to go and got him lowered onto the commode.

"You were completely conked out when I got here," she said, moving around the bathroom to collect what she needed. And she knew where everything was because she used to live here, too—at least part of the time.

"It took *a lot* to wake you," she continued, shaking the can of shaving cream and squeezing the trigger to fill her palm with a heavy dollop of the thick white foam.

Then she began to spread it over his face. Cheeks, chin, above his lip. He let his head fall back and closed his eyes, pretending he didn't want to see the razor in her hand, didn't want to see her using such a sharp implement so close to his jugular.

The truth, though, was that it felt too damn good. It had been months—hell, going on close to a year—since she or any other woman had touched him. The most human contact he'd had since Grace walked out on him was the occasional slap on the back from his friends or a very manly group hug from his teammates when they won a game, complete with uniforms, helmets, sticks, and about ten inches of padding between each man.

Oh, and of course the wonderful poking and prodding from the doctors and surgeons after his injury.

But when it came to gentle caresses or sensual strokes of his skin . . . he'd pretty much been flying solo lately.

He wondered how Grace would react if she knew he hadn't been with another woman since she walked out on him. She would probably roll her eyes and give an unladylike snort. She didn't believe he hadn't been with another woman *while* they were engaged, why should she believe he hadn't been with one since their breakup?

It was true, though, on both counts. Which probably explained why even the sensation of metal blades scraping along his jawline—combined with the soft press of her fingers on the other side of his face—turned his blood warm and sent it flowing in a decidedly southbound direction.

"So if you didn't come over to smother me in my sleep or give me a Colombian necktie, why are you here?"

She hesitated ever so slightly in a downward stroke across his cheek. "Your friends were worried about you," she offered softly.

He arched a brow. "And they sent *you*?" His voice went up at the end in surprise, even though he had to mumble the question because she'd moved to his upper lip.

Wasn't that a bit like sending the fox into the henhouse to check on the chickens? The snake into the sparrow's nest to check on the eggs? Jason Voorhees into the cabin to check on the campers?

"Only as a last resort. They all did what they could

to pry your ass out of this apartment, but that same thick skull that kept you from getting brain damage when your head hit the ice is apparently making it hard for any sense to get through." She waited a beat, tapping the razor on the edge of the sink to dislodge a buildup of shaving cream before adding, "They thought I might have more success getting through to you . . . maybe because I'm less inclined to let you get away with feeling sorry for yourself, and more inclined to inflict physical damage, if necessary."

Of that, he had no doubt. Despite the damage she'd caused to his belongings when she'd gone off the deep end, he actually counted himself lucky to have been in another city at the time.

When he remembered that tumultuous week, he rolled his eyes at the notion that his friends had sent her over to motivate him out of his slump. Luckily, his lids were once again closed, so she couldn't see the gesture. No sense pushing her buttons while he was at her mercy and she was still holding a sharp object uncomfortably close to his throat.

"And you think a shower and shave are going to do the trick?" he asked.

He heard the click of the razor against the sink again, followed by running water. A second later, something hot and wet hit his face.

He opened his eyes to meet her gaze while she stroked his newly shaven cheeks and wiped away stray remnants of shaving cream.

"Getting cleaned up is just the beginning," she told him, tossing the washcloth into the sink basin when she was finished and opening the medicine cabinet to remove a dark brown bottle of Sexy Men aftershave.

His muscles tensed at the sight of it. When they'd first met, he'd been using some cheap, ordinary brand of aftershave and cologne. The stuff you can pick up at Wal-Mart or Rite Aid. He didn't even have a favorite, just used whatever was on sale or grabbed his attention when the old stuff ran out. Brut, Aspen, Old Spice . . . and yes, even Aqua Velva. They all smelled pretty much the same to him.

Then he'd met Grace. No, not just met her, fallen balls over brains in love with her. So when she'd declared that his current brand didn't suit him—he thought he might have been using a mix of Stetson and Old English at the time—he'd been more than happy to let her pick something new. Hell, he'd been as flexible as a Gumby doll, letting her choose his clothes, his shoes, his cologne, his hairstyle.

Not that he'd minded. He'd liked her choices, and hadn't even known some of the stuff existed until she'd introduced him to it.

And if having him smell like a rain forest, pine cone, or ocean breeze turned her on, then he'd been all for it.

She'd had him try Angel Ice, Cool Water, Chrome, Dirty English (which had spurred so many jokes, they'd actually come up with a new sexual position to go with the name), Euphoria, and a few more. He hadn't noticed much difference between them, and only remembered some of the names because the bottles had cluttered the vanity for months on end.

Finally, she'd narrowed it down to the two she liked best—Fahrenheit and Sexy Men. Frankly, he thought the name Fahrenheit sounded more manly than Sexy

Men, but whatever revved her engine was a-otay with him.

She sprinkled a few drops into her palm, then rubbed her hands together before touching them to his cheeks, just the way she used to when they were together. Not every time he shaved, but some of them.

The sweet but musky fragrance tickled his nose and brought back a kaleidoscope of memories—all with Grace at their center, and most revolving around making love to her. They'd done it more than once in this bathroom, against this very countertop.

Something he *didn't* need to be thinking about right now. Not if he wanted to keep from popping a tent under the towel covering his waist and making her think he was either A.) interested in starting up with her again, or B.) he was so hard up, he got turned on by any woman who happened to brush up against him—even one who'd wrecked his ride and stolen his dog.

Locking his jaw and curling his hands into fists, he chastised himself. *Get your big head back in the game, Hoolihan, and your little head off your ex.*

"What do you mean, the shave and shower are only the beginning?" he asked, recalling her earlier remark and suddenly being clear-minded enough to wonder about it.

"You've spent long enough holed up by yourself in this apartment, and enough time ignoring your doctors' orders."

He scowled, brows and mouth drawing down at the direction he suspected this was going. "What business is it of yours?"

"None whatsoever. Not anymore," she replied flippantly, stepping away from him to wash the aftershave from her hands and put away the items she'd used to get him looking a bit less like Grizzly Adams. "Except that your friends seem to think that if I don't sweep in to save you, you're going to turn into some pathetic, housebound slob or end up doing yourself in with the sharp end of a Triscuit."

Without turning her head, she cut her gaze to him, her blue eyes glittering with more than a touch of concern. "You weren't planning anything like that, were you?"

"Suicide by snack cracker? Wasn't part of my upcoming agenda, no." He raised a brow. "So what do they think you're going to do—sweep in with your sunny disposition and turn my world into rainbows and lollipops?"

She chuckled, proving that at least she hadn't lost her sense of humor to all the bile and vitriol that had come to the surface last summer.

"Doubtful. They probably expect me to stick pins in your eyes and set your bedclothes on fire. But they're desperate enough that I guess they're willing to try anything. Or at least look the other way while I whip you into shape."

"No whips," he deadpanned. "I wasn't into that when we were together, and I'm not into it now."

Hitching a hip against the vanity, she murmured, "I don't know. I still say that with enough pleasure thrown into the mix, you can learn to enjoy anything."

Then she pushed herself away from the sink and slapped her hands together, rubbing them as though in anticipation of something truly delectable. "But you're in no condition to fight me, regardless of how I decide to handle your rehabilitation, are you? You're pretty much at my mercy."

Leaning in, she pressed her lips to his ear, her cheek brushing his while her warm breath danced across his skin. He tensed, fighting the shiver that threatened to climb his spine and break out over the rest of his body.

"Be afraid," she whispered. "Be very afraid."

And then she straightened as though she hadn't just delivered a veiled threat. "Now come on. Time to get dressed and get some breakfast before we have to leave."

"Leave?" he asked, letting her drape his arm across her shoulders and hoist him to his feet like he was a child.

Or an invalid.

Or a sack of rotten potatoes.

"Where are we going?"

"*You* have an appointment with your orthopedic surgeon."

Reaching the bed, she turned him around and sat him down.

"I don't think so," he shot back.

"I do."

She moved around in front of his row of dresser drawers for a couple minutes before returning to drop a pile of clothes at his side.

"This isn't up for debate, Zack," she told him in her best no-nonsense tone, hands cocked firmly on hips. "You're going if I have to hit you over the head with a lamp and drag you there by the hair. So you can either dress yourself and go along under your own steam like a man, or you can be a big baby and make me force you to do the right thing. But know this: if I have to do the hit-and-haul thing, you'll wake up looking like a drag queen, and I'll make sure the press has plenty of opportunity to snap your photo."

She stepped away, heading for the closet and rooting around on the floor. "I'm thinking a bright purple bustier, fishnet stockings, and a long black Catherine Zeta-Jones wig."

Turning to face him, she held up a pair of well-worn Nikes. His favorites because they were Rockets blue and red.

"So what's it going to be?" she asked. "Are you going to put on your big boy shoes all by yourself, or do I need to go out and find a pair of size twelve platform stilettos to go with your leather miniskirt?"

Row 7

She hadn't meant to stick around. When Grace had agreed to pop in and check on Zack, her intention had been to do just that—pop in and pop right back out.

She'd forgotten how easy it was to be around him. How comfortable, even with the residual anger and suspicion of his infidelity bubbling at the back of her mind.

Shaving his face herself instead of simply handing him the razor and walking away had probably been a mistake. Maybe not her first one, or the biggest one she'd made that day, but a mistake all the same. It had been entirely too intimate an act, stirring up entirely too many memories of their time together.

The good times, when she'd loved touching him and thought they were going to live happily ever after.

Then they'd gone to his appointment, and her determination to exit stage left at the first opportunity had taken yet another hit. According to the doctor, Zack's recent sloth hadn't caused any additional damage to his injured knee, but he hadn't done himself any favors, either. He was behind on his physical therapy, and it was going to take weeks, possibly months, of intense effort to get him back up to speed. To undo

the atrophy and buildup of scar tissue his couch potato habits had created.

The surgeon had given her a stack of papers outlin-
ing exercises Zack could do at home . . . and that she
could help him with. And his receptionist had set up a
physical therapy schedule at a nearby sports medicine
and rehabilitation facility on Grace's promise that she
would see he attended every single session.

Apparently, they'd gone through all of this with
Zack once before, and had very little faith he'd follow
through this time, either. Grace's presence, though,
had encouraged them to give him another chance.

A couple of the nurses had watched them like a cat
eyeing a goldfish bowl, and she had no doubt that as
soon as they'd left, the gossip had begun.

Were Zack "Hot Legs" Hoolihan and "Amazing"
Grace Fisher back together? Had he really cheated on
her, and if so, had she forgiven him?

If she weren't so busy packing, she would take a
good ten or fifteen minutes to bang her head against
the wall and wonder *why, why, why* her? And *how, how,
how* did she get herself into these things?

But then, she knew how and why, didn't she? Because she had two fickle, devious friends with no com-
punction about throwing her to the wolves. Or at least
in the general vicinity of the wolf.

Grabbing the phone from the bedside table, she
continued pulling bras and underwear, socks, slacks,
and tops from her drawers and stuffing them into an
overnight bag with one hand while dialing Ronnie's
number with the other. The call went to voice mail,
but she didn't let that put a damper on her plans.

"Hey, Ronnie, it's Grace. Just wanted to let you

know that Zack's appointment went well. He has a lot of catching up to do with therapy and the like before he gets full use of his leg back, but the doctor is optimistic. Of course, someone needs to be there to make sure he gets to all of his appointments and does all of his at-home exercises. And who do you think that person might be, hmm? That's right—me! So I just called to *thank you*"—she laced the words with so much disdain, the plastic phone shell nearly melted around her hand—"for getting me into this. And to warn you that if I end up killing Zack, I'll expect you to bail me out of jail. Or if Zack kills me, I'll expect you to cry at my funeral. Really hard. We're talking full-out, inhale-your-tissue, on-the-verge-of-collapse sobbing, complete with a guilt-induced mental breakdown afterward, got it?"

With that, she hung up and punched in Jenna's number, leaving much the same message on *her* voice mail as she moved into the bathroom to collect toiletries.

Nice to know that her two *supposed* best friends were unavailable while she was in the middle of a crisis. She would definitely remember this the next time one of *them* needed something—like a kidney transplant or ride to the airport. As far as she was concerned, unless Jenna and Ronnie found a way to redeem themselves and make her life less of a nightmare right quick, both her car *and* her kidneys were officially off-limits.

Once she had everything she thought she might need for the next few days, she zipped the overnight bag, returned the phone to its charger, and headed into the living room.

Muffin was stretched out full-length along the couch,

snoring gently and leaving a waffle-sized wet spot beneath his right jowl.

"Hey, Muffin! Come here, sweetie."

The giant brown and white Saint Bernard first perked up one ear, then slowly lifted his head. Grace slapped her thigh, and Muffin heaved himself into a sitting position, then dropped his two massive front paws to the carpeted floor, letting his back legs slide off the sofa cushions as he started in her direction.

Poor Muffin might be a hundred and fifty pounds of muscle, but none of it was particularly energetic. Sometimes she thought she could just buy a beanbag chair, stick it in the corner, and get the same amount of activity as she did with Zack's former dog. But then, a beanbag chair wouldn't lick her face, keep her warm on cold winter nights, or inhale leftovers so she didn't have to eat them herself.

"Good boy." Kneeling down so they were eye to eye, she hugged Muffin's neck and gave his furry cheek a big kiss. He returned the gesture with a slobbery lick of her ear.

She giggled at the tickle his tongue caused, then quickly lifted a hand to check her earrings. She'd learned the hard way that kibble and leftovers weren't the only thing Muffin was fond of eating—and that it was not only zero fun, but a thousand percent disgusting to search through Saint Bernard droppings for a missing two-carat diamond stud. *Yerk.*

"We're taking a trip, baby," she informed the panting ball of fur. "Now, I don't want you to get your hopes up. We aren't going to the park or the lake."

Two of his very favorite destinations. One because there were usually other dogs for him to either play with or terrorize, the other because he loved to pretend he was a fish, then climb out and shake half of Lake Erie onto the shore.

Another Muffin-related lesson she'd figured out the hard way—never stand within six feet of a wet Saint Bernard. And never wear anything even remotely considered "nice clothes" while taking one for a walk.

There was now a section of Grace's closet dedicated to Muffin-wear. Grungy jeans and T-shirts, shoes and jackets that could be tossed in the washer or thrown in the trash, depending on the amount of canine destruction leveled upon them.

"You'll remember this place, though," she continued, reaching for a pale pink doggie sweater and fitting it over Muffin's head. She'd knit it herself—along with several more in varying colors—because there was nothing more harsh than Cleveland in winter, and she didn't want her sweet little boy getting chilly.

Never mind that Saint Bernards were cold-weather dogs. The ones that searched out missing hikers in ten feet of snow and brought them brandy in those cute miniature barrels around their necks. Those kinds of endeavors might be fine for other people's dogs, but *not* for hers.

"Lift," she said, and Muffin obediently raised his right front paw, letting her slip on one of the four hand-knit slippers that matched his adorable sweater.

"We're going back to your daddy's apartment," she said as she helped him step into the remaining three slippers, "but I don't want you to get your hopes up. It's okay if you love him and play with him and let him rub your belly, but we won't be staying forever, so don't get too used to having him around. We're only going over there at all because your daddy is a big, fat idiot who can't get himself to the doctor to get his leg fixed. So we have to cook for him and clean for him and haul his . . . *butt* around until he's back on his feet."

Next she circled his neck with a collar about an inch wide and studded with sparkling faux diamonds that spelled out his name in fancy, flirty script. "You'll help me do that, won't you? Won't you, my big boy?"

In response, Muffin's tongue lolled out to sweep a damp path up the full length of her face. A year ago, something like that would have sent her into a tizzy. She'd have bitched at Zack about his disgusting, slobbery dog, then raced to the bathroom to fix her makeup.

Now . . . well, a little puppy saliva and streaked mascara just didn't register on her diva-o-meter anymore. She had more important things to think about. Not to mention a deep and abiding love for the source of that slobber.

"All right," she said, pushing to her feet. "Are you ready?"

Muffin wagged his tail, not just ready, but raring to go. He loved walks, even in the dead of winter. Loved it even more when Grace put on her sweats and took him running.

Alas, there would be no running today. Not unless Zack drove her crazy within the first ten minutes of their forced recohabitation and she ran screaming from his apartment. In that case, though, she probably wouldn't just be jogging with the dog, but racing for the nearest intersection to throw herself in front of a bus.

Clicking a turquoise leash with black paw prints along its length to Muffin's collar, she shrugged into her own long, bone-colored woolen coat, picked up her overnight bag, and said, "Let's go, then."

Zack was slouched on the sofa with his leg propped up on the coffee table, slowly working on more afghan squares and watching *One Life to Live* when he heard a key turning in the lock of the front door.

At first he froze, wondering who it could be. Then he remembered that no matter who might be breaking in or letting themselves into his apartment in the middle of the afternoon, he didn't want them to catch him knitting. So he stuffed his needles and yarn down between the cushions of the couch, making sure everything was completely hidden before folding his arms over his chest, tucking his chin, and staring at the television screen as though that's *all* he'd been doing since Grace dropped him off and left him to his own devices a few hours before.

A second later, the door burst open and a blur of pink and brown and white filled his peripheral vision. He turned his head to get a better look and found the brown and pink portion of the blur barreling toward him.

The blur barked, and he had a moment to breathe "Bruiser" in disbelief before it launched itself at him. A hundred and fifty pounds hitting him square in the chest didn't feel great, but even the twist to his leg as he braced to absorb the impact was worth it to have his face bathed in sloppy kisses.

God, he'd missed this damn dog, he thought as he ruffled the Saint's fur and tried not to drown in doggie drool.

He pretended he didn't; acted like it hadn't bothered him when Grace ran off with Bruiser and refused to give him back. Hey, not having a dog around, depending on him for food and walks, was a good thing, right? Gave him more time to stay out rousing and carousing.

Except that he didn't stay out till all hours rousing and carousing. He'd fucked up his knee five ways from Sunday, which left him stuck in his apartment twenty-four hours a day, with no one to keep him company but fictitious television characters.

He sure could have used a little canine companionship this past month, that was for sure.

"Bruiser," he said again. "Damn, it's good to see you."

Bruiser barked again, then turned himself around and plopped his behind on the cushion next to Zack, tail thumping methodically against the leather.

Zack ran his hand down the dog's back, finally noticing that his dog . . . his big, meaty, *male* dog . . . was dressed in some frilly pink froufrou outfit, complete with diamond-studded collar and— Good God, were those *booties* on his feet?

"What the hell are you wearing?" he asked aloud, the very sight an offense to his masculine sensibilities.

"That's his pink sweater-and-slipper set. Do you like it?"

Zack craned his neck to glance over the back of the sofa. Grace stood on just this side of the kitchen, her hands resting lightly on her slim hips, an innocent smile playing along her lips.

Any other time, he might have taken note that she'd changed from her earlier running outfit into a pair of snug, low-cut jeans and short-waisted, long-sleeved cotton top in olive green that hugged her spectacular figure in all the right places.

Any other time. But at the moment, the only thing he could focus on was the fact that . . .

"He's wearing *pink,* for Christ's sake."

"So? It's my favorite color, he likes them, and they keep him warm in the winter."

A couple reusable canvas totes sat on the counter behind her, and she turned to begin removing items. Groceries, he saw, as she moved around putting things in the cupboards and refrigerator. Healthy groceries, like juice and bananas and salad fixings.

Great.

"He's a Saint Bernard. He doesn't need to be kept warm during the winter. His job is to keep *others* warm during the winter."

She shook her head, sending her loose blond hair swishing around her face as she reached up to slide a box of crackers onto a top shelf. The motion lifted her shirt and flashed him a luscious strip of pale bare skin. For a moment, his mouth went dry and his eyes locked on her midriff.

"That's a barbaric way to think about such a sweet baby," she corrected him. "Besides, the salt and gravel used to treat icy streets and sidewalks is horrible for the pads of animals' feet. It burns and cuts and can cause real damage. You wouldn't want Muffin to get hurt just going on walkies, would you?"

When Grace lowered herself from on tiptoe and her shirt fell back into place, Zack's brain seemed to start functioning again. He replayed what he thought he'd heard her say and blinked. Once, twice, again.

He wasn't sure what was tripping him up more. Her referring to Bruiser as a *sweet baby* when she never used to have a kind word to say about him; the fact that she'd mistakenly called him "Muffin"; or her use of the term *walkies*.

None of it sounded like the Grace he used to know, and he found himself replaying the words over and over in his mind, trying to decide where his side of the argument should start.

Zack faced forward again to keep from getting a kink in his neck, and Bruiser laid his head on his thigh, giving a soft snuffle that caused the big flaps of his upper lips to flutter.

"First of all, his name is Bruiser, not Muffin," he called over his shoulder while he rubbed the dog's head, deciding to address her points from most to least important.

"Second, his feet and every other part of him were just fine when I had him and was taking him out for walks." He stressed the word *walks* just slightly to let her know no respectable parent of a Saint Bernard called them "walkies."

"And third, what the hell happened? You used to hate my dog."

Coming away from the kitchen, Grace rounded the couch from the side farthest from him and sat down on the other end of Bruiser's long, stretched-out pile of fur. Her hands automatically went to the dog's nearest foot and removed one of the pink booties.

"First," she said, moving to the next, "his name *used to be* Bruiser. Now it's Muffin. Second, just because he never required medical attention after you took him for winter walkies doesn't mean you were taking proper care of his paws. Do you have any idea how many moisturizing treatments it took to get rid of his sandpaper skin?"

All four booties were off now and piled on the coffee table, so she reached forward to unbutton the straps that ran under Bruiser's belly to loosen and remove the pussy-pink sweater entirely.

That was something he hadn't tried yet with his knitting—buttonholes. Maybe he should find a pattern and make a dog sweater of his own for *Bruiser* in a color that wouldn't turn his dog gay. Green or black or gray. Or maybe Rockets blue and red. Now *that* would be a manly dog sweater!

After folding the girlie pink sweater and laying it beside the even more girlie booties, Grace leaned back and ran the long, manicured fingers of her left hand through Bruiser's thick brown fur. She didn't even seem to mind that hair was getting on her clothes, something that would have annoyed her to no end a year or so ago.

"And third," she continued, "I never *hated* Muffin, I just didn't understand him. Now I realize what a sweet boy he is, so don't get any ideas about keeping him at the end of this . . ." She waved a hand dismissively in the air. "Whatever this is. I'm here to help you get around and recover from your injury, but after that, I'm going home and I'm taking my dog with me."

"He's *my* dog," Zack retaliated, "and you damn well know it. I had him before we even met. I have the adoption papers to prove it. You *stole* him from me when you got your panties in a twist, and are lucky I didn't decide to call the cops and have your butt tossed in jail."

Over a now snoring Saint Bernard, her eyes narrowed and he noticed the almost imperceptible fisting of her hand in the dog's thick coat.

"Do you really want to go there, Zack?" she asked quietly.

He knew from experience that the low tone of her voice was deceptive. It was like the calm before the storm, and if he answered incorrectly . . . if he decided that he did, indeed, want to "go there" . . . then he could very well be in for the fight of his life.

And in fact, he didn't want to go there. He didn't want to dredge up the tired old infidelity argument. He didn't want to hear any more of her accusations or waste his breath denying them. Whatever she believed, he wasn't going to change her mind at this late date. Better to let the subject drop, at least for now.

He had time. It wasn't like he could jump up and run off with his dog, even if he wanted to. Not with his knee in this kind of shape.

But if Grace was going to be around for a while, and Bruiser was going to be with her, then there was a chance he could come up with some sort of wicked, devious dog-napping plan of his own. Maybe he could even rope Dylan and Gage into becoming accomplices.

"No, I guess I don't," he told her, even as his mind was filtering through possible scenarios that would get his dog back to him for good.

For a second, Grace merely stared at him. He wondered if she'd been expecting a fight, gearing up for it, and it amused him a bit to have taken the wind out of her sails.

Taking a deep breath, she nodded. "Good. Then how about telling me what you want for dinner."

"Pizza," he said without bothering to think about it.

Her nose wrinkled. "I have a feeling you've been living on pizza and assorted other garbage long enough.

Time to get healthy. Muffin and I stopped for groceries on the way over and picked up some foods that are actually good for you."

Releasing her grip on *Bruiser*—God, he hated hearing her call him "Muffin"—she pushed up from the sofa and got to her feet. "We'll start out slow, though. I wouldn't want your body to go into shock or anything."

She smiled at her own joke. He smirked. *Ha ha, very funny.*

"How does salmon and asparagus sound?"

Actually, not half bad. He loved seafood, but was too lazy to fix it for himself. And lately, he couldn't stand long enough to fix himself a bowl of cereal, let alone a decent meal.

But for her benefit, he shrugged a shoulder and blandly replied, "Fine."

She inclined her head ever so slightly, tugged the hem of her top down to meet the low waist of her faded jeans, and turned to saunter back to the kitchen.

This time, Zack risked a crick in his neck to watch her go. He couldn't help it; he was a man, after all. And Grace always had looked as good going as she had coming.

Once she'd disappeared from view and he started to hear the telltale signs of dinner prep, he twisted back around. The TV was still on, but sometime during his showdown with Graoo, *One Life to Live* had ended and *General Hospital* had begun.

Shit. He wondered if Grace had noticed what he'd been watching when she arrived. He hoped not. But then, he could always claim he'd been flipping channels when she'd barged in and interrupted him, right?

Grabbing the remote, he flipped automatically to ESPN. There was auto racing on, which he didn't particularly care for, but at least it sounded more macho than the ongoing melodrama of Port Charles.

On his lap, Bruiser shifted slightly and let out a snuffle. Zack glanced down, continuing to knead the dog's ruff.

"What do you think, buddy?" he asked, leaning down to whisper in the Saint's ear. "Should we let her stick around a while?"

Bruiser's chest expanded as he inhaled a deep breath, which set his nose to twitching. Zack took a whiff of his own, already smelling a hint of grilled fish and other delectable scents. His stomach growled, and he suddenly realized how starved he'd been for real food.

It didn't hurt, either, that a beautiful woman was in his kitchen cooking it up for him. Insane ex or not, he could just imagine Grace gliding from sink to counter to stove, her slim fingers peeling potatoes and chopping vegetables, her lips pursed as she hummed a little tune to keep herself company.

"Yeah," he said, as though the dog had answered his earlier question and they were in agreement on the subject. "But just until after dinner, then we'll have to reevaluate."

Row 8

On Monday, they had grilled salmon and asparagus spears in a garlic butter sauce.

Tuesday and Wednesday it was pot roast, complete with carrots, onions, and those little baby potatoes he loved.

Thursday, she put together a lasagna that lasted through the weekend and would have made all of Italy weep in envy.

After weighing everything else Grace put him through that week against the same number of incredible, out-of-this-world meals, Zack decided it was totally worth it.

Being awakened at the butt crack of dawn every morning to get dressed and take Bruiser/Muffin for a walk . . . Well, she and the dog walked while pushing him in his wheelchair, injured leg sticking out in front of them like a divining rod. But she insisted that the fresh air would do him good, and if *she* had to wake up early for "walkies" . . . a word that still made his molars grind together . . . after exhausting herself taking care of him the rest of the day, then he could get up and go along to keep them company.

Not exactly something he would have expected

from the woman who'd trashed his life and threatened to have him castrated only a year before if he ever came near her again.

Being dragged to some sort of medical appointment or another every single day . . . She made him go to physical therapy three times a week, and to checkups with the doctors in between.

Last but not least, being pummeled twice a day . . . Normally, he'd be all kinds of agreeable to having a beautiful woman touching him. But Grace made it clear that just because she had to touch him during his exercises to get him walking again, she didn't have to enjoy it.

And she was none too gentle with him, either. After inviting him to step out of his pants and lie down on the bed—an invitation most men would be happy to accept—she would climb up beside him . . . and proceed to crank his leg up, down, left, right, forward, back.

Oh, she claimed to be helping him. Assured him that everything she did was prescribed by his doctors and outlined in the stack of photocopies they'd given her. But since he had yet to get a good look at those diagrams, he wasn't sure he believed her.

The problem was, he *was* feeling better.

With the amount of food she was shoveling into him, he didn't think it was possible to lose weight, but according to his doctors, he'd already started to shed a few pounds. Must be the difference between broccoli calories and Doritos calories. Though he still preferred the Doritos, truth be known.

And though he'd been so sore after his first visit to physical therapy and his first round of at-home exercises with Nurse Grace Ratched he'd had to double up on painkillers just to get through the night, he hadn't needed a pill in . . . going on three or four days now. His knee wasn't nearly as stiff as it had been, he had more range of motion, and he was beginning to need the wheelchair less and less. The doctors were even talking about switching him to crutches soon.

So now he was faced with the realization that though he'd brushed off his friends' concerns and protested that he was fine and needed no one—not them, not the doctors, not his fellow Rockets—he had maybe been a little off the mark. A week with Grace back in his life and he was feeling better than he had in a long, long time.

He wasn't sure what that said about his emotional foothold. Although things had been rocky for quite a while after she'd walked into that hotel room and found another woman in his bed, he really had thought he'd gotten over her, gotten on with his life. He'd come to terms with the fact that the woman he loved didn't trust him and didn't even love him enough to listen to his side of the story.

Then again, it might not be Grace at all. It could just as easily be Bruiser's presence that was raising his spirits and helping his body to heal.

He glanced down at the brown bag of fur currently drooling on his jean-clad thigh—sans the ridiculous rhinestone "Muffin" collar Grace put on him whenever they went out. He damn well loved this dog, and still planned to find some way of shanghaiing him back before Grace could run off with him again.

"You hungry?" she called from the kitchen, as though his impure thoughts about keeping his dog in his possession had psychically caught her attention.

"I could eat," he called back, envisioning a culinary concoction worthy of a five-star restaurant.

Two minutes later, Grace appeared at his elbow. She was wearing a pair of black leggings today that left absolutely nothing to the imagination. Her sunflower-yellow blouse fell off one shoulder and showed more than a hint of eye-catching cleavage. If he didn't know better, he would swear she was flaunting her amazing body to tempt him.

She flounced around the arm of the sofa and plopped down on one of the thick, overstuffed cushions before handing him a platter of raw celery sticks. He stared at the dull green vegetable strips like they were a pile of squirming worms.

Celery? She cooked like an Iron Chef, and her idea of a decent midday snack was *celery sticks*?

"Do we have any chips?" he asked, still holding the plate a good six inches away from him.

"Baked beet and turnip chips that I picked up at the nature store," she supplied, snatching a strip of celery for herself.

He made a face. Suddenly the stringy green strips didn't look so bad.

"Where's the remote?" she wanted to know. "There has to be something better on."

Yeah, *Guiding Light,* but he hadn't been able to catch up on his stories since Grace's arrival. He'd had to settle for half-hour sitcoms and repeats of old game shows like *Family Feud* and *Who Wants to Be a Millionaire?*

Searching the area, she finally found the remote tucked between Bruiser's rump and his thigh. He'd known it was there, but had kept his mouth shut out of fear for what she might decide to watch instead of 1967 episodes of *Let's Make a Deal*.

Her fingers brushed his leg as she retrieved the clicker, and a zap of electricity shot through the rest of his body. It settled low in his abdomen and groin, sending heat and a long-absent arousal rippling out into his torso and limbs.

Breathing carefully through flared nostrils and making a concerted effort *not* to glance in Grace's direction, he did his best to ignore the sensation. It was an involuntary response, that's all. Nothing to do with Grace and everything to do with the fact that he hadn't gotten laid in half a year. Which, frankly, was beginning to feel more like half a decade.

She was flipping channels, completely oblivious to the semi throbbing away behind his fly.

"Oh, I love this movie," she said, grabbing another handful of celery and wiggling around until she found a comfortable position in the corner of the couch.

Her bare feet were tucked close to her side, the remote resting on the arm of the sofa, well away from him, her free hand absently petting Bruiser's head. She chomped happily on the raw veggies, eyes glued to the television screen.

It took him a minute to figure out what they were watching, but when he did, he groaned.

"Come on," he complained. "You aren't going to make me watch this, are you?"

She shrugged a shoulder—the one without a stitch of fabric covering her smooth, porcelain skin. "Why not?"

The slope of that shoulder and the rise of full,

perky breast it led to might make his mouth water, but it didn't distract him from the subject at hand. "Because it's a sappy chick flick."

"It's a sweet romantic comedy," she corrected. "It's Julia Roberts and Hugh Grant. What could be better than that?"

"Chuck Norris kicking ass. Tom Cruise on some impossible mission. Even Harrison Ford being heroic and adventurous in some far-off country."

She chuckled, but shook her head all the same. "I'll stick with *Notting Hill,* thank you very much."

He rolled his eyes and let out a long-suffering sigh. "Why do you get to decide what we watch?"

"Because," she said . . . as though that were answer enough. Then she turned her head, tilted it to one side and batted her lashes. In a soft, superficial near-drawl, she added, "I'm just a girl, sitting next to a boy, telling him his opinion doesn't matter worth a hill of beans."

For a second, he simply stared at her, not knowing whether he should laugh at her droll wit, cry at her poor Julia Roberts impression, or be pissed off at her lack of interest in his entertainment wishes.

He settled on amusement, because she really was a candy-coated pill. "You do know you're not only slaughtering that line, but mixing your movie quotes, right?" he asked with a chuckle.

She shrugged again, sending the silky yellow material of her top sliding a few centimeters lower down her arm . . . and therefore lower on her chest. His gaze followed the slippage, but only for a split second. Before she noticed his distraction, he forced his attention back to her face.

"You get the gist, though, right?" she asked, taking

a bite of celery and chewing methodically. "We're watching *Notting Hill* now. Later, when I go to start dinner, you can watch whatever you want."

Another snap of her pearly white teeth at the tip of her veggie stick, followed by the widest shit-eating grin he'd ever seen. "Even your soaps."

His hand on Bruiser's back froze while the heart in his chest stopped pumping.

"What?" he nearly croaked.

She laughed, tossing her head back and sending her Goldilocks curls bouncing. "So when did you get hooked on the stories, Hot Legs? They don't seem like the sort of thing a big, brawny hockey player like yourself would care about."

Pulse still pounding a mile a minute at his temples, Zack weighed his options. He could play dumb and deny what she was saying, or he could come clean. She sounded pretty confident, though, which meant denial would only make him look more guilty—and give her more to rub in later.

"How did you find out?" he asked in a low voice.

Still chuckling, she said, "Your DVR is littered with them, they're circled every day in your *TV Guide,* and when I turned the TV on yesterday, it was already on the SoapNet channel. Way to cover your tracks, Columbo."

"Shit," Zack muttered, which only sent Grace into another spate of giggles.

"I can't believe it," she muttered on a gasping breath. "Big, bad Zack Hoolihan hooked on daytime television. If I didn't know better, I'd think you were turning into a girl." She turned teasing blue eyes on him and whee-dled, "You aren't turning into a girl, are you, Zackary?"

"Screw you." He knew it was mean and childish, but the words slipped out before he could stop them.

Rather than be offended or annoyed, she simply grinned and tossed back, "Not anymore."

That only made his frown deepen. Slouching down on the sofa, he crossed his arms over his chest and bit his tongue to keep from saying something even ruder.

"Oh, don't pout," she told him, uncurling her legs and leaning to reach across Bruiser's stretched-out length and punch him in the arm. "I won't tell anybody. Not unless . . . you know, you do something stupid to piss me off."

He rolled his eyes in her direction. "Oh, good. Because you're so hard to rile, and we both know there's *no chance* I'll ever do anything you consider stupid or annoying."

For the space of one whole heartbeat, they both managed to keep straight faces. Then their gazes met. Zack wasn't sure what kind of expression he was wearing, but Grace's eyes danced and her lips pursed as she fought her amusement. Suddenly he shook his head and they both broke out laughing.

They were apparently being too rowdy for poor, delicate Bruiser, because he lifted his head, gave them each a dark look, and lumbered off the couch to find another place to sleep.

Probably the middle of his bed, Zack thought wryly. Even though he had his own giant Rockets throw in the corner, the dog seemed to take great delight in climbing up on the center of the mattress just before Zack got there so that Zack had to contort himself into a pretzel just to find a half-decent position for the night.

He wondered if Grace had the same problem with the much smaller guest room bed she'd been staying in the past week, or if Bruiser cut her some slack now that he had bigger, softer options to choose from.

Turning to make use of the extra space now that it was no longer occupied by a hundred and fifty pounds of Saint Bernard, Grace stretched out, her bare feet with their seashell-pink tips coming to rest mere inches from his left thigh.

"So how did you get hooked on soaps?" she wanted to know.

Not feeling quite as defensive now that they'd both had a good laugh over his secret pastime, he rolled his shoulders and said, "It just sort of happened. I was home all day, stuck on the couch because of this bum leg, and there was nothing else on. Then I started to get kind of caught up in the storylines."

"Which is your favorite?"

He hesitated, not sure he should admit quite *that* much to an ex-fiancée who still had wrath and revenge on her mind . . . or at least the potential for wrath and revenge.

But as they said, in for a penny, in for a pound. And chances were, she either already knew or could figure it out, just by scrolling through his DVR recordings again.

"I like *All My Children* and *One Life to Live*, but I think *Guiding Light* is probably my favorite."

"Me, too!" she cried, slapping the top of her leg with the open palm of one hand.

"Wait a minute." He pulled back, startled, eyes narrowing as he studied her. "You watch *Guiding Light*?"

She watched soaps at all? How could he have been engaged to her for so long and not known that, not had a clue?

"Well . . ." She tipped her head, her mouth pulling into a self-deprecating moue. "Not so much anymore. I'm too busy with the show. But I do have a small television set in my dressing room, and I will admit to turning it to a certain channel at a certain time each day if I'm in there."

He readjusted his seating on the sofa, using his hands to lift his leg from the coffee table and set his foot carefully on the floor. His knee still didn't bend all the way, so the angle was awkward, but it was sure as heck better than a week ago.

"I think I'm feeling better about you knowing one of my secrets," he said with a grin. "Especially since I now know one of yours."

"Gonna hold it over my head and threaten me with exposure if I don't lighten my touch during your exercises?"

There was an idea. "I'm not sure a woman watching soaps carries quite the same stigma as a guy who does."

She seemed to brighten. "True. And if word got around, I might even be able to score a guest role on one of the shows."

Without turning his head, he slanted a curious glance in her direction, wondering if she realized or even cared that she was completely missing the movie she'd fought so hard to get to watch.

"You angling for a daytime TV career now?" he asked.

She wrinkled her nose. "Probably not. I don't really think of myself as an actress as much as a talk show host. It's much easier to sit and chat with someone like they're sitting in your living room with you than it is to memorize lines and pretend to be someone else."

"And to put together a seven-layer wedding cake, fix the carburetor on a '76 Mustang, or rewire a ceiling fan on live television," he added, reminding her of only a handful of the other things she did on *Amazing Grace*.

"Yeah, well," she said as though none of those were any big deal, "that's just following directions. I've also got a lot of people on set to tell me what to do, show me what to do, and make sure I look good doing it. Besides, the show is taped, not live, so if I screw up, there's always a retake."

Retakes were nice. He only wished they could be applied to real life as easily as they could in a television studio. There were certainly more than a few times—most of them in recent memory and involving her—when he'd have liked to yell "Cut!" and start a conversation or situation over again.

Her easy dismissal of her on-air accomplishments made him wonder, though. Was she just being modest, or did she truly not realize that much of what she did on a regular basis really was amazing? He also knew for a fact that many of the segments and show topics that appeared on *Amazing Grace* were her brainchildren.

When they'd been dating and engaged, she would often hop up during dinner or roll over in bed to find a piece of paper and a pencil so she could make notes about some idea or another that had popped into her head. Or she would use him as a sounding board while she worked out the details of a concept before taking it to her writers and producers.

Truth be told, he'd always thought she was kind of brilliant. She was both beautiful and brainy, and he'd considered himself one lucky son of a bitch to have her at his side, willing to marry a plain old jock and spend the rest of her life with him.

And most of the time, he still wondered how he'd managed to screw that up.

Oh, he was aware of the technicalities of their breakup. But knowing the facts rather than the fiction both Grace and the media had blown out of proportion, he didn't understand why he hadn't been able to put things back together again.

In the beginning, it was those regrets that had kept him up at night. And it had taken him a while to get over it, to come to terms with her being gone and not coming back.

Later, though, it was the knowledge that he would probably never find another woman as smart, sexy, or suitable for him as Grace that made him want to crawl into a bottle and not come out.

It wasn't that he couldn't find another woman. Hell, if he wanted, he could have a different babe in his bed every night of the week. God knew they threw themselves at him often enough.

After practices, when he was out with the guys, sometimes while he was simply walking down the street. The best, though, was after games. Whether they were playing at home or away, whether they won or lost, the heat and excitement of the game got the chicks all worked up, and they seemed to come out in droves. Sometimes they weren't even Rocket groupies, but fans of the other team who wanted bragging rights to bagging an opposing player.

And B.G.—Before Grace—he'd had no reason not to accept just about every offer he got. No red-blooded, heterosexual male in his right mind would turn down a set of double Ds being pressed to his chest and the promise of strings-free tail, after all.

Especially when the bunnies shaking those tails made him feel like a god—or a rock star. It was pretty damn intoxicating.

Women of all shapes, sizes, and walks of life had thrown themselves at him, and he'd been only too happy to catch.

And then he'd met Grace. Not his finest moment, since it had involved being the shooter of a puck that had flown into the stands and whacked her in the head. Then later, at the end of the game they were playing for charity, and after she'd recovered from her injury, he'd skated across the ice to apologize and crashed right into her.

They'd both gone down like a ton of bricks, Zack landing flat on top of a dizzy and breathless Grace. She'd opened her dazzling blue eyes, staring up at him in astonishment, and a second later they'd both been laughing their asses off.

It had been one of those "when we met" stories he'd thought they would be telling their children and grandchildren someday. The story of how Daddy/Grandpa had quite literally knocked Mommy/Grandma off her feet.

Looking at her now, just as cute—and yes, smoking hot—as she'd been the day he'd slap-shot her in the noggin and then steamrolled her, he wished it still were.

But *if wishes were horses,* right?

At least his dog was back. Not forever, unless he figured out a way to snatch him and hide him away until Grace lost interest, but something was better than nothing at this point.

And at the rate she was riding him, he might also be able to regain his mobility and get back on the ice sooner than he'd ever thought possible. In time for this season's playoffs? Probably not. But it was looking good for next season, no doubt about it.

The irony was that it had taken the woman who wanted him drawn, quartered, and sterilized to get him on track and make him realize he actually *wanted* to get better and get back on the ice.

He wondered if she'd figured that one out, too. And that she hadn't threatened his life or manhood in nearly a week.

Or if she still considered her stay with him simply the easiest way to get her friends off her case—and get him back to the peak of health so she could run him over with her car and kill him clean. (Because hitting him while he was in a wheelchair or on crutches just wouldn't be enough of a challenge for her, he was sure.)

She laughed at something taking place on the TV screen, absently leaning over and resting a hand on his good knee while she reached for another celery stick.

Yeah. He needed to get back on his feet, back on the ice, and then back into the dating game before his feelings for Grace started clawing around in his chest again and he fell into the trap of thinking there might be a chance of reconciliation.

The only problem, he thought as he forced himself to turn his attention on the chick flick, was that there was a strange warmth already niggling behind his rib cage, making him uncomfortable.

He hoped to hell it was indigestion from too many raw vegetables, because if it wasn't. . . .

If it wasn't, he was in trouble.

Row 9

Grace was beginning to feel like a housekeeper—or a house*wife*. Especially since, with her moving in to take care of Zack, Magda's once-a-week visits weren't necessary for the time being.

She cooked three meals a day, plus snacks.

She did laundry and dishes and kept the apartment neater than Zack ever had.

She walked the dog, chauffeured Zack back and forth to appointments, and made sure he did his exercises in between.

She should be going stir-crazy . . . pulling her hair out . . . bubbling over with resentment. Instead, she thought she might actually be . . . enjoying herself.

Even though she'd cut back her hours at the studio, relying on repeats of her show to make up for the filming of fewer new episodes, it was still slightly exhausting to juggle both her regular job and the care and feeding of her ex-fiancé. And yet she popped out of bed each morning feeling refreshed and ready to greet the day.

She preferred *not* to think it had anything to do with spending her days with Zack, but that it had more to do with the change in routine and feeling as though she were truly making a difference.

That difference being Zack himself.

It had taken a few days for him to get with the program, but once he'd figured out she wasn't about to leave him alone to wallow in Cheetos and self-pity, and that he could either go along with her plans willingly or risk having his penis Super Glued to his leg in the middle of the night, he'd really come around.

He went to physical therapy without complaint, and reminded her when it was time for his home exercises rather than making her drag his butt off the couch with threats of excessive poking with pointy objects or the poisoning of his pork chops for dinner. He was also getting around pretty well on crutches now instead of relying on someone to push him in the wheelchair.

She was actually, maybe, almost . . . *proud* of him. He might have hit a rough spot and not had much motivation there for a while, but he'd really turned things around. In another month, she expected him to be off the crutches almost entirely. And a month or two after that, he'd probably be back on the ice.

She had to be careful not to let that slip, though.

Often while they were working on his stretches or when he moved faster during one of their walks with Muffin than he had the day before, she found her mouth opening to compliment his progress. Whenever she realized what she was about to do, she would quickly snap her teeth together and keep her jaw tightly locked.

She was supposed to hate staying with him, be resentful that she had to babysit him through his recovery from his injury. She was *not* supposed to be feeling at home in his apartment or falling back into the comfortable, pleasant routine of living with him again.

But she was. It felt like old times, and it was . . . *curses* . . . nice. She even caught herself—more often than not—forgetting that she was mad at him, that he'd betrayed her.

Once, for only a second, the thought had even run through her head that she should forgive him, give him another chance, and that they should maybe try again to make things work.

It was a stupid idea. She'd been right to end things, even if she'd maybe gone a little overboard in the *how.* And she was definitely not the type of woman to be used and abused, then go back for more.

No, thank you. She'd rather walk barefoot over broken glass, eat a bowl of wiggling worms mixed in with her Chinese noodles, or go an extra month without having her roots done.

But he did look sexy slouched down on the couch, bare feet propped on the low, glass-topped coffee table, Muffin's wide snout resting on his denim-clad thigh. A ripple of awareness . . . okay, she could admit it, *attraction* . . . curled through her belly.

Eight or nine months ago, she'd have responded to that burst of desire by pushing her chair back from the dining room table, sauntering silently across the bare oak floor, and crawling onto his lap. She might have had to share that space with a snoozing pooch, but it would have been worth it. And she'd have bet her favorite pair of Jimmy Choos that after she kissed him, pressed her soft curves to his firmly muscled planes, and whispered a few sweet nothings in his ear, he'd have been only too happy to push the Saint Bernard aside and let her take the dog's place.

That wasn't going to be happening today, though. Instead of pushing away from the table, she stayed where she was, reviewing the script for an upcoming show about children who exhibit signs of obsessive-compulsive disorder. That would be followed later in the same hour by a segment about homemade Valentine treats. She was set to decorate cookies and cupcakes and make ladybugs out of gumdrops and black licorice.

Over the dialogue of a new episode of *General Hospital*—which he'd gone back to watching (along with all of his other stories) since she'd caught on to his big, bad secret—she heard a loud, obnoxious ripping noise.

"Good God, Zack," she said, her brows knit and her mouth open in disgust.

"Wasn't me," he called back. Then a second later, he started waving a hand in front of his face to dissipate what—from the sound of it—had to be a horrific odor. "Whoa, Bruiser, that was toxic! Must be the green beans you served for lunch," he tossed back over his shoulder. "They were a bit *al dente*."

She'd long ago given up correcting him when he referred to Muffin as Bruiser. For a while, they'd done the battle of wills thing, but she'd soon realized it was a lost cause. So now Zack called him Bruiser and she called him Muffin, and she only hoped the poor dog didn't develop multiple personalities because of it.

Of course, she still dressed the Saint in his warm, fuzzy pink sweater, booties, and rhinestone-studded

"Muffin" collar when they went out, and she'd still won the ultimate battle of having the dog fixed.

Oh, Zack had thrown a fit when he'd figured that one out, but Grace knew it was more for manly, macho appearances and the need to maintain a bit of clout over his former dog than anything else. Because he, too, believed in spaying and neutering to cut down on the pet overpopulation; he'd simply wanted to be the one to have it done.

But he'd procrastinated too long, and since she'd had Muffin (née Bruiser) at the vet for shots and a checkup, anyway, the smart thing had been to have that taken care of at the same time.

"I'll be happy to turn the meal prep over to you, if you like," she replied, tapping the end of her pen against the papers in front of her. "Besides, I'm not the one who feeds him from the table."

"He likes it." Zack continued to defend, and continued to use his arms in an attempt to clear the air around him. "And it's not like you can exactly hide food from him. He sits a full six inches taller than the tabletop."

"You spoil him."

"So do you, you're just sneakier about it, and slip stuff to him when you think no one's looking."

Grace wrinkled her nose, glad he was facing away from her. He had her on that one. The pony-pup apparently had them both wrapped around his gigantic paw.

She opened her mouth to fire back another witty retort . . . because she *couldn't* let him have the last word—she never had before, and was darned if she'd start now . . . when the phone rang.

She jumped a little at the unexpected buzz, but stood and went in search of the cordless that never seemed to be in the same place twice.

"I'll get it."

She found the phone, punched the talk button, and said, "Hello?"

"Grace! My lovely, my darling, my doll!"

Rolling her eyes, she couldn't help but chuckle. "Hello, Quentin," she greeted her flamboyant, often over-the-top agent.

"Hello, hello. Do you realize, sweetie, that you've just answered the phone at your ex-boyfriend's apartment?"

Now that he mentioned it . . . "Yes," she said slowly, drawing out the single word. "But how did *you* know I would be here?"

He only even had this number because she'd given it to him when she'd started spending as much time at Zack's place as at her own and wanted him to be able to reach her wherever she might be. It had seemed like a smart idea at the time, but now she wondered if she should be regretting that decision.

"A little cockatiel told me that you and your estranged hubby-to-be have been seen together about town, and I wanted to find out for myself if it was true. Is it possible that your broken heart has mended, and that bad-boy ex of yours has changed his evil ways?"

"No," she answered quickly, firmly, as much to assure him as herself that there was no reconciliation going on whatsoever.

"So you and the blond Adonis haven't been tripping the light fantastic together?" he asked, but she could hear the note of suggestion in his tone.

"You're the only one tripping, Quentin, as usual."

It was his turn to chuckle.

With a sigh, she moved into the kitchen, farther away from Zack and his television program, and said, "I'm just helping him out. He hasn't been doing very well since he hurt his knee, and he needed someone to kick his butt, get him to his appointments, and see that he does his physical therapy. That's all."

"Too bad," her agent replied.

"What is it, Quentin?" she asked, knowing there had to be more. He wouldn't have called, especially on Zack's line, unless he had something important to say.

"Oh, nothing but the opportunity of a lifetime. Remember that endorsement deal the Insides Out clothing company offered last year? The one that involved both print and television ads for you and Zack."

Grace's heart gave a little ping. She remembered. Getting that phone call had been one of the most exciting experiences of her career.

Insides Out Underwear (also known as I.O.U.) produced some of the finest, sexiest undergarments in the business. They'd begun branching out into other types of clothing recently, but their reputation was still that their bras and panties, boxers and briefs were so nice, they could be worn on the outside of any outfit and still look amazing.

She loved them and had been wearing their stuff for years, even before they'd come to her with a deal so sweet, it had made her want to weep. And when they'd tossed "free undies for life" into the mix, she had.

Of course, that was before she and Zack had split. Because Insides Out's offer had hinged on them being a couple, and after the breakup it had all gone away.

"Well, they just called and are interested again. They got wind that you and that 'Hot Legs' hottie of yours might be back together, and they're putting the offer back on the table. Provided you are—back together, I mean."

The ping in her chest turned to a full-fledged pain.

Great. It wasn't enough that she'd been guilted into moving back in with her ex after he'd maybe, probably, most likely cheated on her. Or that she'd been relegated to chief cook and bottle washer. Or that she'd been forced to cancel the tapings of several shows in order to play nursemaid to her cheating ex.

Oh, no, that could never be enough. Life had to eat a big bowl of refried beans and then take a dump on what was left of her happiness and self-esteem.

She swallowed hard, the words she had to say lodging in her throat like a giant, uncoated pill. "Sorry, but we're not. I almost wish we were, though, for an offer like that."

Never one to take no lightly, her agent's enthusiasm remained the same as he said, "You're sure? Because we're talking nearly a million dollars here for you and the hottie both. Nationwide print ads and commercials. And because they know how cause-oriented you are, they're also still offering to give a portion of future sales to the charity of your choice, up to a quarter of a million. That's a hell of a deal to walk away from."

"Are you *trying* to make me cry, Quentin?" she asked, and was only half kidding. She really was near tears at the thought of having to pass on something so amazing.

"You're making *me* cry, doll." He let out a ragged

sigh, sounding just as disappointed as she felt. "At least tell me you'll give it some thought. Sleep on it. And then, if the spirit moves you, sleep on Zachariah so we can tell Insides Out you're an item again and will be happy to become the poster booty for their products."

Was it wrong that she could imagine doing just that . . . jumping on Zack, stripping him down to his own Insides Outs, and "convincing" him to partner up with her—in more ways than one? And that it sent a little thrill rippling out from her solar plexus?

Bad idea. Bad, bad, bad.

Talk about mixed signals. She'd already shown up on his doorstep to play Nurse Betty only months after going postal on nearly everything he owned, and threatening forms of bodily harm that would make Lorena Bobbitt toss her cookies.

Snuggling up to him now just because her juices were flowing and there were a million tiny temptations singing in her ears would only confuse Zack and let him believe there was a chance they might reconcile.

"I'll think about it," she agreed, ignoring the rest of Quentin's suggestion, "but don't get your hopes up."

"Sometimes hope is all I've got," was his melodramatic reply. "Let me know what you decide."

For better or worse, she'd already decided, but nodded all the same, even knowing he couldn't see. They said good-bye and she clicked off the phone, setting it beside the stovetop.

"Who was that?"

Eeep! Stomach lurching into her throat, she jumped, squeaked, and whirled around.

Zack was standing directly behind her, leaning only slightly on a pair of apparently stealth crutches.

"Jesus, Zack!" Hand on her heart, she fell back so that the edge of the counter bit into her spine. "I'm going to break your other knee just so I can hear you coming."

Rather than being offended, his mouth curved into a patented I'm-so-cute-girls-fall-at-my-feet grin. She had no intention of falling at his feet, but in all honesty, he *was* cute, and other women's brains did tend to become the consistency of blueberry Slushie when he was around, so she supposed his cockiness was justified.

"You're the one who's been hauling me to physical therapy so I can get better. Guess you've got no one to blame for my new catlike grace but yourself. *Grace*."

Shaking her head, she fought a grin of her own, linking her arms loosely beneath her breasts. Zack crutched past her, opening the refrigerator to retrieve a cold Miller Lite, which he was allowed to have now that he was off the painkillers (at least on a regular basis) and she was no longer concerned that he was trying to crawl inside a bottle so he wouldn't have to deal with the outside world.

He opened a drawer, removed a bottle opener, and popped the cap before tossing the opener back and closing the drawer with his hip. She watched every movement, feeling her body warm with a feminine appreciation of the pull of strong male muscle beneath his loose T-shirt. Today's wardrobe selection was black with white lettering that said NATIONAL SARCASM SOCIETY. LIKE WE NEED YOUR SUPPORT.

Handsome face, rock-hard body, and razor-sharp

sense of humor—it was a combination she'd found irresistible from the moment they met.

And it was no less resistible now, she realized as the urge to reach out and touch that flexing bicep caused her thighs to squeeze together and warmth to blossom in her bikini zone.

Uh-oh. *Bad hormones, down!* No driving down that street. It was not only a dead end, but a steep drop-off, as well.

Taking his weight off the crutches, Zack leaned back against the section of counter running perpendicular to her. He tipped his head, the cords of his throat working . . . and drawing her eager eye . . . as he gulped down several swallows of beer.

"So," he said, straightening, tongue darting out to lick away a drop of moisture stranded on his bottom lip.

Whimper.

"Who was on the phone?"

It took a minute for her fuzzy mind to register what he was asking. And another few seconds to mentally kick her own butt for being distracted by her ex's amazing physique and scrumptious mouth.

"Oh," she replied, striving for nonchalance while her insides continued to jitter and jump like they were dancing to *Disco Inferno.* "It was just Quentin."

The pale slash of brow over his right eye veed upward. "He called here? What for?"

Zack knew Quentin from their goin'-to-the-chapel days, not to mention the fact that Quentin had attempted more than once to talk Zack into accepting his representation, too. Actors, musicians, writers, sports figures . . . If one was a public figure and had a career that needed to be managed, Quentin was more than happy to help—for a hefty commission, of course. But then, he was very good at what he did, and nine times out of ten, well worth the percentage.

Zack had always passed on Quentin's offers. Personally, she thought he might be a tad homophobic and feared receiving phone calls from a man who referred to him as "babes," "luv," or "Hot Buns."

That sort of thing didn't bother Grace because those calls usually went something along the lines of "Have I got a deal for you, luv!" or "Babes, I've been trying to reach you all day. Wait until you hear this!" As far as she was concerned, he could use whatever endearments he liked as long as he kept her working, kept her name and face in the public eye, and kept those checks rolling in.

Seconds ticked by while she debated sharing the reason for Quentin's phone call with Zack. It probably didn't matter one way or the other, but she was afraid that bringing up the Insides Out offer would also bring up memories of their past together and things better left buried and forgotten.

Then again, what did it matter? He already knew Quentin had called her on *his* phone line rather than her cell, and she couldn't take the deal even if she (really, really) wanted to.

"We've apparently been spotted together on the street and word is getting around that we might have patched things up."

A shadow seemed to slip across his light blue eyes, but otherwise, he remained perfectly still, cradling his bottle of Miller Lite against his stomach, crutches still propped under his armpits.

"And that would be Quentin's business why?" he asked.

With a negligent shrug, she did her best to keep the disappointment from her face. "Because Insides Out came back with the same offer as before—but only if we're a couple again."

"That million-dollar endorsement deal?" he wanted to know. "The one with the newspaper and magazine ads, television commercials, and charitable donation?"

She swallowed, then rubbed her lips together, surprised he remembered so much about it. He hadn't seemed to care one way or the other the first time they'd come knocking at her door. He'd agreed to do it, said it sounded like fun, but hadn't seemed overly interested in the money or added recognition it would bring him.

He hadn't cared what it would do for him, but was willing to do it for *her*.

Funny how she hadn't realized that until now. She'd been so wrapped up in herself, so excited about moving to a new level of her career, that she hadn't noticed the role Zack was playing—his true role—in all of it.

"That's the one," she said, and even to her own ears, her voice sounded thin and strained.

He lifted a shoulder, let it drop again, took a quick sip of beer. "So what's the problem?"

She gave a snort—not the sharpest or most ladylike comeback ever, admittedly—and pushed away from the counter. Their arms brushed as she opened the refrigerator door to grab a beer for herself, and little tingles of electricity danced along her skin.

"The problem," she explained as she returned to her spot against the opposite counter, "is that we *aren't* together anymore. Or again. And Insides Out only wants me—us—if we are."

For a minute, silence surrounded them. Silence broken only by the muted hum of the television and the occasional snoring dog snuffle coming from the living room.

But in the kitchen, it was as though a bubble surrounded them, cutting them off from everything else. An underlying crackle of tension buzzed between them.

Or at least she thought it did.

Maybe not. Maybe she was the only one with a slow trickle of warm honey filling her belly, the only one clamping her thighs together to keep the sharp stabs of arousal at bay.

In a tone normally reserved for small children and the mentally challenged, Zack said, "I repeat: what's the problem?"

With a frustrated growl and eye-roll, she just barely managed not to stomp a foot against the smooth white linoleum floor. In a truly juvenile attempt to get through his thick skull exactly what "the problem" was, she set the untouched bottle of beer on the counter and began a one-sided game of charades.

She tugged the waistband of her panties up out of her jeans so he could see them. "Underwear company," she said in her best Tarzan of the Apes impression, "want you"—finger point at Zack—"and me"—point-point at herself—"to be *mmwaa-mmwaa-mmwaa*." She wrapped her arms around herself, closed her eyes, and made big, wet, exaggerated kissing noises.

"You"—jab-jab at Zack—"and me"—index finger to her chest . . . ouch, that hurt; she was going to have a bruise in the morning—"no *mmwaa-mmwaa-mmwaa*"—more disgusting kissy noises—"so underwear company"—a bruise on her chest and a wedgie up her bum; she was going to need tweezers to recover the damn things if he didn't catch on soon—"no want Zack and Grace."

Point-point, darker bruise, another eye-roll, and a fed-up sigh as she returned to the counter, popped the cap on her beer (the old-fashioned way, by propping it against a hard surface and smacking it with the heel of her hand), and took a long, much-needed swig.

When she returned her gaze to Zack, he didn't look enlightened, but he didn't look insulted, either. No surprise there; it took a lot to offend Zack, and treating him like a dumb jock didn't even make the list.

He'd told her once that he actually enjoyed people labeling him with that stereotype, and often played into it. Why? Because dumb jocks could get away with stuff smart, sophisticated guys couldn't.

No, he wasn't offended. He was amused.

His lips were curved in a grin, his eyes dancing with barely suppressed mirth.

"I liked that," he responded eventually. "Do the *mmwaa-mmwaa-mmwaa* thing again. That was hot." He waggled his brows and affected a lascivious leer that was actually kind of sexy.

Her feminine, internal muscles gave an involuntary flutter, and she nearly moaned.

Bad cootchie—stop that! she ordered sternly. *If you settle down and stop throbbing after the man who cheated on us and broke my heart, I promise to go home later and give you a little alone time with the Bunny* (her bright purple jackrabbit vibrator). *Please, please, please, please, please.*

"Ha-ha, very funny," she said, because it was literally the best she could do. As it was, her voice rasped, her fingers clutched the cold brown glass of the beer bottle like a lifeline, and she teetered on the jagged edge of coming in her high-climbing panties.

"What I *meant*," he continued, as though she weren't Sarcasmo, Queen of the Derisive Rejoinder, "is that if it's something you really want, and that's the only thing getting in the way, you should go ahead and accept the offer."

"You want me to lie?" she chirped, startled into sounding like a cartoon chipmunk. Just call her Alvin, Simon, or Theodore.

"Lie, comply . . ." He raised his arm and took another sip of Miller Lite. "It's a good deal, and I know how important that charity money was to you. So why not play along? Consider it an acting gig, like when you have neo-Nazis on your show and have to pretend you don't want to pull a Geraldo and bash them over the head with a folding chair."

She studied him closely, wondering exactly when it was that he'd lost his marbles. Maybe he was still on those painkillers, after all, and mixing them with alcohol made him seven kinds of stupid. Because there was no way anyone with functioning brain cells would be standing across from her suggesting what he was suggesting.

"And what do I do at the photo shoots when they're expecting us to pose as a couple and I show up alone?

Throw on a hockey jersey and grow a pair of testicles?"

He threw back his head and gave a deep, rolling laugh, the solid wall of his chest rising and falling with his amusement. "Now that's something I would definitely pay to see."

He straightened, his sea-blue gaze locking on her and causing a heated hair-to-toe flush to break out over her body.

"The testicles part," he clarified. "I've already seen you in one of my jerseys."

Oh, God. No rabbit vibrator needed. She was totally going to orgasm standing right here in his tiny, pristine, rarely-cooked-in kitchen.

"No," he went on, as though she weren't squirming inside her skin, struggling to keep him from seeing how close she was to flying apart. "I figured we could pretend to be back together long enough to get through the contractual requirements, then have yet another very ugly, very public breakup."

Row 10

Grace's eyes went wide, her mouth flopping open like a flycatcher.

Yeah. Zack kept his expression carefully blank, but felt pretty much the same.

Brightest idea ever? Probably not. He couldn't even say what made him think of such a thing, let alone why he'd allowed the words to slip past his lips.

"You would do that for me?" she asked, regaining a bit of her equilibrium.

A fist-sized ball of emotion clutched at his gut. She had no clue what he would do for her. Once upon a time, he'd have done anything, said anything, gone anywhere to make her happy.

Pretending to be a couple again so she could settle a business agreement just didn't seem like that big a deal. Not when they were going to be together—physically speaking, at any rate—for a while, anyway.

But rather than tell her that, he set the empty brown bottle of Miller Lite on the counter, rearranged the crutches under his arms, and started to slowly hobble away. Casual indifference at its finest.

"I'm okay with it, if you are." Even though she was in her stocking feet, he heard her following him back to the living room. He rounded the end of the sofa and dropped down on his usual cushion. Bruiser lifted his head, gave a long sigh, and shifted slightly so that he could rest his chin on Zack's thigh.

"It might be fun," he added. "And it could be a good way to keep my name out there, keep me in the public eye until I can get back on the ice."

Crossing in front of the television on the other side of the low coffee table, Grace folded her legs beneath her and took a seat on the opposite end of the couch.

"What if someone finds out?" she asked, worrying her bottom lip the way she always did when she was mulling over an idea. Especially one that made her nervous and didn't fit into a nice, neat little package.

"Finds out what?"

"That we aren't really back together. That we're just pretending to be . . . in love again for the sake of a business deal."

"A damn good business deal," he pointed out. "And nobody's going to find out. Even if they did, or if they suspected something, we could claim to be going through a rough patch. Fighting about dinner plans, or how many guests to invite to the wedding, or where to go on our honeymoon."

It wasn't easy to utter those words, to talk about an imaginary wedding and honeymoon that had been real at one time.

She shook her head, adding a thumbnail to the biting of her lip. "I don't think it's a good idea. I mean, we'd have to pretend to be in love. To be engaged again, and most likely living together."

He raised a brow and shot her a humorous glance. "News flash, princess. I don't know if you've noticed or not, but we pretty much *are* living together. You've been here going on a month now, and we've been seen out and running around together—without you trying to kill, maim, or castrate me even once. I'd say we're already doing a decent job of convincing people we're on friendly terms again. All we have to do is keep that up, smile for the camera, and *not* get into a sparring match in public, and we're golden."

"Golden, huh?" she repeated, her mouth curving in the hint of a grin.

His own lips itched to lift in a matching smile. "Okay, bronze, then. My point is, it's no big deal. We play the lovey dovey couple for a while, and everybody gets what they want. You get your big break. Quentin gets his big commission and another feather for his big, gay hat. And Insides Out gets a gorgeous spokesmodel for its new line of fancy underpantsies."

Grace turned slightly, her luminescent blue eyes meeting his.

It was no wonder Insides Out wanted so badly to have her as the face—and body—of their new intimates line. She really was incredibly beautiful.

The flawless, porcelain skin, long lashes, and lush lips. The sexy, platinum-blond Marilyn Monroe curls. The Venus de Milo figure—with arms, thank goodness—in designer clothes.

If ever there was a perfect woman walking the earth, it had to be Grace Fisher. Minus the mean streak that occasionally reared its head when she believed she'd been wronged.

It definitely wouldn't be easy to pretend to be in love with her without *actually* falling in love with her again. Or to live with her without wanting to partake of all the living-with perks.

Not easy at all, if the low-level thrum behind his fly was any indication.

But he'd opened his mouth and blurted a heck of an idea . . . well, it had seemed like a good idea at the time . . . and it was too late to back out now.

"And what do you get?" she asked, still pinning him with that clear, intense gaze.

The pleasure of her presence for a while longer.

More time with his dog.

Maybe a bit more recognition for his own career, which he hoped to get back to as soon as his knee was strong enough.

But what he said was, "Free underwear?"

She broke out laughing, the sound washing over him like a warm waterfall, but making Bruiser jerk.

"If your underwear collection is anything like it was when I left, you could definitely use them," she told him. "And if we go through with this . . ."

She paused a moment, shaking her head in indecision. "I don't know yet. I'm going to have to sleep on it, think about it a while. But if we do, I'll make sure you get lots of free underwear in whatever styles and colors you like."

He wondered if she was picturing him in any of those fancy designer Underoos the way he was picturing her in hers. And out of hers.

Maybe he'd even get the chance to see her in some of them while they were playing house and pretending to be Mr. and Almost Mrs.

A guy could hope, right?

"Fair enough," he responded, nodding solemnly, as

though a dozen Grace-related Victoria's Secret fashion-show fantasies weren't strutting through his mind—high boobs, firm buttocks, feathered angel wings and all.

For the longest time, neither of them spoke. But they couldn't seem to break eye contact, either.

"I should get back to work," she said finally, reluctantly unfolding her legs and climbing to her feet. "Do you need anything while I'm up?"

"No, thanks. I'm good."

Better than good, he thought. He was almost . . . excited. Anticipation of following through on his little plan—provided Grace was willing to go along with it—coursed through his veins the same as before a big game.

He hadn't felt this way in a long time, and realized now that he'd missed it. Even if this time around, it meant having his picture taken in his BVDs—or I.O.U.s, as the case may be—and then printed in every major newspaper and magazine in the country, and plastered on billboards in major cities and along major highways.

Not exactly his first choice of national advertising exposure, and he knew he'd get his fair share of ribbing from his teammates. But if it made Grace happy, and got her a deal she wouldn't be entitled to otherwise, then he was willing to flash his ass in front of the entire world.

He tipped his head to look at Grace, who was sitting stiffly at the dining room table, exactly as she'd been before the phone had rung an hour earlier.

A slow smile spread across his face as he studied her, unaware that he was watching her.

Yeah, he'd flash his ass, if that's what it took. But he'd rather see her flash hers.

The next morning, Grace sat across from Zack while he scarfed down enough eggs, sausage links, and heavily buttered wheat toast to feed a small Ethiopian village.

She didn't always cook him such a large breakfast, but she'd been feeling generous . . . and slightly guilty. After all, what he was offering to do for her was worth a few grease burns and whisk-related wrist sprains.

"You're sure about this?" she asked, cordless phone in her hand, her own empty plate—because she hadn't refilled it three times—in front of her.

"Yep," he said around a mouthful of sausage, to which he quickly added a bite of toast. After washing it all down with a gulp of orange juice, he added, "It's okay with me, if it's okay with you and the man in charge."

She started to dial Quentin's number. "Just, please don't embarrass me," she said, knowing even that was sometimes too much to ask of Zack. Not that he could help it. He was like a five-year-old hopped up on Pixy Stix, and she could have sworn the term *Peter Pan complex* was created with him in mind.

"Believe me," he said, mouth still full, "no one will be embarrassed when we get to the photo shoot and my pants come off."

Shaking her head again, she refused to respond, focusing instead on the ringing at her ear. Quentin's receptionist came on the line, and Grace gave her name, asking to speak to Quentin if he was available.

Half a minute later, she heard her manager's exuberant greeting.

"Hello, my Amazing Gracie. What can I do for you this fine morning? Might I hope that you've had a change of heart about the Insides Out offer?"

Taking a deep breath, heart thudding behind her breastbone, she prayed she wasn't making a giant mistake, and said, "Actually, yes."

A beat of complete and utter silence passed, and Grace realized she had stopped breathing. Although it made her light-headed and caused her heart to pound so hard it felt ready to burst out of her chest, she couldn't seem to inhale.

"Yes, I can hope? Or yes, you've changed your mind?" Quentin asked . . . very, very hopefully.

Finally, she opened her mouth and sucked oxygen into her sadly deprived lungs and diaphragm. Swallowing hard, she put the poor man out of his misery.

"Both. Or rather, you don't need to hope any longer because I *have* changed my mind."

One final glance in Zack's direction, checking to make sure he was still ready, willing, and able to do this. He nodded, wide jaw continuing to chomp away at his breakfast.

Another deep breath, and rip it off like a Band-Aid. "I'll do it."

The pressure in her chest and at her temples eased. The stress that had been eating away at her mind and raising her blood pressure lessened.

It didn't disappear entirely because she still had to get through the photo and commercial shoots and pretend to be re-engaged to Zack for the next . . . oh,

God . . . year, at least. But it lowered to a more manageable level.

And while she was enjoying the lack of knots in her stomach, Quentin was apparently tap-dancing on his desk. Enthusiastic yeses and *whoo-hoo*s filled the air, spilling out of the phone so that she had to move the earpiece to arm's length or risk a loss of hearing. Beside her, Zack raised his brows and shot her an *I-told-you-so* half-grin.

When Quentin's celebration died down—or at least pulled back to a dull roar—she heard his out-of-breath huff and the squeak of his chair as he sat back down.

"All right, all right. Enough of the partying during work hours—that's what Saturday nights are for."

She grinned, picturing her slightly short, slightly pudgy agent with his slightly thinning hair and penchant for dressing in pastels boogying down on the dance floor. Something she had seen on more than one occasion when they'd attended the same events. If he weren't so charming and accomplished the other ninety percent of the time, she would have been seriously concerned about allowing him to represent her.

"What about Zack?" he asked, his sharp mind quickly getting back to the business at hand. "Is he on board? Because I.O.U. is only interested if they can have both of you. There's no offer if it's one or the other."

"I know," Grace assured him. "Zack is in, too."

Her gaze slid to the man in question, who was chewing and bobbing his head—chew, chew, bob, bob—aware of the conversation taking place and the part he played in it, but not overly interested in the particulars.

"So you two *are* back together?" Quentin wanted to know, and she thought he sounded . . . suspicious.

Not that she could blame him. Yesterday she'd been adamant that she and Zack were *not* an item. Today she was claiming she was ready to accept a million-dollar endorsement deal that hinged on the fact that they were.

"Yes, we're back together."

She cut her gaze to Zack as the lie rolled off her tongue, and at her words, he froze with the fork half-way to his mouth. Only for a second, though. Then he inclined his head, as if granting his approval of her fib, before continuing with the last few bites of his meal.

"I have to admit, I'm surprised to hear that," Quentin said. "You seemed awfully against the idea last night."

"I know, but as you suggested, I slept on it. Our breakup was so ugly and public that we weren't eager to let people know we're trying to work things out. I didn't think Zack would be willing to advertise our relationship quite so soon, but after discussing it with him, we've decided the opportunity is too good to pass up. The charitable donation really tipped the scales for us," she added, hoping that would make her sound a little less greedy, and praying God wouldn't strike her dead for the web of lies she was weaving.

Whether he believed her story or not, it took Quentin less than a nanosecond to jump on board. "Excellent. I'm very happy to hear it and will call the I.O.U. rep to iron out the details. I'll be in touch, okay?"

With a nod she knew he couldn't see, she said, "You can reach me here or on my cell."

"Will do, doll. Congratulations, by the way. This is a really important step for you."

A lump formed in her throat, and it was all she could do to push out a guilt-ridden, "Thank you."

"I'm happy to hear you and Zack have worked things out, too," he added. "You two make an absolutely scrumptious couple, you know. And if wedding bells start to ring again, darling, be sure I get an invite."

She almost chuckled at that, but it came out as more of a strangled croak. "I will."

They said good-bye, and Grace hung up, carefully laying the phone down on the glass-topped dining table.

"So how'd it go?" Zack asked, pushing away from his now (finally!) empty plate. Then he gave a low snort and said, "Like I need to ask."

"He's very happy we've decided to accept the Insides Out offer," she told him. "And he wants to be invited to the wedding, if we decide to take another stab at that."

It was the first time either of them had mentioned the big W-word since before their breakup, and she found herself tensing, waiting for his reaction. Would he be hurt? Sad? Angry? Upset?

She was a little of everything, she realized, uncomfortable even talking about it. It brought up too many memories, both pleasant and painful, and reopened a wound she would prefer to keep tightly closed.

But instead of responding in any way she might have anticipated, Zack simply said, "He just wants the chance to be one of your bridesmaids so he can prance around in a frilly pink dress."

For a minute, Grace sat perfectly still, struck dumb by his statement. Then her imagination took over, creating a picture of her manager wearing a Pepto-Bismol-colored gown with a thousand obnoxious ruffles and matching hat, strutting down the aisle dropping rose petals. And later, at the reception, cutting a rug at the very center of the dance floor.

It was too much, too goofy, too over-the-top. And too darn funny.

She started laughing and laughing and laughing until tears rolled down her face and she was holding her stomach, gasping for breath. Zack was laughing with her, enjoying the heck out of his little joke.

"I really shouldn't laugh," Grace said after a few moments, wiping the corner of her eye. "That's not nice at all."

"Oh, come on, you know I have nothing against Quentin. He's an okay kinda guy. But I have to rag on him once in a while at least—it's part of the Man Handbook. Besides, pink really isn't his color anyway."

They both chuckled again, but seemed to keep themselves more in check this time around. Still, sitting here, laughing with Zack, was the most fun she could remember having in ages. It was relaxing, and comfortable, and for once not underscored by the tension of anger and betrayal.

Before she could second-guess herself, she reached out, covering his hand with her own, and gave it a small squeeze. His skin was warm beneath hers, his fingers large and rough and familiar.

"Thank you, Zack," she said softly, meaning it with every fiber of her being. "Thank you for this."

He stared at their hands, then swallowed, causing

his Adam's apple to move up and down the center of his throat. Keeping his eyes down, he nodded.

"So when do we get started?" he asked a moment later, his voice rougher than she suspected he would have liked.

Slowly, reluctantly, she pulled her hand away from his and sat back in her chair. "I don't know. Quentin is working out the details, but since they wanted us for this last year, I assume they'll want to get started on the campaign as soon as the contracts are signed. Is that all right with you?"

Leaning back in his own chair, adopting a negligent posture, he checked his watch. "Sure," he drawled. "In the meantime, though, we should probably get ready for my physical therapy session."

She glanced at the clock on the far wall and realized he was right. With a nod, she stood and pushed in her chair, then grabbed his crutches and handed them to him.

"I'd better take Muffin out for a quick walk before we leave. Meet you back here in ten?"

"Sounds good," he agreed.

Good, yes, great. So why wasn't she moving? Why did her feet feel glued in place?

She licked her lips as her mouth suddenly went dry. Yet her palms were sweating.

Maybe she was coming down with something. A cold or the flu.

Or raging hormones, a tiny voice at the back of her head offered. An evil voice. One dressed in a fuck-me red vinyl catsuit and platform stiletto thigh-high boots. With horns growing out of the sides of her head, a tail twitching at her rear, and a sharp, three-pronged pitchfork in her fist.

It was Devil Grace. She had Angel Grace gagged and hog-tied, and wanted Grace-Grace to do very bad things. Things like forgiving Zack, forgetting what he'd done and how much pain he'd caused her, and then jump his sexy bones like Muffin on a dropped Cheerio.

Standing there, being pulled in two different directions, she felt Zack's heated gaze sizzling over her.

DO IT.

No.

GO AHEAD, DO IT.

No.

YOU KNOW YOU WANT TO.

Well, yes, but— No!

A struggling Angel Grace got one hand free, then the other, then released her feet. Without bothering to remove the gag from her mouth, she lowered her shoulders, got a running start, and tackled Devil Grace. Devil Grace went down, the air being driven from her lungs as Angel Grace hit her point-blank in the sternum.

The hold Devil Grace had on Grace seemed to snap, and she took a big, indrawn breath, shaking off whatever brain-freeze anomaly had kept her immobile.

"Right," she said, as though her bizarre behavior required explanation. "Walk Bruiser. Muffin. Walk the dog."

Aack! She mentally whacked herself in the head. *Dumb, dumb, dumb. Stop acting like the biggest idiot in the village and start moving.*

"Okay, well . . ." She actually did start moving, and inside her head, Angel Grace gave a little cheer. "See you in a bit."

Crossing the room, she grabbed Muffin's collar and leash, called the Saint Bernard's name, and hustled out of the apartment before Devil Grace could regain consciousness and convince her to be wicked and do what she most wanted to do—throw her arms around Zack and kiss him till they both turned blue.

Row 11

It took the better part of a week to get the particulars ironed out with I.O.U., and another week after that for the contracts to arrive at Zack's apartment by messenger.

Not that Zack just sat around twiddling his thumbs while they waited. Oh, no.

Somewhere around the breakfast when Grace called Quentin to accept the endorsement deal, he'd realized that Grace was no longer furious at or apathetic toward him. That she might even still be ... *attracted to? Interested in?* him.

How else could she explain the light touch she'd laid on his hand, and the heavy, heated glance she'd raked him with before taking Bruiser out for a walk?

There was no mistaking the look she'd given him. Uh-uh, no way. He'd seen it a million times before.

It was the same sultry, sexy look she used to flash at him from across the table at dinner, or from across the room at fund-raisers when neither of them could wait to get away from the same old boring people telling the same old boring stories and rip each other's clothes off. It was a look that promised hours and hours of white-hot passion between cool black sheets.

And it gave him hope that things between them might not be as dead and buried as he'd believed.

He certainly hadn't been thinking along those lines when she'd first showed up to shoehorn him off the couch and back into some so-called quality of life.

For a while, he'd considered using Bruiser as a food taster for fear she was going to poison his meals or drinks. If he didn't love the damn dog so much, he probably would have.

And for longer than that, he'd seriously considered wearing a cup inside his jeans, never quite sure she wasn't planning a sneak attack that would leave him with either one giant, swollen, ruptured scrotal sac or no sac at all.

When she hadn't tried to kill him or cripple him even worse than he already was, he'd begun to relax and think that if they weren't going to be a couple, maybe they could at least be friends. They were getting along well enough, after all, and it would be nice if they could go back to running in the same circles, having civil conversations that didn't turn into knock-down-drag-out fights, and sitting down for a beer at The Penalty Box with Gage and Jenna, Dylan and Ronnie.

But now . . .

He whistled as he *tu-thump-tu-thump*ed his way to the kitchen for a bag of Sun Chips and a Diet Coke. He'd rather have a real Coke and a bag of deep-fried, fully salted Any Brand potato chips, but Grace had gone grocery shopping without him this last time, so he was stuck with her idea of snack foods.

Not that he minded all that much. Not now that he realized there was a chance he could get her back, that they could work things out.

There was still that pesky infidelity issue to get past, but since Grace was no longer bringing it up or calling him a "cheating bastard" every five seconds *and* he knew she was still attracted to him . . . hell, she was hot for him, no doubt about it, he thought with a grin . . . he truly believed they could get past it. That he could convince her of his complete and total innocence.

The *how* part was a little more up in the air, but he'd come up with something.

He never thought he'd see the day, but Quentin was turning out to be Zack's fairy godfairy. Maybe he'd buy the guy a nice paisley tie or two to go with his pastel suits as a thank-you.

"Hey, Zack?"

Grace called to him from the other side of the apartment, bringing his head out of the refrigerator. He smiled, both because he'd forgotten what a sweet voice she had—when she wasn't screaming epithets at him or cursing him to the bowels of hell—and because he was confident in the knowledge that she was going to be his again very, very soon.

"In the kitchen," he called back. "You want a soda?" he asked, setting a can for himself on the counter while he used his crutches for balance and scrounged in one of the overhead cupboards for the chips.

"No, thanks," she said, coming up behind him.

He hadn't heard her, but he'd sensed her, so her sudden appearance didn't startle him. Finding the chips, he turned, leaning against the counter while he opened the bag and popped a flat yellow crisp in his mouth.

Oh, yeah. This was going to be fun.

He'd forgotten how much he enjoyed the thrill of the chase. Grace hadn't exactly been easy, but they'd met in such a peculiar way that they'd never gone through the normal dating rituals.

From the time he'd concussed and flattened her, then asked her out to dinner in an effort to make amends, they'd just sort of meshed and ended up hanging out together as much as possible. Having a mutual group of friends had helped, and before either of them realized what was happening, they'd fallen into bed, then love—or maybe it had happened the other way around, to be honest—then being engaged.

It had been easy and comfortable, but also scorching enough to singe him to the bone.

He hadn't had to chase Grace, though. She hadn't played hard to get.

Now, there would definitely be a chase. No way would Grace fall back into a relationship with him without a fight. And she wouldn't just be *playing* hard to get, she would *be* hard to get.

Given the deck stacked so very high against him, it might be darn near impossible, but there was nothing Zack liked more than a challenge. And in this case, at least, the prize was definitely worth fighting for.

From his spot beside the refrigerator, he studied her where she stood just inside the kitchen entry. She hadn't come closer and was worrying one side of her bottom lip, so he knew there was something on her mind.

The only thing on *his* mind, though, was her tall, lithe, well-stacked body. She was still wearing the khaki-green sweatpants and camouflage top she'd been in when they walked Bruiser first thing this morning. Both garments hugged her shapely figure like a second skin, and the top—with flat silver grommets in the shape of a winking, feminine skull and crossbones—was so short, it bared a good two inches of her flat midriff every time she moved.

Reaching up to tighten her ponytail—which was also sexy as hell—he got a glimpse of much more than just two inches, as well as another flash of silver.

His throat went dry, despite the waterfall of Diet Coke he'd been pouring into it, and his mouth fell open, causing the fizzy brown liquid to trickle down his chin and onto his T-shirt.

"Shit!" he swore, righting the can, closing his mouth, and swiping embarrassingly at his damp chest.

Grace lowered her arms and studied him with concern, brows furrowed.

His own lips dipped in a frown as his eyes zeroed back in on the region of her belly button.

"When did you get that?" he grated.

"Get what?"

"That." He pointed at the center of her stomach, even though the camo material was now lowered and covering what had captured his attention and was making him drool. "The piercing."

Tipping her head to follow the direction of his gaze and index finger, she lifted the hem of her shirt to reveal a sterling silver navel ring with a sparkling diamond on one end and a couple of tiny butterflies dangling from the other.

"Oh." She shrugged a shoulder and let the top drop.

It was all he could do not to stalk across the kitchen, hike up the shirt again, and look his fill. He couldn't remember ever getting turned on at the sight of a butterfly before, but there was a first time for everything, judging by the sudden semi stirring to life between his legs.

"A few months ago. The girls and I decided to go out for a tattoo-and-piercing night."

The brow over his right eye shot up while his left eye narrowed. "Tattoos *and* piercings?" he croaked.

If his throat had been dry before, it was now in stiff competition with the Gobi Desert, and his dick was quickly making progress in its quest to point due north.

Oblivious to the level of his suffering and arousal, she nodded. "Jenna wanted to get a tattoo to surprise Gage, so Ronnie and I offered to go along and get something done, too. I decided on a belly button ring. I've always wanted one."

He didn't know that. If he had, he'd have taken her himself—and spent an inordinate amount of time playing with it while they made love.

"So what kind of tattoo did Jenna get?" he asked. Not really caring, but feigning interest while his attention remained riveted on her abdomen.

Her nose wrinkled. "I don't know if she'd appreciate my saying anything, but if you asked Gage, I'm betting he'd tell you, so . . ." She blew out a breath and said, "She got a badge similar to the Cleveland Police Department's on her butt that says 'Property of Gage Marshall.' "

Zack's mouth twisted in appreciation. "I'll bet Gage liked that."

"According to Jenna the next morning—yes," she replied cheekily, shooting him a quick grin.

"And Ronnie?"

Uh-oh. Her bottom lip disappeared between her teeth again. A sure sign that she had something juicy to reveal.

"I'm not sure she'd want me sharing that."

"Must be good if you'll tell me about your belly button ring and Jenna's tattoo, but not Ronnie's . . ." He trailed off, thinking for a minute, then blurted out, "Nipple ring."

It was a wild guess, but he didn't think Grace would hesitate to tell him about a nose, brow, or tongue piercing. And if she was willing to talk about Jenna getting a tattoo on her ass . . . well, where else could Ronnie have gotten one of those that would be so hush-hush?

An amused, I-know-something-you-don't-know smile tugged at the corners of Grace's mouth, and then she said softly, "Lower."

He thought about that a minute, silently stripping *Grace,* not Ronnie, and taking a mental inventory of her fever-inducing body parts from the breasts down. Well, okay, he got stuck on her breasts for a good thirty seconds.

Not nipples, although that was kind of a sexy thought. Nothing between those and the belly button to pierce, and it couldn't be the belly button or Grace would have simply told him.

A little lower, and . . .

His eyes widened and he jerked his gaze up to hers.

"No," he said, truly and thoroughly shocked.

She chuckled, her lips spreading into a full-fledged grin. "Uh-huh. I couldn't believe it, either. She said it hurt like a son of a bitch, but Dylan had once teased her about being too chicken to do something like that, and you *know* how she is about his dares. Even now that they're an item, they can't seem to break the habit of goading each other."

Zack's attention trailed back down the line of Grace's body, getting stuck in a fantasy that Dylan apparently got to live every freaking night. Lucky bastard.

"So did you . . ." Zack half asked, half suggested.

Two long-fingered, pink-tipped hands shot down to cover the area he was trying damn hard to burn the clothes away from with the heat of his gaze.

He now knew what power he would want if he ever got the opportunity to be a superhero, even for only a day—X-ray vision. Definitely, one hundred percent, without a doubt—X-ray vision.

"No!" she yelped, then jerked sideways when his concentration never wavered. "And stop staring at me like that. Geez!"

The view of her rear was almost as good, so it was hard to peel his gaze away, but he managed . . . barely.

"It's not like I haven't seen it before," he remarked, surprised at how normal his voice sounded when his heart was thudding inside his chest like a heavy-duty subwoofer amplifier, and every drop of blood in his veins had descended to fill his aching cock.

"Yeah, well, you aren't going to see it again," she shot back, "so stop trying to visualize it."

Too late. He'd done just that any number of times since their broken engagement.

And I wouldn't be so sure of that, he thought, in response to the first part of her statement. He wouldn't say it aloud, of course, because that might tip his hand

and alert her to his nefarious plans—as well as earn him a kick to the nads.

No, he'd wait, and bide his time, and visualize her naked as much as he darn well pleased. She didn't have a say over his brain cell activity, thank goodness, and as long as he didn't start drooling like a horny teenager, she wouldn't even know that he was mentally filming *Inspect Her Gadget* with her playing the lead.

"Sorry," he apologized, even though he *sooo* was not. All part of his master plot to get her to lower her guard. Then he would pounce.

In an effort to appear blasé, he grabbed a handful of chips, shoved them into his mouth all at once, and washed them down with a swig of cola. His cock still throbbed in sync with his heartbeat, but she didn't need to know that—not when the chip bag made such a great shield.

"I didn't come in here to talk about tattoos and body piercings, you know."

He raised an eyebrow, continuing to chew while he waited for her to tell him why she had come in here.

"I just got off the phone with Quentin," she murmured reluctantly.

"Problem?" he asked.

"Not a . . . problem," she said slowly, making him think that's exactly what it was. "More like a special request from Insides Out that I'm not sure you'll be willing to go along with."

He lifted one shoulder in a careless gesture and let it drop again. "So spell it out for me, and I'll let you know."

"All right." Taking a deep breath, she said, "Instead of sending a photographer and film crew here to shoot the ad campaign and commercial, I.O.U. wants us to fly to New York and spend a few days there to get everything done."

He bit into another chip, waiting for her to get to the part he wasn't going to like. When she didn't, he prompted, "And?"

"I told them no."

Though he didn't let it show, he was surprised. This entire thing was a huge opportunity for her; he would have thought she'd be bending over backward to do whatever Insides Out asked of her.

"What's the big deal?" he asked. New York wasn't that far away. "Can't you get enough time away from the show?"

She frowned, her lashes fluttering as a short burst of confusion played across her features.

"No," she replied. "I mean, yes, I could get the time away if I needed it. I turned them down because of you."

"Me?" This time he was sure his shock registered clearly on his face. He pulled back, shaking his head. "Why me? I've got nothing keeping me here right now."

Of the two of them, he was the one most able to just pick up and take off, with no boss to make excuses to or obligations to put off. It was just one of the perks of being on medical/lame duck leave.

"Because of your knee," she said, cocking her head in that direction. "There's no way you could tolerate traveling that distance on a cramped airplane."

For several long seconds, he stared at her blankly, trying to register her words. She was fighting the endorsement company's request *for him*? Because she was worried about his knee?

Was this the same woman who had driven one of his hockey trophies through the wall and turned his Hummer into a pile of scrap metal?

Couldn't be. Either she'd been possessed then, or she was possessed now—once by the devil and once by a saint.

On the other hand, her concern was encouraging. If she didn't care, if there wasn't a possibility she still had feelings for him—or could be convinced to let herself have feelings for him again—then she wouldn't have bothered one way or the other. She'd have said yes to I.O.U.'s request, and told him to suck it up, folding him like a cheap sweater and stuffing him into the overhead compartment if she had to.

Part of him wanted to hop over, wrap his arms around her, and kiss her smack on the lips.

Hell, a bigger part of him wanted to throw her down on the floor and do a lot more than that.

But his dick didn't always get its own way—more's the pity—so he tamped down both urges and stayed where he was, knowing she wouldn't welcome either advance. Not yet.

"You didn't have to do that," he told her carefully. "I don't mind flying." It wasn't his favorite thing in the world, but he'd survive. It also wasn't that long a flight from Cleveland to New York City, and if his leg got stiff, he could get up and pace back and forth along the aisle on his crutches for a while.

"No," she said adamantly, shaking her head. "Your leg is getting better, but it's still too much for you at this point. Not to mention dealing with the crowds and airports."

"What are you going to do?" he wanted to know.

"Blow the whole deal because you don't want me to aggravate my injury?"

"If I have to." Her mouth flattened into a mulish line and she stuck out her chin, daring him—or anyone—to argue with her.

That was a look he'd seen a million times before, too. One that said *I'm prepared to be as stubborn as it takes to get my own way, so don't even* think *about trying to change my mind.*

"Seems a little silly to me," he murmured, "to get this far, have such a great deal in your pocket, and then blow it over a minor geographical detail."

"You won't think it's so minor when your knee pops or swells up and you're in agony again," she threw back.

She had him there, but he still believed there had to be some happy medium they could find to give everybody what they wanted.

"Any room for compromise?" he suggested.

Her gaze skittered off to the side and her tongue darted out to wet the soft, glossy swells of her lips. "I did tell Quentin that we might be able to drive."

As soon as the words were out, she fixed him with a glare that was part hopeful, part dare, part nerves over how he would respond.

"That's a hell of a distance to drive," he said. Not awful, but definitely longer than it would take them to fly.

"I know, but if we take your Hummer, you can put the seat all the way back and stretch out your leg, and we'll stop whenever you feel like you need to walk around and work out the kinks. We'll give ourselves plenty of time to get there, too, so we won't feel rushed.

And we can even take Muffin along, which we wouldn't be able to do if we flew. He'd have to go to a kennel or something, and you know how much he'd hate that."

Her mention of his brand-new Rockets-blue Hummer sent a stab of icy fear skating down his spine. He barely heard the rest of what she was saying for the loud *whoosh* echoing through his brain.

The last time she'd gotten near his vehicle, she'd completely destroyed it. She'd gone medieval, breaking out the windshield, side, and back windows. She'd flattened the tires with God-knew-what and shredded the upholstery. Smart money was on a pocket knife or box cutter for that one, but he wouldn't have been surprised to learn she'd used her bare, taloned hands.

After that little incident, he had personally paid to have security cameras installed in his apartment complex's underground parking garage.

So the idea of letting her within a thousand yards of his new Hummer—let alone behind the wheel— pretty much gave him the shakes and shrank his teabags down to the size of Milk Duds.

The rest of her proposal . . . once his heart had started beating again and his brain had regained enough oxygen to interpret her words . . . did make sense, though. A road trip would take longer than flying, but then *a road trip would take longer than flying.*

A lot longer. And rather than dealing with crowded airports and crowded planes, they would be alone for days . . . and nights . . . on end.

Just him, Grace, and a snoring, sometimes flatulent dog. Alone in the car, and then again in a hotel room each night.

So maybe the danger to his vehicle wasn't as important as the chance to get Grace alone—*really alone*—and out of her comfort zone. And that was what car insurance was for, right?

"You think we can find hotels that will let Bruiser stay with us?"

A hint of excitement turned Grace's blue eyes sapphire sharp. "I'll make sure of it. I'll tell Quentin it's a deal-breaker, and have him call ahead to set up everything."

Zack took a slow sip from his can of soda, letting the carbonated liquid roll down his throat while he weighed his options and played it all out in his head.

"Okay, I can see the sense in that." And the bevy of opportunities to charm Grace out of her silky French underwear.

"So I'll do it," he said, watching her face light up with happiness, only to have her go pale a second later as he added, "On one condition."

Row 12

She should have known.

Things had been going so well. They'd been getting along. He'd even offered to put himself out and fake a resurrected relationship in order for her to accept the Insides Out deal, which she'd taken as not only a good sign, but a very kind repayment of how she'd put herself out to move in and take care of him.

But, of course, it couldn't last. She should have known Zack would find some way to fuck it up.

He was probably ready to ask something truly vile of her, too. Some sick, perverse sexual favor. And he was going to dangle the I.O.U. photo shoot over her head like a thick, juicy carrot until she agreed.

Any modicum of appreciation, or even enjoyment, she'd found herself having by being in his company again vanished, and she straightened, crossing her arms beneath her breasts, regarding him with a stern, even hostile gaze.

"And what might that be?" she asked. As though she didn't already have a pretty freaking good idea.

"I want you to start calling 'Muffin' "—he used two fingers of each hand to make air quotes sarcastic enough to match his tone—"Bruiser again."

She blinked, wondering if she'd heard him correctly. "That's it? You just want me to start using the name Bruiser instead of Muffin for your"—oops—"my"—still not quite right—"*our*"—*grr,* what was wrong with her today?—"dog?"

No requests for naked table dancing? No favors that involved knee pads, lockjaw, or positions that only streetwalkers and contortionists were usually willing to perform?

"He's a boy dog," Zack explained, as though she didn't know that and hadn't been the one to drag the massive Saint Bernard to the veterinarian to have his nads chopped off. "He should have a boy name."

"Muffin isn't a boy's name, huh?" she asked with a slight curl to her upper lip.

She was still having trouble wrapping her mind around the fact that this was the only thing he wanted when he *could* have asked for so much more. Was he being sincere, or simply biding his time, softening her up for some bigger, more squirm-worthy proposition later on?

Zack frowned, his light blond brows dipping down. "Definitely not."

"But what about all the adorable accessories I've bought for him that already say Muffin?" she asked, fighting the smile that tugged at the corners of her mouth. It was cruel to tease him this way, but she couldn't seem to help herself.

She could almost hear his teeth grinding together before he said, "I'll pay you back. And buy new."

"But if you buy him all new stuff, it will be in Rockets red or blue, or some other ugly, manly colors."

"I don't know what's so wrong with manly colors,"

he grumbled, turning his head down and to the side for a brief second. Then he raised his gaze to hers once again and grated out, "You know how much I hate that frilly, girly shit you put on him. You painted his nails red, white, and pink for Valentine's Day, for Christ's sake. But if you let me change his name back to Bruiser—and use it yourself—" he stressed, "then you can continue to dress him up however you like. I won't say anything about the pussy sweaters and booties, or even the nail polish and trips to the doggie day spa."

Grace was torn. Letting him change her sweet bran Muffin's name back to Bruiser was a small price to pay to get him to let her drive him to New York instead of flying . . . not to mention his agreement to go along with the deal in the first place when he didn't have to.

But yanking his chain was so damn fun!

"Okay," she agreed, deciding to let him off the hook. "It might take me some time to get used to the idea and remember to start calling him . . ." She let out a put-upon sigh. "*Bruiser* again, but I'll try."

He inclined his head, apparently willing to accept that as good enough for him. "Then set it up. We'll drive to New York for the photo and commercial shoots. Not like I have anything better to do until I'm fit to get back on the ice, anyway."

"Thank you." Without thinking, she stepped forward, closing the distance between them and going up on tiptoe to press a kiss to his slightly stubbled cheek.

Her hand brushed down the hard line of his forearm as she shifted away again, her heart racing and her stomach doing cartwheels as she both realized what she'd done . . . and realized how much she'd missed touching him, kissing him, being close to him.

She started to retreat, hoping he wouldn't read too much into her actions or think the one quick peck meant more than it did, when he grabbed her by the elbows and hauled her against his chest. Her eyes widened in surprise a fraction of a second before his mouth swooped down to capture hers.

The kiss was electrifying. Like a direct lightning strike, it zapped her from head to toe and scalded every centimeter, every cell, every nerve ending along the way.

His lips were soft but firm, just as she remembered them. Also just like she remembered, he didn't bother keeping them closed to tease and tempt, but immediately used his tongue to delve into her mouth.

She let him wrap his arms around her waist and tip her back, one of his wide strong hands at the very base of her spine. Let him tangle his tongue with hers, swirling, sucking, exploring.

Let him? *Ha!*

Everything he did to her, she did right back. Her hands drifted up to lock behind his neck, fingers braiding into the longish strands of his sandy blond hair.

Her brain told her to pull away, to slap him for his boldness and storm off before he got any other funny ideas.

But her body . . . oh, her body didn't agree with her brain at all. Her bones were melting under her skin, everything turning thick and hot and flowing like molten lava through her veins.

She moaned and made tiny mewling sounds that she would kick herself for later. He tasted so good, though. Of salty chips and the sweet, fizzy bite of cola, making Grace's stomach growl. She was suddenly ravenous, either for food or—much more likely—what Zack, and only Zack, could give her.

Running a hand over the swell of her bottom, he cupped one of the rounded cheeks and squeezed, drawing her even closer so that she could feel the hard ridge of his erection low against her abdomen.

She wanted to reach down and stroke him through the thick denim of his jeans, but was too busy stroking his neck and toying with his hair. So she settled instead for rubbing herself up and down the length of his body like an amorous cat, adding extra pressure where she knew he would appreciate it most. Where *she* needed it most, the gentle friction making her wet and completely willing.

With a low groan, Zack grasped her waist and turned her so that she was the one with her back to the counter. His crutches clattered to the floor and he leaned into her, deepening the kiss . . .

And then pulled back, sucking in a sharp breath as he cursed, his face contorted in pain.

"Shit. Shit, shit, shit." Balancing on one leg—his good leg—he gripped the counter on either side of her, knuckles and lips going white.

Though her chest was heaving, heart fluttering like a hummingbird and lungs gasping for air, she moved quickly, darting under his arm and grabbing the crutches. She shoved them at him, helping him to get propped and steady before whispering a quick, "Hold on," and rushing into the other room.

She returned less than a second later with a chair from the dining room set and arranged it behind him, helping him to carefully lower himself onto the cushioned seat.

Moving the crutches out of the way again, she hunkered down beside him while he rubbed his knee.

"Are you all right?" she asked, still slightly out of breath and thoroughly concerned.

"Yeah," he grated, sounding both pained and annoyed. "I put my weight on it. Too much too soon, I guess."

"Maybe we should call the doctor. You might have torn something or caused further damage. You could need X-rays or more surgery."

Lifting his head, he shot her a half-amused, half-annoyed glare. "Way to look on the bright side, Pollyanna."

She licked her lips and made a concerted effort to steady her breathing. "Forgive me for being concerned," she shot back. "You've been doing so well, though. And a setback will cause even more problems with the I.O.U. deal and the advertising shoots in New York."

In all honesty, those were not the biggest worries currently topping her list, but she was already starting to feel awkward and regretful of the kiss.

The Big Kiss.

The Bad Kiss.

The Kiss That Never Should Have Happened Even Though It Turned Her Brain to Mush.

The Kiss That *Would Not* Happen Again. Ever.

Better to let him think she was only being overly

cautious out of fear for how his condition might impact her career.

"I'm fine. A couple aspirin, an ice pack, and a nap on the couch should fix me right up."

"And if it doesn't?" she pressed.

"Then we'll call the doctor, and you can take me in to get checked out," he acquiesced. With more than a hint of mockery in his tone, but he acquiesced. "Happy, Nurse Ratched?"

"If I were playing Nurse Ratched," she tossed back, "I'd be kicking you in the knee and withholding pain medication. Not getting you a chair and hovering over you like an anxious mother."

"You're right," he agreed. Quickly enough to make her suspicious. "You're definitely more the Florence Nightingale type. Care to tuck me into bed and mop my brow?"

He flashed her one of his charming, disarming grins, shifting on the chair so that he leaned forward a bit, bringing their faces closer together.

"If you're not careful, I might push you out the window instead."

Rather than putting him in his place, her threat only widened his grin. "Goddamn, I've missed you," he murmured.

For a moment, she thought she'd misheard him. But those had seemed to be the words his mouth formed, and he still looked inordinately pleased with himself.

She swallowed hard and pushed to her feet, nervously wiping her palms up and down her thighs.

Maybe this had been a mistake. Coming here, taking

care of him, getting him involved in the Insides Out deal.

Letting him kiss her.

Kissing him back.

Oy. No maybe about that one. Of all the stupid, idiotic, boneheaded things she'd done in her life, it ranked right up there.

"Don't get up on my account," he said as she started to move away.

He waggled his brows, and she had to bite her tongue to keep from laughing out loud. Leave it to Zack to crack jokes and have sex on the brain while she was in the middle of a crisis of conscience.

"This was a bad idea," she said—for his benefit or her own, she wasn't sure.

"A woman on her knees in front of me is never a bad idea," he quipped.

She frowned. "Keep it up, Hoolihan, and you'll be walking with a limp for another reason entirely."

"No doubt. And you know I've never had a problem keeping it up."

He was still wearing that shit-eating grin, thinking they were joking around. Thinking that because of the kiss, and her response to it, their relationship had moved to a new level. One where he could flirt and tease, and she'd take it all good-naturedly.

Unfortunately for him, she *so* was not there yet.

"Is that what you told the bimbo in your hotel room?"

The question was spoken in a low tone, as short and cold as she felt. And it wiped the smile from Zack's face faster than a bucket of cold ice water down his pants.

Sitting up straighter, he scrubbed a hand across his eyes and muttered, "Jesus, are we back to that?"

Back to it? He'd ripped her heart out and stomped it into the ground. That wasn't exactly something a woman got over or moved on from in the space of only a few months . . . or a few centuries.

"I wasn't aware we'd ever left," she told him truthfully.

He muttered a few more creative oaths beneath his breath, injured leg stretched out in front of him, but forgotten in the seriousness of the matter at hand.

"I swear to God . . . to Buddha, to Allah, to the god of ice hockey and the Stanley Cup, that I didn't know she was in my room. She wasn't there when I went into the bathroom to shower, and the first time I saw her was right after you did. What the hell is it going to take for you to believe I didn't cheat on you?"

"I don't know," she answered honestly, moving back a few steps to lean against the refrigerator door, arms across her chest. And for the first time since it had happened, she admitted, "I don't know if I'll ever believe you. If there's anything you could say or do to make me believe you."

"So my word means nothing," he challenged. A statement, not a question.

"I guess not," she admitted. "I wish it did, but how many cheating spouses do you think there are out there who swear their infidelity meant nothing and promise it will never happen again? Of course it does, because once a cheater, always a cheater. They just learn to become better liars and pray they won't get caught again."

"And what about the poor schmucks out there who

are faithful to their wives and girlfriends, but find themselves in dubious situations that make them *look* guilty when they're not? They just—what?—have to pay the tab for the guilt of others and their partners' suspicious minds?"

He was right. Put that way, it sounded decidedly unfair. But every time she thought about it, remembered and relived it, she kept coming right back around to being the betrayed party, and not knowing what to think or believe.

And when it came right down to it, fair or unfair, she chose to err on the side of caution because she was *not* going to be hurt again. She was *not* going to be some man's patsy or doormat. She was not going to be blind, deaf, and dumb to reality, the "little woman" who stayed home while he was out banging anything that moved.

She'd seen enough of that in her lifetime. Being a victim might have been good enough for her mother, but it sure as hell was not enough for her. She would rather be alone than be with someone who didn't truly love her, didn't respect her, and wasn't willing to forsake all others to be with her.

"I don't know what to tell you," she said with a shrug, not quite able to meet his gaze. "I guess the answer is yes. Unless I can be absolutely, one hundred percent certain you've never cheated on me, I can't live with the question mark. And I'm not sure how you could ever assure me of that without taking a polygraph test or something. And the kiss . . ." she added, almost as an afterthought. "That can't happen again, either."

He didn't respond, merely stared at her as though

the intensity of his ice-blue gaze could burrow beneath her skin, into her heart and soul, and change the way she felt.

"If you're still willing to drive to New York, I'll call Quentin and get things set in motion."

Jaw set, he nodded, just one short jerk of his head.

"I've got a knitting meeting tonight at The Yarn Barn, too. The girls will probably go for a drink afterward at The Penalty Box, so if you'd like to get together with the guys, I'd be happy to drop you off there on my way."

Clearing his throat before he spoke, Zack said, "I'll have to call Dylan and Gage, see if they're interested."

It was her turn to nod. "Just let me know."

Turning, she opened the freezer door and took out a bag of frozen peas. As she passed, she set them carefully on his swollen knee, waiting to let go until he took hold of them himself so they wouldn't slide to the floor.

"Make sure your knee is up to it, though," she told him. "I wouldn't want to be responsible for a setback in your recovery."

Row 13

"It's good to see you, man."

"Yeah. For a while, we thought we were going to be stuck buying rounds for ourselves."

Zack shot his friends a crooked *ha-ha* smirk, but deep down, he appreciated their concern. If they hadn't been so worried about him, they wouldn't have gotten Grace involved, and he wouldn't be sitting here now.

He'd missed this place, he realized. Missed feeling more alive than dead, being with his friends, getting around—more or less—on his own two feet.

But he'd really screwed the pooch where Grace was concerned. He'd thought they were getting closer, getting past some of the things that had come between them to begin with.

And the kiss . . . Holy Moses, the kiss had been amazing. Any hotter and smoke would have poured out of his ears. For all he knew, it had, and he just hadn't noticed.

She'd been into it, too. She could deny it now all she wanted, but he knew damn well that if he hadn't twisted his freaking knee and cried out like a pussy instead of pushing through the pain, she'd have let him peel down her pants and take her right there against the counter, pounding into her with six months' worth of pent-up passion.

God, how he wanted that. Had wanted it, did want it . . . He could make love to Grace twenty-six hours a day, eight days a week, and never get tired of it, never get tired of her.

Yet she still believed there was a possibility he'd cheated on her.

She'd have a better chance of going out to Lake Erie and walking across the water without getting her feet wet.

The kiss had seemed like a good idea at the time. And, Jesus, he'd wanted it more than he'd wanted his next breath.

But he admitted now that he'd rushed it. He should have held back, waited until they were on the road and had spent time together in the *really* close quarters of his Hummer and a hotel room or two.

So he had some making up to do. Some backtracking and reassessing. He would have to tread lightly for a while, lull her back into a false sense of security. And most importantly, seduce her into being with him again.

Of course, there was still the small matter of her distrust of him, so he would have to come up with a way of convincing her he was trust*worthy* and hadn't betrayed her with another woman.

Not such a tall order. He should be able to squeeze it in between devising a plan for world peace and inventing a cheap, alternative fossil fuel to gasoline.

A waitress, dressed in the skimpy Penalty Box "uniform" of blue hot pants and tight white tank top with red lettering, stopped at their table to take their orders. She tossed her long brown hair and batted heavily lined doe eyes at first Zack, then Gage, and finally Dylan.

Not that Dylan was the ugliest of their bunch by any means. He just happened to be the boy-next-door type while Zack was a local celebrity with a very recognizable face, and Gage was built like a professional wrestler with the face of a cover model. So while he got noticed, it just maybe wasn't first when the other two were nearby.

This wasn't the waitress's lucky night, though, because Gage and Dylan were very firmly taken . . . so taken that even the brunette's firm ass and double Ds, which she was doing her best to shake right under their noses, didn't turn their heads.

And though Zack noticed—he, after all, was not taken, though not for lack of trying—they didn't really turn his head, either. He had someone else's tits and ass on his mind at the moment.

They ordered a pitcher of beer to split between them, and because it was Zack's first time at the bar— hell, out of the apartment—in quite some time, the guys even let him pick the brand. Nice, since the three of them had three different preferences, and normally they'd have argued a bit, then resorted to flipping a coin or playing a quick round of rochambeau.

"So tell us what's been going on with you," Dylan pressed once the waitress had sauntered off to fill their order. "Last time we saw you, you looked like something the cat had hawked up. Now you look great. And you're getting around a lot better on that leg."

"Yeah." He ran a hand absently over his knee. It

was still a little sore from the incident in the kitchen, but they were right about it being a lot better than before. Not a hundred percent better, but hovering around eighty or ninety, that was for sure, at least when compared to where he'd been only two short weeks ago, or where he might be now if it hadn't been for Grace's interference and cattle-prod mentality.

"Sending Grace was a good idea, then, I take it?"

The question was tentative, as though Dylan expected Zack to lay into the both of them for first getting on his case, then abandoning him, and finally sending his ex in to whip him into shape. And if they'd showed up a day or two into Grace's visit, that's probably exactly what he would have done.

But how could he be upset or hold anything against them when A.) they'd had his best interests at heart and B.) it really had been what he'd needed?

So he could be stubborn and didn't always know what was best for himself. Or maybe he did, but didn't always want to admit it.

"Yeah," he told them, not too proud—not anymore, at any rate—to come clean. "It was a good idea."

Without a word, Gage reached into his front pocket, pulled out a folded twenty-dollar bill, and tossed it across the table to Dylan.

Zack regarded them curiously. "What was that for?" he asked, though he had a pretty clear idea.

"We had a wager going over whether you'd be okay with Grace moving in or be ready to take our heads off."

"You bet on decapitation, I take it," Zack replied dryly to Gage.

The waitress returned with their pitcher of Sam

Adams draft and three empty glasses, pouring the first round for them.

After she wiggled away, Gage said, "I was kind of expecting you to take a swing at us with your crutches when you first arrived."

"To be honest, so did I," Dylan said. "Except that Ronnie's been hovering by the phone ever since she and Jenna badgered Grace into going to see you, and since Grace never called either crying or screaming, I figured you must have worked out some sort of truce."

"Why would I need to beat you with my crutches when I've already flattened all your tires and filled your cars with dead fish?" he asked, raising his glass to his lips for a first, long sip.

"You know," Dylan said, "I'd almost believe you if Ronnie hadn't dropped me off on her way to The Yarn Barn."

"Same here."

Zack chuckled. "God, we're a bunch of pussy-whipped losers," he muttered. "At least I've got a decent excuse for having a woman drive me to my favorite watering hole." He slapped the side of his bum leg in emphasis.

"Speak for yourself," Gage told him. "Having Jenna drop me off is the smart move. It gets her here after her knitting meeting, and gets a few drinks into her so she's feeling all mellow and receptive by the time we get home." One corner of his mouth lifted. "That's even worth riding around town in her damn tiny tuna can of a car."

Gage lifted his beer at the same time Zack lowered his.

"You need to knock her up already so you have an

excuse to upgrade to a minivan or something, man," Zack offered.

At that, his friend's mouth stretched into a full-blown smile . . . or as much of a smile as Gage ever shared, anyway. "I'm working on it. And enjoying every minute of it, believe me."

"Tough job," Dylan put in.

And then all three of them together: "But somebody's gotta do it."

That got them all laughing and bumping knuckles for a few minutes, and Zack thought he might have just managed to slip under the radar of his eagle-eyed friends and their earlier topic of conversation.

He should have known better.

"Back to the important stuff, though," Dylan put in, making him once again feel like a bug under a microscope. "You've gotta tell us how things are going over at Casa del Hoolihan. We've been watching the news and reading the papers, but we haven't seen any domestic disturbance reports. No Hummers being violated. No clothes flying from windows or hockey trophies being mounted headfirst through walls."

His friend's lips twitched with amusement, and Zack burrowed his face back into the foamy head of his beer to hide his scowl.

That was the problem with having two such close buddies, he thought. They knew too much about his personal life and weren't afraid to bring up things that might be private or uncomfortable, or pester him when they wanted further details.

There was no getting out of it, either. They'd hound him until he was tempted to snatch the hair right out of his head, and he wasn't exactly up to running away.

With a sigh, he lowered his beer to the table with a clink and sat back in his chair, adopting a negligent hunch that allowed him to stretch his injured leg a bit more.

"What do you want to know?" he asked, resigned.

Dylan and Gage exchanged a surprised glance.

It was something, at least, catching them off guard. He was sure they'd expected him to be tight-lipped and make them fight to drag the information from him.

But what was the point when he'd end up telling them everything eventually, anyway? Either they'd wear him down and he'd spill because he couldn't take the endless interrogation any longer, or he'd end up needing their advice and would have to fill them in to get it.

"Would I sound like too much of a girl if I said 'everything'?" Dylan asked.

"Yes," Zack and Gage both responded at the same time.

"All right, then you ask him something," he said, gesturing to Gage with his glass before taking a drink.

The bigger man thought for a minute, tapping the side of his thumb on the tabletop. When he finally spoke, it was in a low voice and with a completely straight face. "How's your dog?"

Both Zack and Dylan stared at him as though he'd just asked if Zack was wearing women's underwear. Then a round of chuckles went around the table, punctuated by a couple of good-natured curses from Zack. His friends really could be jerk-offs sometimes.

"Bruiser's great," he told them, and realized how happy it made him to say that, to have the Saint Bernard back in his life again. He'd missed the big, furry drool factory.

"And it *is* Bruiser, by the way," he added, knowing that his friends would appreciate that piece of information, since they'd been the ones to inform him when Grace changed the dog's name to Muffin to begin with.

Muffin—*God.* It still sent ice chips through his blood to think of it. What *had* she been thinking?

"Wow." Dylan's eyes went wide. "How'd you get her to agree to that?"

"We hammered out an agreement," he said, and then filled them in on everything that had been happening.

"You've got a hell of a lot going on for a guy who only a month ago couldn't be bothered to move off the couch unless he needed another bag of cheese balls," Gage said after they'd taken a moment to absorb his little tale.

"Cheetos," Zack corrected.

"So do you think there's a chance you two can work things out?"

This from Dylan, who'd been there when Grace had flipped out and gone running from the hotel, thinking he'd been banging other women while he was on the road and away from her.

Unlike Grace, however, Dylan *didn't* believe he'd been messing around. Aside from being one of his best friends, and therefore most likely aware if he was stepping out on his fiancée, he'd also done the math and realized that Zack wouldn't have had the time to do anything inappropriate since they'd parted company and headed for their separate rooms on different floors. At least not anything interesting or that could qualify as truly unfaithful.

And though Zack had pretty much written off ever being in the same zip code with Grace, let alone *being* with her again, Dylan hadn't given up on them. He'd constantly offered encouragement and suggestions for convincing her that Zack hadn't cheated.

None of those suggestions had worked—possibly because Zack had never followed through on any of them—but it had been nice to have at least one person in his corner, unwilling to believe he was the horned beast from hell everyone else made him out to be.

Okay, two people. Gage had been on his side, too. He hadn't been there the day Zack's world came crashing down around him, so he hadn't known the details or had his own eyes and ears to go by.

But he'd listened to both Zack's and Dylan's version of events, then asked Zack flat-out—*Did you cheat on her? Did you know that woman was in your hotel room? Have you* ever *fucked another woman while you were involved with Grace?*

Zack may have been drunk at the time, his mind sluggish and vision blurry with lack of sleep. But he'd looked his friend straight in the eyes and answered with one hundred percent, cross-his-heart, God-strike-him-dead honesty. No. No. And absolutely not.

That had been good enough for Gage, whose background as a police detective and undercover cop gave him better skills than most in spotting deception.

And though they'd never come right out and told him so, Zack suspected both men had slowly, subtly begun sharing their opinions of him with their significant others—Grace's best friends. Maybe not singing his praises to the heavens, but stating a few facts about his behavior both that day in the hotel and in the past. Letting them know how broken up he was at losing Grace and having his entire life turned upside down.

He should probably be upset about that. Pissed that they'd been talking behind his back, sharing things that he considered private and very, very personal. But not only had they been doing what they thought was best *for him*, to help him, it had also paved the way—eventually—for Grace's reappearance in his life.

Without Dylan and Gage defending him to Ronnie and Jenna, he had no doubt the two women would have gone to their graves before ever speaking a kind word about him again.

Instead, they'd apparently (either directly or indirectly) rehumanized him to Grace. No way in hell would she have ever shown up on his doorstep otherwise. Not without her friends' soothing, encouraging, prompting.

That was reason enough for him to be buying the drinks tonight.

Even though their glasses were still full, the pitcher wasn't, and he signaled the waitress to bring them another.

"I'm still not real sure how she feels about me, but I think it's safe to say she's no longer burning me in effigy."

"I don't think she ever did that," Dylan assured him.

"But she did have a voodoo doll," Gage remarked.

Zack's lips twisted in self-deprecation. "I guess that explains the knee and my shitty performance leading up to it."

"Did you get a lot of stabbing pains in weird areas after the two of you broke up?" Dylan wanted to know.

"Or just the usual itching around your crotch and burning when you pee?"

Gage's face remained impassive, his delivery of the question as flat and serious as if he were pulling over a speeder and asking for the driver's license and registration.

"You're a laugh riot," Zack told him without a hint of actual amusement. "You should take your show on the road."

Along with a fresh pitcher of beer, the waitress brought bowls of pretzels and peanuts. Gage grabbed a handful of the nuts, popped them in his mouth, and said, "That's the plan."

Right. Putting Gage on stage as a comedian would be sort of like putting a couple of Cleveland Browns linebackers in tights and tutus and asking them to dance *Swan Lake*.

Zack took a couple of pretzels for himself, biting into them and chewing slowly, then washing down the salty snack with a swallow of beer.

"If it were just a matter of seducing her," he said, getting back to the matter at hand, "I think I'd be okay. I could just grab her up, kiss her stupid, and carry her off to bed."

"Yeah, if you can keep from putting any weight on that knee," Dylan quipped, rubbing Zack's nose in his earlier admission of blowing things with Grace by forgetting that he was half crippled and couldn't exactly cart anyone off to bed. At least not without the aid of a wheelchair or little red wagon.

"You know, maybe it wasn't my knee that's kept me from hanging out with you two the past couple of months. Maybe it's because you're shitty friends and I'm sick of you."

The other men exchanged glances, made funny faces, then turned back to him, lips twitching.

"We're so sorry," Dylan apologized—not meaning a single word of it, Zack was sure. "Please go on. We'll try not to interrupt you again, since you've always been so kind and sympathetic with us when we were going through hard times."

At the reminder, Zack cringed. Okay, so maybe he deserved a bit of ribbing, considering some of the things he'd said to each of them in the past.

He recalled referring to Ronnie as "The Ice Queen" when Dylan had first begun showing an interest in her, and remarking that he'd likely need the Jaws of Life to pry her legs apart.

When Gage and Jenna had started trying to work things out after their divorce, he definitely hadn't said anything so crass—mostly because he was afraid of what his teeth would taste like after Gage rammed them down his throat. But when they'd first broken up, and his friend had been suffering the pains and resentments of freshly signed divorce papers, he'd done what any good friend would—called the ex a bitch, claimed Gage was better off without her, and offered to buy him a few hours with the call girl or stripper of his choice.

"Time for some payback, huh?" he asked, knowing he deserved it.

Dylan shrugged, raising his glass for a sip. "Just a little."

"We'll be gentle, though," Gage told him. "We wouldn't want to make you cry."

Lip curling, Zack flipped them off.

They shared another brief laugh before Zack admitted, "The attraction is still there, but I don't think she'll ever let herself trust me again until she's absolutely sure I didn't cheat on her. And how the hell am I supposed to prove that?"

"Time machine?" Dylan suggested *ever* so helpfully.

"Yeah, or a lie detector test," Zack scoffed, remembering Grace's comment. "Like I can just run to Wal-Mart and pick one up the next time I run out of milk or need a pair of eight-dollar shoes at three in the morning."

Seconds ticked by with only the sounds of the bar around them filling the silence at their table. A hockey game on one of the large-screen TVs—thankfully not a Rockets game or Zack seriously thought he might have wept with homesickness—and some random sports show on another. The clink of glasses, the hum of voices, the occasional shout of victory or hiss of disapproval as somebody's favorite team either scored a point or didn't.

Normally he'd have had one eye glued to the game himself, but he just wasn't into it tonight. He had other things, more important things, possibly life-altering things on his mind.

And then Dylan chimed in, breaking his train of thought.

"You definitely can't pick up a polygraph machine at Wal-Mart," his friend said slowly, turning his glass back and forth on the table, creating wet rings of condensation. "But maybe if you knew somebody with access to one . . ."

He let the words trail off, and Zack almost piped up with, "Gee, thanks for the insight, Sherlock Holmes."

But then Dylan's statement registered. It wasn't much of a statement, after all, he realized. It was a hint, a suggestion, a verbal elbow to the ribs, nudge-nudge.

His head snapped up and he stopped chewing the pretzel he'd just tossed in his mouth. Swallowing quickly, he gave a small cough and directed his gaze at Gage.

"That's right. All I need is someone with *access* to a lie detector test to help me out. You know anybody like that . . . Gage?"

It took as long for Gage to catch his meaning as it had for him to put two and two together on what Dylan was saying. When he did, he sat back with a jerk, eyes going wide.

"What? No way."

"Come on, man," Dylan cajoled. "You're a cop. The only one we know. You can't tell us the department doesn't have a polygraph machine and an operator on the payroll."

"Well, of course they do," he shot back, "but it's not a toy. It's used on murder suspects and pedophiles to bolster the DA's cases, not to settle marital disputes or help you get out of the doghouse with your ex."

"It's more than that and you know it," Zack said quietly.

Their gazes met and held, neither saying anything for several long minutes. Gage's lips flattened and his jaw worked as though he were clenching it in indecision. Zack simply gripped the edge of the table, knuckles going white, while he held his breath waiting.

"We'd do it for you," Dylan put in barely above a whisper.

But it seemed to be what Gage needed to hear and what pushed him over the line from by-the-book cop to bend-the-rules buddy.

"Dammit," he muttered. And then, "All right, fine. No promises, and I'm not losing my job over this, but I'll see what I can do."

The air left Zack's lungs in a rush. "That's all I ask. Thank you."

If Gage could get him access to a lie detector and someone to run the test, then maybe he could convince Grace once and for all that he hadn't done anything with that puck bunny who broke into his hotel room.

He raised his glass to his mouth and took a long, quenching swallow, lips curved in anticipation.

Oh, yeah. Things were looking up already.

Row 14

Even before she walked into The Yarn Barn for her weekly meeting with the other Knit Wits—a cutesy name created by Jenna's aunt Charlotte for their small group of knitters—Grace braced herself for a modern-day Spanish Inquisition from her friends.

She'd spoken with them on and off during her stay with Zack, but very briefly. And since he'd been within earshot most of those times, she hadn't been able to tell them anything good or important or juicy.

Of course, up until this morning, she hadn't had anything particularly juicy to report.

Now, she did. *If* she could bring herself to tell them about the kiss in Zack's kitchen.

Her cheeks flared at the memory, heat washing over the rest of her body by slow degrees.

She should be furious with him. Their relationship was definitely not a touchy-feely one . . . not anymore. And she wasn't there to get cozy or shack up. She was there to nurse and take care of him, help him get back on his feet.

So the fact that he'd grabbed her that way, kissed her, run his hands along her waist and breasts and back . . . She should have slapped him, or at least stepped away before things got carried away.

Unfortunately, the second his lips had touched hers, she'd gone boneless and breathless and brainless. The three Bs of the lonely, horny female.

Those were the only reasons she could think of for why she'd capitulated so easily. She'd been spending too much time alone lately, not dating, not going out, only going to work, knitting meetings, and for Girls' Night Out with Ronnie and Jenna once a week.

Not that she didn't have plenty to keep her busy. Between walking, entertaining, and knitting a whole new wardrobe for Muffin—whoops, it was back to Bruiser now—and reviewing her notes and scripts for upcoming shows, she was never bored, never sat around feeling sorry for herself.

But maybe, without even realizing it, she'd been missing a bit of *male* companionship. Lord knew her apartment had been almost cemetery quiet since she'd broken up with Zack. Even though they'd split their time between their two places when they were together, no matter which apartment they were in at any given moment, the television had almost always been turned to a sports channel, filling the rooms with too-loud arena or stadium noises and commentaries.

She still had her television, of course, and could put it on any channel she liked, but it wasn't quite the same. There was no six-foot-four blond Adonis sitting on her sofa yelling back at the screen or calling for her to bring him a beer, even though he knew darn well her response would most likely be, "What, are your legs broken? Get it yourself."

Then there were the times when she'd bring him a

drink willingly and sit down to watch a game with him. Or when she was able to convince him to snuggle through a movie or show of her choosing.

And the bedroom ... oh, the bedroom was the worst. It had taken her months to get used to sleeping alone, *knowing* she wouldn't soon be sleeping with Zack at her side. To fall asleep on her own, without resorting to a late-night cocktail, over-the-counter sleep aid, or simply crying herself into exhaustion.

So perhaps Zack had just caught her at a weak moment. Maybe he'd been studying her and noticed her vulnerability, then picked the best time to strike.

That would be just like a man. And even more like Zack.

Besides, believing she'd been needy and he'd been a cad was a far sight better than admitting that she'd enjoyed the kiss because it had been Zack, and because she still had feelings for him. She wasn't sure *that* was a road she wanted to traverse just yet.

Setting her knitting tote on the seat of an empty chair, she shrugged out of her long ivory wool coat and draped it over the back of her seat.

"Hi, everybody," she greeted those who were already there.

They smiled and said hello while digging out their own knitting projects or getting a drink from the small refreshment area the craft store provided for meetings just like theirs. Because it was so cold outside, most of the ladies opted for hot coffee or tea, but there were also bottles of water and soda for those who were courageous enough to brave the chill.

A plate of homemade banana bread sat in the center of a small, round coffee table at the center of their circle of mismatched armchairs, and though she shouldn't have, Grace sneaked a slice.

"Mmm, this is delicious," she moaned, practically inhaling the dessert and reaching for a second slice.

Geez, what was wrong with her tonight? She'd eaten dinner before changing into nice clothes and leaving for the meeting, so she shouldn't be hungry. Not that anyone would believe her, given her stomach's sudden growling and hunger pangs.

Maybe she was PMSing. Or maybe she was stressed to the max by that kiss and all the questions that were now flooding her brain about what it meant, how she felt about it, what *Zack* was thinking about it. And her hormones had apparently decided that if she stuffed herself with enough banana bread, those questions might be answered . . . or at the very least, she'd be too fat and too nauseated to worry about them any longer.

"I'm glad you like it, dear," the mop-headed Charlotte beamed from a chair directly across from Grace. She had her knitting out already, size-ten needles clicking and crossing as she added stitches to the sleeve of the navy blue cardigan she was working on, no doubt with yarn spun out of fibers from her very own herd of alpacas.

"I should have known you were the one to bring treats," Grace said. "You're so good to us, Charlotte."

If possible, Charlotte's smile stretched even wider. Her bright orange beehive was particularly high and fluffy tonight, making Grace wonder just how much hairspray the woman went through in a month. And if she measured the coiffure with a ruler, striving each time to get it taller than the last.

Her short, squat body was squeezed into clothes one size too small—black polyester slacks and a long-sleeved turtleneck covered in a dizzying black, yellow, red, and green floral pattern. She was wearing a truly hideous pair of purple fake Ugg boots, but had already taken off her coat—a lime-green monstrosity that made her look like a crazed leprechaun.

Despite Charlotte's terrible fashion sense, she was one of the sweetest people Grace had ever met, and everybody in the group loved her. She was Jenna's aunt by blood, but treated every single one of them like a beloved niece or daughter, bringing them home-made goodies and homespun skeins of yarn.

"You know how much I love to bake," Charlotte said, "and I certainly don't need all those calories calling to me at home."

Finishing off a final bite, Grace reached for a napkin to wipe her hands, and then stood, crossing to the tiny kitchenette for a Constant Comment teabag and mug of hot water. She would fill up on liquids rather than fattening desserts, and then, if she was still feeling guilty on the way home, maybe she would also stop off for a case of Slim-Fast and stick with that as sustenance for the next ten or fifteen days.

Returning to her seat, she left her tea to steep on the table in front of her while she dug around in her bag for needles and yarn. There were a couple different choices in her tote this week, and she couldn't quite decide what she wanted to work on. Glancing around the circle and tuning in to the different conversations taking place with half an ear, she noticed the others were knitting scarves, boas, slipper socks . . . Melanie was even trying her hand at a complete layette set in the lightest of pastel baby colors for a friend who was expecting her first child.

"So tell me, dear," Charlotte said to her from the other side of the circle. "What did you think of that yarn I gave you? Have you made anything wonderful with it yet?"

Uh-oh. Grace paused with her hand on an olive-green vestlike sweater she'd begun, then lost interest in.

She'd forgotten all about the skein of bright pink yarn Charlotte had given her after their meeting . . . gosh, it had been months ago now. Not so surprising, considering all that had happened since then—Zack's accident, Grace's moving in with him, the Insides Out offer . . .

But Charlotte was such a sweetheart, and she tended to take the appreciation and use of her yarns seriously. Grace remembered when she'd given Ronnie and Jenna each balls of "very special" yarn—skeins Charlotte had apparently been quite fond of for some reason. Charlotte had hounded them for weeks to find out how they liked it, if they'd started knitting with it yet, what they were making . . .

If she discovered that Grace had forgotten all about the skein she'd given her, Grace was worried Charlotte would be both hurt and offended, and she would never want to make the woman feel either of those things.

Pasting an overly bright smile on her face, Grace said, "Oh, yes, it's wonderful."

She dug around in her bag, trying not to draw too much attention to her actions while she frantically searched for the yarn in question.

Please let it be in here, she thought. *It has to be in*

here. This is the same bag I bring to every meeting, and I don't think I took it out.

From the corner of her eye, she spotted a flash of pink and sent a prayer of thanks heavenward. Next up, she needed a story that would sound logical, as well as appeasing and pleasing to Jenna's aunt.

"I've actually been saving it because I wanted to make something really special with it, and I wanted to have all of my other projects out of the way first."

She drew the yarn out of her bag and set it on her lap while she rooted around for two needles in the same size she thought would do for the project she was thinking about starting on the fly.

Charlotte frowned. "Oh," she said, disappointment clear in her tone. "I expected you to have used it already."

Crap. She was a terrible friend.

"I'm going to," she assured the woman. "Right now. I told you, I've been saving it. I'm very excited about making it into a new sweater for Muf—" *Hmph.* "Bruiser."

Zack would shit a brick when he found out she was knitting yet another girly pink outfit for his "boy dog" instead of something dark and manly and dirt-colored, but what could she do? Charlotte was staring at her with such a sad but hopeful expression, and she'd made so many doggie sweaters over the past months, it was the one pattern she knew best and by heart at the moment.

"Did I just hear you call your dog Bruiser?" Ronnie asked, breaking off from a conversation she was having with the spiky-haired young woman to her left and leaning to her right instead, toward Grace. Grace glanced from Ronnie to Jenna, who was sitting on her other side, before lowering her gaze and hoping they wouldn't notice the flush of embarrassment she was sure stained her cheeks.

"Oh, my God," Ronnie exclaimed. "He actually got you to change the dog's name back."

This was going to get rough, she could tell. Grace was not one to back down once she'd made up her mind, to lose once she'd set her cap for something, or to not get what she wanted in any given situation. Her friends had probably expected to see her go goth before they would have expected her to ever give in to something her "cheating bastard" ex-fiancé wanted.

With a sigh, she unwound a good bit of Charlotte's fluffy-soft pink yarn and began casting on, loop after loop after loop. In the back of her head, she was counting, but her frontal lobe was busy deciding what to say, how to respond, how much to tell her friends, and how much to tell her best friends in front of the others, who were more acquaintance-friends than deepest-darkest-secrets friends.

Everyone in the circle knew about her engagement and subsequent breakup with Zack. How could they not? It had been such a public spectacle, she wouldn't be surprised if monks in Budapest who had taken vows of silence and didn't have running water, let alone electricity or cable, knew about the split.

But not all of them knew that she'd moved back in with Zack to help him while he recuperated from his injury. Briefly, she filled them in on that, and then explained about the Insides Out offer.

Ronnie and Jenna knew the truth—that I.O.U. had

been interested in doing a major campaign with both her and Zack while they were together, but had then withdrawn the offer when they were no longer a couple. The others didn't, however, so she let them believe it was something new.

Fudging a bit on the details—which she would clear up later for Ronnie and Jenna only—she told them that she and Zack were back on speaking terms . . . not romantically involved, not even close friends, but getting along well enough that they had mutually accepted the I.O.U. offer.

"And letting him change Muffin's name back to Bruiser was part of the deal we worked out about driving to New York for the photo and commercial shoots instead of flying," she finished with a half-hearted shoulder shrug.

"Wow. The things I miss when I don't come every week," Melanie, one of the gals who'd been attending the Knit Wits meetings since their inception, said. She was young, in her early thirties, and married with two small children, so she didn't make it as often or religiously as some of the others. "I've really got to find a more reliable babysitter."

Because there wasn't much more to tell that she wanted the whole world to know, Grace did her best to change the subject, asking about the others' weeks and following up on some of the things she knew were going on in their lives. Thankfully, everyone took the hint and filled the rest of the hour with easy banter and the *clickety-clack* of needles putting together an assortment of interesting items.

As the meeting wrapped up, and they all stood to put away their knitting and shrug into their coats and gloves, Grace asked Ronnie and Jenna if they were heading to The Penalty Box straight from The Yarn Barn.

For the three of them, going for drinks after their knitting meetings was almost a given. But after she'd left Zack, the practice had become a bit hinky, because the Box also happened to be the guys' favorite hangout. Which meant that either Grace had to take great pains never to be there at the same time as her cheating scumbag ex or she and her friends had to hole up in a far-far corner booth, as far away from the men as possible.

Unfortunately, since Ronnie and Jenna were now both seriously involved with two of the three men, asking them to avoid their significant others like the bubonic plague was kind of like asking the sun not to rise in the east every morning.

So instead of making her friends feel as though they had to choose between their men or her, Grace had suddenly become very, very busy and begun making excuses for not going out for drinks after their meetings.

She was sure her friends knew they were just that—excuses—but they'd played along. And truth be known, Grace had gotten a lot of extra work done in the time she wasn't spending gossiping like a Desperate Housewife and sipping Limoncellos.

But she'd missed the weekly ritual, too. Missed the sense of decompression the tradition brought, as well as simply chatting with Ronnie and Jenna.

Which sort of made her peace treaty with Zack worthwhile. It meant that she could go to The Penalty Box again without worrying about bumping into him or feeling the overwhelming urge to throw a drink in his face. And without making her friends feel awkward or torn between two loyalties.

Chalk one up for waving the white flag of surrender. Something she never would have considered doing before, and especially wouldn't have thought she'd end up being grateful for.

Look at me, she thought with a silent chuckle and a grin she didn't let reach her mouth, *making all kinds of personal growth without breaking out in a cold sweat.*

Well, a moderate amount of personal growth, anyway. She still enjoyed thinking of it as maturity with a side of snark.

"Yeah, we're going," Ronnie said, slipping her arms into her calf-length, leopard-print coat and slipping the black buttons through their holes from bottom to top. "We've gotta pick up our guys before some other skanky hos do."

Grace and Jenna both raised similar brows.

"*Other* skanky hos?" Jenna asked pointedly, pretending to be insulted.

Ronnie laughed and rolled her eyes at her own gaffe. "You know what I mean."

To be polite, they asked if any of the other ladies from the group wanted to join them, just as they always did. Thankfully—or at least Grace was thankful—most of them passed. The knitting meetings ran late enough, making the older women and those with young children want to get home.

"I can spare another hour or two," Melanie said.

And Charlotte added, "I still need to get home to feed my babies, but I'd love to join you for a glass of wine."

They agreed to meet at the bar, whoever arrived first promising to find and save a table for the rest.

Fifteen minutes later, Grace walked into The Penalty Box behind Jenna and Ronnie, who both made a beeline for their beaus. The men were seated at a small round table near the front of the room, so they weren't hard to spot.

Melanie waved to them from a booth at the back of the bar and Grace held up a finger, signaling that they'd join her in just a minute. Following her friends, she said hello to Gage and Dylan, trying not to act like she was overly concerned about Zack, even though she kept him in her peripheral vision the entire time.

She had to admit, he looked quite happy and comfortable. No doubt the past months hadn't been any easier for him than they had for her.

Admittedly, before now, she hadn't cared much what he'd been going through or how rough a time he was having. If anything, she'd have been delirious knowing he was miserable and suffering.

But now, being on a slightly different level than before . . . personal growth and all that . . . she realized that the same press that had hounded her had likely hounded him. The same outrageous headlines that had embarrassed, pained, and infuriated her had likely embarrassed, pained, and infuriated him. And if she had avoided people, places, and things for fear of running into him, then he had probably done the same to avoid a confrontation with her.

Recognizing those facts somehow made her feel a tad more sympathetic toward him. Not forgiving, not wipe-the-slate clean, but the other side of the coin was starting to become a little clearer when she hadn't even noticed there was another side before.

"How's your knee?" she asked quietly, sliding into a free chair between Zack and Dylan, who had Ronnie perched on his lap. Across the table, Jenna was sitting on the edge of her own chair, but she was leaning so close to Gage that she might as well have been in his lap.

"Good," he responded. "Better."

"Will you be in good enough shape to leave for New York on Monday?"

"Should be, as long as I don't try to do any more heavy lifting," he said.

At his words, she cocked her head and gave him a very pointed *Excuse me?* look. First Ronnie called her a "skanky ho," and now Zack was calling her "heavy." Much more of this kind of treatment from her so-called friends and she was going to develop a complex.

Zack's mouth twisted half up in self-deprecating amusement, half down in remorse. "You know what I mean."

She made a noncommittal noise. "Uh-huh. I suggest choosing your words more carefully from now on. Unless, of course, you want to make the trip to New York tied to the roof of your Hummer."

This time, the lift of his lips was one hundred percent humor. "I forgot how vicious and bloodthirsty you could be."

She smiled back. The smile of a cat who's just picked the lock on the canary's cage and swallowed his last yellow feather. "No you didn't."

For a second, he didn't respond. And then he threw his head back, letting out a deep, belly-rumbling laugh. Dylan, Ronnie, Gage, and Jenna all whipped around, staring at them as though they'd just sprouted wings and cloven hooves, and the rest of the Box patrons followed suit.

Rather than being embarrassed, Grace thought it was funny. Every single person in the bar knew who she and Zack were, she was sure. She was also fairly certain everyone was well aware of their nasty breakup and the turbulent state of their relationship since then. Because of that, they had to be scrambling to figure out what was going on with the two of them sitting so close and *laughing* together.

She wondered how many would be on their phones within the next minute or two, calling and texting their friends or passing the information on to contacts they might have in the media.

"Good comeback," Zack said, paying zero attention to the eyeballs still riveted on them from every direction. "Definitely deserving of a drink. Can I buy you one?"

Throwing her shoulders back and casting a glance toward the bar, she said, "Sure. I'll have a Cosmopolitan. You can have it sent over to me at that table." She pointed a finger in Melanie's direction, then slid her chair back and got to her feet. "Come on, girls, let's get away from all this testosterone and go have a few frilly, girly umbrella drinks."

Ronnie and Jenna both stood, but before she'd completely slipped off Dylan's lap, Ronnie muttered, "I don't know, testosterone does have its merits."

Then she pressed a quick kiss to his cheek, as did Jenna to Gage's, and the three of them headed to the back of the bar.

Row 15

"What was *that* about?" Ronnie wanted to know the minute they hit their seats at the back of the bar, well out of earshot of the guys.

"What was what about?" Grace asked, though she had a pretty good idea what her friend meant.

"The laughing. The grins. You and Zack acting like you're old buddies and maybe . . ." She waggled her brows and then finished suggestively, "more?"

"I heard that," Melanie said. "I thought I was hallucinating. Either that, or you were about to stab a fork into his thigh to teach him a lesson about being overly amused at your expense."

Grace shrugged, folding her coat over the back of the booth seat and setting her purse at her feet. "Inside joke," she said, unwilling to elaborate. "Besides, I told you at the meeting that we're getting along better. I no longer fantasize about using him as a dart board."

A waitress appeared with a pitcher of pretty pink liquid and four empty martini glasses. "Cosmos," she announced, "courtesy of that table over there."

She gestured toward Zack, Gage, and Dylan, and when they all turned in their direction, the three men raised their glasses of beer in salute.

"Well, that's awfully nice." Melanie remarked.

"Yeah. Wonder what made them feel so generous all of a sudden," Ronnie added in a much wryer tone, as though she had some suspicions of her own about what had caused one of them, at least, to spring for their first round of drinks.

Ignoring both women, Grace lifted her attention to the waitress and said, "We're expecting one more person, so we may need another glass. Unless Charlotte would prefer wine or something."

The young woman in the skimpy shorts and tank Penalty Box uniform nodded. "Can I get you ladies anything else?"

The four of them exchanged glances, then responded in the negative. "Nothing right now, thanks," Grace said.

A second after the waitress moved away, Charlotte bustled through the front door. She stood a few steps in for a moment, scanning the crowd until she spotted them, then made her way around tables and other patrons until she reached them. She struggled out of her bulky, oversize coat—the green so bright, it burned Grace's retinas—before sliding into the booth beside Melanie, who scooted over to give her room.

"You've started without me, I see," Charlotte remarked, but without a hint of disappointment or censure.

"The guys sent us a pitcher of Cosmopolitans before we even had a chance to order," Jenna supplied. "We didn't know if you'd like this or a glass of wine instead."

"Hmm." Charlotte studied the pink concoction in the pitcher and their four funnel-shaped glasses while she wiggled around, trying to find a comfortable position for her well-padded bottom. "I think I'll go with a nice glass of red wine, thank you. You girls enjoy that."

As soon as their waitress came into view again, they waved her down so Charlotte could place her order, then turned back and settled in for a friendly, relaxing chat about nothing in particular.

Or so Grace thought. She'd expected—apparently prematurely—that whatever curiosity had been roused about her and Zack by the round of free drinks had been forgotten with Charlotte's arrival and the change of subject.

"So," Jenna threw out, aiming her question at Grace and Grace alone before anyone else got the chance to speak, "*is* there anything more going on with you two?"

"All right, all right," she relented on a long-suffering sigh. "But you have to swear . . . *swear* . . . 'cross your hearts, hope to die, stick a knitting needle in your eye' swear . . . that you won't breathe a word of this to anyone. Not your husbands, lovers, best friends, priests, or clergy of your choice."

She narrowed her eyes and stared down each and every woman at the table. "Swear it, or you can go right on wondering and speculating until monkeys take over the world."

There was murmuring, whispering, bent heads, and intense expressions. Finally they all looked at her, and Ronnie—who had apparently appointed herself spokesperson for the group—nodded. "We swear. Cross our hearts . . ." Each and every one of them began going through the motions of the old childhood pledge. "Hope to die. Stick a knitting needle in my eye."

That was about as good as it was going to get. So now she either had to come clean or back out and risk having four drinks—with glasses—launched at her head.

Taking a deep breath, she counted to ten and clutched the stem of her martini glass until her knuckles turned white. Then she blurted out what had been squeezing her heart and scrambling her brain for the better part of the day: "He kissed me."

"Oh, my God."

"Oh, my *God*."

"Oh, my goodness."

"Oh, my."

Blurted exclamations went around the table like toppling dominoes. Grace could feel her face heating, her stomach doing somersaults while they regarded her with wide eyes and even wider mouths.

"Wait, wait, wait," Ronnie said. She slapped the tabletop with a flat palm, tossed back the last of her drink, and refilled her glass, then gulped down another good portion of that. "Go back. Start at the beginning. We need details."

Grace didn't want to, but since the cat was out of the bag, she didn't seem to have much choice.

"We were in the kitchen, talking about our trip to New York, and he just leaned in, grabbed me, and started kissing."

"And I'm sure you remained stiff as a board, not kissing him back the least little bit, right?" Jenna pressed, a teasing note to her tone.

"I wish," Grace said, letting out a baffled breath

and making herself admit to her true reaction to The Kiss. "The minute his lips touched mine, it was like my brain melted and dribbled right out my ears. If he hadn't twisted his knee, I probably would have stripped him down and done things with him that would have put him back in his wheelchair."

Ronnie gave a low whistle, while Jenna chuckled even as her cheeks pinkened, and Melanie *whoo-hoo*ed. Only Charlotte remained silent, though her eyes sparkled and the corners of her mouth twitched merrily.

"So did you?" Melanie asked. "Jump his bones, I mean?"

Jenna elbowed her in the side. "She just said she didn't. But only because he hurt his knee."

Melanie blinked, looking slightly dazed and disconcerted. "Oh, right. I guess I got a little carried away imagining all that hot sex."

"What's the matter, Mel? Things running a bit on the cold side at home these days?" Ronnie queried.

The brunette rolled her eyes heavenward. "You try finding time to get naked and nasty when you've got two small kids underfoot twenty-four hours a day."

"Aw, poor Melanie," Ronnie said with a chuckle. "But think how much hot, sweaty sex you got to have before the munchkins came along."

Melanie's expression turned vacant and she tilted her head with a sigh. "Ahhh, those *were* the days."

Grace remembered. Not the "before kids" part, but definitely the hot, sweaty sex. She remembered, and she missed it, which was probably why Zack's kiss had turned her so upside down and inside out.

"What are you going to do?" Jenna asked her,

toying with the stem of her glass, but not touching the Cosmo that still rose almost to the rim.

"About what?" Grace asked.

"About Zack. Do you think there's something there? Do you think there's any chance the two of you can work things out and get back together?"

The question caught Grace off guard, though maybe it shouldn't have. Wasn't that the exact same question that had been running through her head ever since The Kiss had taken place?

She might not have acknowledged it or let herself wonder about it too closely for too long, but it was there, floating in the ether and tugging at her like an invisible thread.

A week or two ago, the answer would have been simple. She'd have responded with a resounding *NO!* No way, no how, not in this lifetime.

But, oh, how things could change in the space of only a week, or a day, or an hour. Now, she just didn't know.

Which was what she told her friends, very frankly.

"Do you still have feelings for him?" Melanie asked softly.

"Of course," she responded truthfully and without having to think about it for even a second. "But I'm not sure they're all *good* feelings. Am I still attracted to him? Sure. Do I want to be with him again? I honestly don't know. Am I still angry with him? Yes and no. I'm not sure I know *how* to feel about him these days, because it all depends on whether or not he cheated on me back in Columbus or before, and I don't know what the hell to believe about that anymore."

Feeling more frustrated than ever, she picked up her Cosmo and gulped, enjoying the warm sting of alcohol sliding its way down her throat to pool in her belly.

Ahh, vodka, the perfect cure-all. If only it lasted more than a few precious hours.

"Well, I, for one, hope you do get back together," Melanie said with conviction. Cosmo-bolstered conviction, maybe, but conviction all the same. "I thought you made a great couple, and a big part of me wants to believe that Zack *didn't* cheat on you."

Though Grace had never put her exact thoughts into words before, she found it effortless to do so now. "Me, too," she admitted.

"So maybe you should give him a second chance," Ronnie suggested.

At Grace's sharp look, she said, "I know, I know, it won't be easy. But I've grilled Dylan within an inch of his life, and if he knew or even suspected Zack had truly been unfaithful, he'd have said so by now."

Even though Grace wasn't at all sure it was the right thing to do or if she had the resolve to follow through on it, she made herself open her mouth and say, "I guess I could try."

"There you go," Ronnie chimed cheerily. She even leaned into Grace, nudging her harder than necessary with her shoulder.

Grace only wished she felt the same level of enthusiasm. Instead, a lump the size of a hockey puck seemed to have wedged itself solidly behind the wall of her chest.

"Wait a minute." The now-empty drink pitcher gave a clunk as Ronnie set it back in the center of the table. She glanced around, brows drawn down in a frown.

"What's the matter?" Grace asked.

Pointing her finger at each of the women in their party, Ronnie said, "Charlotte had wine. The rest of us had Cosmos, and I've refilled almost everyone's glass at least once. Everybody's but Jenna's."

All eyes turned in that direction. The petite, dark-haired woman blushed and shrank back slightly against the bench seat. Sure enough, her martini glass was still full and pushed a few inches farther away than one might expect.

"I'm not thirsty," she said, but the excuse sounded lame even to her own ears, if her downcast glance was any indication.

"Would you like something else?" Grace inquired, a sneaking suspicion beginning to play through her mind. "A soda, maybe? Or just plain cranberry juice?"

Jenna's head jerked up, her wide eyes making her look decidedly guilty . . . of something.

"Oh, my God!" Ronnie exclaimed. "Oh, my God, oh, my God, oh, my God!"

Grace's mouth curved in a sly smile.

"You're pregnant!" Ronnie's exclamation was nearly loud enough to echo off the walls and be heard over the rest of the din filling the bar.

"*Shhhhhh,*" Jenna hissed, cringing as she whipped a worried glance in the direction of the men's table. "I haven't told Gage yet, and he would kill me if he found out he wasn't the first to know."

"Ohmigod, ohmigod, ohmigod," Ronnie said again, this time in a stage whisper that wouldn't be overheard by anyone who wasn't at their table, let alone across the room. "This is wonderful. I'm so happy for you. Congratulations!"

Which pretty much summed up everybody's feelings, but they each added their own exuberant wishes, either hugging her or reaching out to squeeze her arm, depending on where they were seated around the table.

"When did you find out?" Grace asked, beaming. Despite the mess her own life was in at the moment, she was thoroughly delighted for her friend.

Jenna had been wanting a baby ever since she and Gage married the first time. Though he'd been on board at first, something along the way had changed his mind, and that change had caused them to split.

They were married again, thank goodness—if any two people had ever belonged together, it was Gage and Jenna—and this time, they were both on the same page about starting a family. In fact, according to Jenna, Gage had been almost single-minded in his intention to knock her up. Either that, or he just really, really liked making love to his wife.

Grace supposed that was the real motivation behind his attentiveness . . . and the trying-for-a-baby thing was just a nice side benefit and excuse for getting vertical as often as possible.

"Last week," Jenna told them. "I want it to be a surprise, though, so I'm planning to tell him this weekend before we go house hunting. He's going to flip," she said, and it was her turn to beam.

Row 16

Grace and Zack spent the rest of the week and weekend slowly packing and making arrangements for being out of town, then set off first thing Monday morning for New York. Being behind the wheel of his big, blue Hummer was kind of like driving a tank, Grace thought, and for the first hour or two of their trip, she had an overwhelming urge to put on camouflage and combat boots.

But the ride was smooth and comfortable, even for Bruiser, who sat like a third passenger on the floor of the backseat, head hovering between them. Thank goodness she'd given him one of his special breath-freshening bones before they left, otherwise the Saint Bernard's heated panting would have knocked them out within the first five minutes. As it was, every once in a while he would slap his lips together, and she and Zack would both be sprayed with little dots of doggy slobber.

Grace was surprised, actually, by how comfortable the drive turned out to be. She'd expected at least a modicum of uneasiness after the kiss, especially considering her mind-set when she'd left The Penalty Box Wednesday night. But Zack had been in such a good mood all week, she found his upbeat demeanor infectious.

Was he so chipper because he thought she was going to let him kiss her again? Or worse yet, that he might get laid?

Or was he simply feeling better and feeling more relaxed around her?

That would be okay, she decided. She was starting to feel more comfortable around him, too. And she was trying, really trying, to take Ronnie's advice and give him another chance.

Not that she'd printed up some giant banner or made a flowery speech to alert him to her latest resolution. No, she was going slow, playing it smart.

She was going to try her best not to constantly think of him as a cheater or the man who'd betrayed her, letting that perception color her every interaction with him. She was trying to go into this with a blank slate, treating him the same as she had when they'd first met and begun dating.

Or trying to, anyway. Because Ronnie and Jenna and Melanie were right—if he hadn't cheated on her, it would be a true shame and the biggest regret of her life for them *not* to be together.

Traveling the straight shot of Interstate 80 through Ohio and the entire length of Pennsylvania, they stopped regularly at rest areas and fast food restaurants so Zack and Bruiser could both stretch their legs. Though Grace could have gone much longer, she didn't mind the frequent breaks, and took the opportunities to walk around or use the restroom, too.

They took turns staying with Bruiser and picking where to eat. It was all very amicable, almost as though they'd never separated. She imagined if they'd taken road trips together while they'd been engaged, they would have been just like this—slow and easy and even fun.

It was dark out, already seven or eight o'clock, and Bruiser was sound asleep stretched door to door on the backseat when she asked Zack to dig out the Map-Quest directions she'd printed that would get them to their hotels each night. Turning on one of the overhead interior lights, he studied the pages and started telling her where to turn until they reached the parking lot of a Holiday Inn Express right off the main highway.

Twenty minutes later, they were checked in, and she'd made a couple extra trips to get all of their luggage to the room while Zack stayed in the suite with Bruiser. She'd allowed Quentin to talk her into sharing a room and a king-size bed with Zack at each of their stops along the way, her agent's rationale being that if word got out they were traveling together, but staying in separate rooms, no one would believe they were *really* a couple again and Insides Out might get nervous about the deal they'd struck. A deal with very meticulous, very precarious clauses, of which I.O.U. could renege at any time if they discovered claims she and Zack had made or agreed to within the contract were false.

She didn't think sharing a room and a bed made much difference in the scheme of things. After all, they were both adults, and because they'd been involved once before, they were used to sharing a bathroom and close quarters.

And as far as sex went, she knew her mind well

enough to be sure that if she wanted to make love with him, a wall, door, or even floors between them wasn't going to stop her. In the same vein, if she didn't want to be with him, then the fact that they were only a few inches away from each other under the same sheets and covers wasn't going to give her a sudden case of brain fever and cause her to do anything she wasn't one hundred percent willing to do.

Even so—even though she'd agreed to go along with everything the endorsement deal required—she didn't particularly want to advertise her association with Zack to the general public just yet. They might be traveling together and sharing a hotel room, but she'd asked Quentin to make their reservations under a different name, and the fewer people who recognized her or Zack and put two and two together, the better.

Thus her desire to check into the hotel at night, with a hat and sunglasses still on, and to park at the back of the building where she could move all of their things in and out on her own.

They were pretty much sneaking Bruiser in and out, too, since pets weren't normally allowed, and the fact that Bruiser spent a lot of time drooling on his own paws and sniffing, licking, or leaning against the walls precluded him from passing as a seeing-eye dog.

She didn't know how much money or how many firstborn children Quentin had had to throw at the hotel managers to get them to let the Saint Bernard indoors, but he'd managed. Just one more reason he was such a good manager, and why she kept him on the payroll.

When she returned to the room a final time, slightly out of breath from toting suitcases up four flights of secluded back stairs, Zack was seated on the end of the bed, left leg propped out in front of him. Bruiser, of course, was stretched full-length across the wide, king-size mattress, taking up seventy-five percent of the plain maroon spread.

It was going to be interesting to see if they could get him to stay on the floor when they were ready to climb into bed themselves. Even though they'd brought his favorite blanket—a thick, soft throw with the Rockets emblem that was large enough to cover a small sofa—Bruiser was a dog who preferred his creature . . . scratch that . . . *human* comforts. And since he weighed in at a hefty, often immovable hundred and fifty pounds, she wouldn't be surprised if *they* ended up sleeping on the floor and letting Bruiser take the bed.

"Sorry you got stuck doing all that yourself," Zack said.

"That's all right, I don't mind," she told him, moving things around, finding places to lay down and open their luggage. Since they were only staying the one night, it didn't seem worthwhile to unpack anything but the bare necessities. "This was my idea, after all. I'm the one who talked you into letting us drive instead of flying, and it's my fault I forgot to ask for a ground-floor room."

"I don't mind."

His voice was low, and she glanced at him in the process of pulling a pair of pajamas and some toiletries out of her suitcase. He looked earnest and a little contrite, and she smiled to let him know she didn't hold the manual labor against him.

"How's your knee feeling?" she asked him.

"Fine. Great, actually," he said, flexing it a bit to show her that it hadn't stiffened up on him in the car. "You were right about driving, I think. I can't imagine it feeling this good after a few hours crammed on a plane, even in first class."

She gave a small nod, still smiling. "I'm glad. Mind if I use the bathroom first?"

He shook his head. "Help yourself. Bruiser and I will get comfortable and see if there's anything on TV."

"Bruiser's already comfortable," she told him. "Good luck finding room to stretch out on there with him."

Zack's chuckle followed her as she stepped into the bathroom and closed the door. She sank back against the thick metal panel and let out a long, shuddering breath.

Oh, man. Maybe this hadn't been such a good idea.

She'd been fine all week, staying in Zack's apartment and making plans for this trip. She'd been fine all day, riding in the close confines of the Hummer with him. She'd even been fine in the small hotel room, contemplating the evening ahead and having to share a bed with him. Through all of that, she'd been fine, fine, fine, fine, fine.

Then he'd looked at her in just that way he had—that soft, dark, kind of smoldering way that made her knees weak and dampened her panties.

Not that it was the first time she'd been turned on by Zack—before or after their breakup—or any other man. She wasn't exactly a stranger to sexual arousal or how to handle it when it struck.

But then his low, throaty chuckle had joined the flashing eyes and sultry expression, and she'd felt as though an atomic bomb had detonated inside her chest. It stole her breath, knocked her back a step, and filled her with so much pent-up longing, she'd nearly moaned aloud.

Which would be bad, of course. No doubt if she gave Zack even the tiniest hint that she was still attracted to him, he'd be on her like a moth on a bug zapper.

Hiding out in the bathroom was definitely the best plan of action. And if she could find a way to sleep in the tub without waking up with the mother of all neck cramps, she might just do that, too.

When she could breathe again and her knees had stopped knocking, she set her things on the sink countertop and started getting ready for bed. After taking as long as she could to shower and wash her hair and face without prompting Zack to come check on her, she closed her hand over the round silver doorknob, inhaled as deeply as she could, and steeled herself for what was to come.

She needn't have worried that Zack would be stripped down and ready for action, or have the lights off, the room bathed in flickering candlelight and strewn with rose petals. He hadn't been *that* kind of guy even when they were engaged.

No, Zack didn't do candlelight and romantic dinners he'd cooked himself. He didn't do candy for Valentine's Day or cards for birthdays.

He was more about the big gestures. The ones that came less often, but definitely had a larger impact.

When he'd proposed to her, he'd been sweaty and stinky from hours on the ice. But the Rockets had won the game, and immediately afterward, he'd skated up to the first sports reporter he spotted who had a camera and microphone, and started talking about Grace, and their relationship, and how he'd promised himself if they won that night's game, he'd do something he'd been contemplating for the past couple months. Next thing Grace knew, he'd been on one knee in front of her, camera and microphone in tow, asking her to marry him.

Their pictures, his question, and her answer had flashed across the giant overhead monitors for the entire stadium to see, followed by massive coverage on every sports channel and news segment in the country.

Thank goodness she'd loved him and been more than ready to say yes, otherwise the entire event could have been hugely embarrassing.

For Valentine's Day, he bought her diamond earrings. For her birthday, he flew her to the Bahamas. For Christmas, he made her go on a scavenger hunt all around town to find her gift, which was usually something gigantic and hugely expensive.

At first, everything with him *seemed* simple and easygoing. A small box, plain wrapping, no bow. But then whatever was inside turned out to be something amazing, like an autographed first edition of *To Kill a Mockingbird* or an emerald necklace that was worth twenty-five thousand if it was worth a dime.

His presents and his idea of romance were a lot like Zack himself: calm and unassuming on the outside. But inside, pure gold.

She'd forgotten that about him until just now. Forgotten how thoughtful he could be underneath the rough jock exterior, and how there were times when he'd treated her like an absolute princess.

Provided he *hadn't* cheated on her, hadn't been a wolf in sheep's clothing, she could definitely see herself going back with this man. Marrying him, even. *If* . . .

At the moment, he wasn't trying to seduce her. Probably wasn't trying to impress her at all, unless he had a mariachi band stashed under the bed ready to pop out and serenade her.

Instead, he was lying on the bed, using Bruiser as a pillow. His head was propped on the dog's belly, the Saint draped full-length across the top of the mattress just in front of the real pillows. Zack's fingers were linked together on top of his flat, T-shirt-covered stomach, his heavy-lidded gaze locked on the television screen.

"Find something to watch?" she asked in a low voice.

He blinked and rolled his head in her direction. She expected him to answer her with a drowsy "yep" or simply the name of the show.

But he didn't. He didn't say a word, just stared at her, eyes wider now than they had been before.

He raked her from head to toe, his look so heated that she glanced down at herself, wanting to make sure she hadn't accidentally forgotten to put on pants or something.

She hadn't. She was fully dressed, and not in her usual choice of nightclothes.

The one thing she'd gotten from her mother, without a doubt, was überfeminine genes and a love for slinky, sexy things. At home, she wore satin nighties and matching robes. Heeled slippers decorated with brightly colored feathers or sparkling rhinestones.

But since she hadn't wanted Zack to get the wrong idea—or any ideas at all—when she'd moved in to his apartment to help him get better, she'd left the Hollywood starlet wardrobe in her closet and opted instead for a few sets of nice, sturdy, flesh-covering pajama sets. The one she was wearing now had long legs and long sleeves. The bottoms were a thin flannel material in vertical rainbow sherbet stripes. The top was a solid lavender to match one of the wide stripes in the pants. She was even wearing a bra and panties underneath because she hadn't wanted to risk erect nipples peeking through the fabric or shadows in the wrong places as she moved around.

"The bathroom's all yours," she said, because she couldn't stand the silence anymore, or the way his hot stare was, indeed, making her nipples bead.

Zack blinked, swallowed, tore his eyes away as he rolled to the side and reached for his crutches.

"Right," he said, climbing to his feet. He went to his own suitcase, which she'd arranged on top of a round table in the far corner, and began to gather a few items.

As he hobbled past her on the way to the bathroom, she said, "If you need anything, let me know."

He gave a sharp nod, but kept walking, and she didn't let out her pent-up breath until she heard the bathroom door click closed.

Okay, he might be in trouble here.

More trouble than in his last game when he'd gotten dog-piled while his leg went one way and the rest of his body had gone another.

More trouble than when Grace had first showed up at his apartment and dragged him out of bed, announcing that she was there to whip him into shape and get him back on his feet—literally.

Possibly even more trouble than the day Grace had walked into his hotel room in Columbus to find a strange woman in his bed.

Because he was very much afraid he was falling back in love with Grace.

Despite everything they'd been through. Despite the fact that he'd broken down and lost himself for a while after she'd left him, then pulled himself up by his bootstraps and decided he could and would move on without her. That he'd be all right without her.

His resolve had gotten a bit shaky when she'd suddenly reappeared in his life, but he'd handled it well, he thought. Even after the kiss . . .

Oh, man, that kiss had rocked him to his very soul. Turned him on harder than he could ever remember being turned, and made him want to sink to the floor and slide into her right then and there.

It had aroused him and brought up a lot of old memories, yeah, but even that hadn't caused his head to spin quite as much as it was doing at this very moment.

And he wasn't sure why. All he knew was that the minute Grace had stepped out of the bathroom and he'd turned his head to look at her, every cell of his being had seized up, frozen, refused to function. His lungs burned, his vision turned hazy, and his blood burned so hot, he wouldn't have been surprised if steam started to seep from his skin.

The funny thing was that he shouldn't have had

that reaction given Grace's appearance. It wasn't like she'd sauntered out of the bathroom like Jessica Rabbit, in high heels, thigh-high stockings, and a barely there teddy. No, she was very conservatively dressed in plain cotton winter pajamas. Cute pajamas, but not exactly the stuff of wet dreams or even a Victoria's Secret catalog page.

How she could knock him for such a loop while covered from head to toe, hair still damp from her shower, pink-tipped toes bare, he would never understand. And yet she had. He'd taken one look at her and felt his stomach drop, felt his groin tighten . . . felt his heart melt, slide around in his chest cavity, then re-form in the shape of Grace's beautiful face.

Oh, yeah, he was falling, and falling fast. Falling hard, too. It was going to hurt like a son of a bitch when she let him know, in no uncertain terms, that he didn't have a shot in hell and he hit the pavement three million stories below.

Ouch. Lifting a hand to his chest, he rubbed the spot over his already aching heart.

This was going to be brutal. Losing her the first time around had been nasty enough, but now he felt as though he'd been given a second chance . . . or at least a shot at a second chance.

But Grace's mind was set where he was concerned. She thought he was a cheater, and nothing short of a message from God or Gage coming through with that lie detector idea—and Zack wasn't holding his breath on either count—was going to change her mind.

So here he was, locked in the crapper of a Holiday Inn Express in Bumfuck, Pennsylvania, afraid to go back out into the other room because Grace was there.

And if he saw her again, he'd want to touch her, hold her, tell her things that would only make his life miserable in the long run.

Leaning heavily on his crutches, he dumped his things on the closed lid of the toilet and began to undress. Once he was naked, he stepped carefully into the shower, crutches and all—though, thankfully, there was a safety bar along the wall that he could hang on to—and flipped on the water.

It was a cold shower for him tonight, unfortunately. Because if he didn't get his johnson under control, when he did go back into the other room, there would be no need for words. Grace would take one look at him and know exactly what was on his mind. Exactly what her presence did to him.

Then there would be a need only for explanations and possibly the ducking of objects flying at his head . . . or lower. It would be like opening Pandora's box . . . or a big, fucking can of worms he just did not want to deal with.

So he let the water run, standing under the icy fall until he was clean, but shivering, and everything that should be drooping instead of standing at attention had dwindled back into place.

Please let her be asleep, he thought as he climbed out of the tub and started to dry off. *Please let her be buried under the covers up to her neck, with a hundred and fifty pounds of Saint Bernard conked out between her and his side of the bed.*

Otherwise, there was a good chance certain parts of his anatomy would start pointing north again, and that would be bad. Very, very bad.

Row 17

Grace wasn't asleep, and the covers most definitely were not tucked up to her chin.

Damn.

The television and all the lights were still on, and she'd somehow managed to manipulate Bruiser to the foot of the bed so that she could turn down the sheets and the spread. Her damp hair was pulled back into a ponytail, and pillows were propped behind her against the headboard so that she could sit up straighter, legs out in front of her and crossed at the ankles. Her feet were still bare, the painted nails both adorable and sexy at the same time.

She was knitting. Something pink and girly—Jesus, not again—and in an indiscriminate shape, at least to his eyes. But it was coming along. The needles were clicking and clacking, and yarn was floating like a leaf on the wind as she wound it around her finger and one of the needles over and over with each stitch.

And just that quickly, he needed another cold shower.

Seeing her on that bed did things to him, made his mind wander in all sorts of directions it had no business wandering. Stirring up memories it had no business remembering.

Same went for his cock. If he didn't rush across the room and dive under the covers like he was trying to stop a puck from hitting the net, he was going to be in big trouble. Ten inches of big, throbbing trouble.

Doing his best to angle his body so that she didn't notice what was going on behind his blue striped boxers, Zack hitched his way across the room to the other side of the bed. Because, of course, she'd taken the side closest to the bathroom, closest to safety and concealment.

"You got him to move, I see," he said once he'd turned around and dropped onto the white-sheeted mattress.

"I promised him smoochies and lured him down there with some doggie biscuits slathered in peanut butter."

"You brought peanut butter?" he asked with a short chuckle, hoping the conversation and her knitting were enough to distract her while he eased his injured leg onto the bed and pulled the covers up to his waist.

There. Success. He was safe, as long as he kept his other leg bent so she would think *that* was the only thing tenting the sheets.

Pay no attention to the "little man" behind the curtain, he thought, the scene from *The Wizard of Oz* playing through his mind. Nothing to see here, nothing to worry about. It's just a knee.

Yeah, right.

"I brought *everything*," she told him without looking up from whatever it was she was knitting. "Three quarters of my luggage and what's packed in the car is for Bruiser."

He waited a beat, considering that. And then he said, "You're a good doggie mama, you know that?"

Her fingers slowed, and she cocked her head, watching him for a moment before replying. "Thanks," she said softly, a slow smile slipping over her face.

Okay, compliments were a bad idea. Or at least saying stuff that would make her smile like that was a bad idea.

Because now there was a fist-sized knot of desire sitting in the pit of his stomach, his balls were tightening, and he wasn't sure a knee the size of the biggest ball of twine in Minnesota was going to distract her from noticing the occasional wiggle around the area of his lap.

Yet even knowing all that, and mentally reciting hockey scores, couldn't keep his next words from tripping right off the tip of his tongue.

"A good nurse, too."

Damn tongue! Not good for anything but sucking his foot into his mouth. And, okay, yeah—once in a while, cunnilingus.

"Thanks," she said again, looking slightly confused now.

Join the club, he thought.

All right, time for a much-needed change of subject.

"So what are you knitting?" he asked.

Her lips twisted. "I don't want to tell you," she said, sounding oddly reluctant.

He snorted. "Why not? Is it something slinky and sexy . . . or naughty and embarrassing?"

Shit. Why the hell couldn't he shut up? Why the

hell did he keep muttering such suggestive stuff, when all it did was put pictures in his head? Dirty, naked pictures that were *not* helping the situation down below.

Grace laughed and reached out to elbow him in the arm without ever dropping a stitch. "No, nothing like that, you big perv."

Oh, if she only knew.

"I'm just afraid you'll be upset when you find out."

He turned his head, studying what she was doing more closely. What would he be upset about?

It was a pretty, Necco-wafer pink, which was quickly becoming one of his least favorite colors, thanks to how often she dressed his dog—his big, tough, *male* dog, thank you very much—in sissy outfits of that shade.

But other than that, he couldn't figure out why he would care what she was making. Unless it was a jock-strap or banana hammock or something equally embarrassing that she expected him to prance around in.

"Sorry," he said, shaking his head, "I don't get why that thing—whatever it is—is supposed to bother me."

Taking a deep breath, she let her hands and the yarn fall to her lap. "Promise not to be angry," she said.

Um . . . yeah, he could pretty much guarantee that one, since he was sitting here as clueless as an earthworm.

"I won't be angry," he assured her.

"All right," she said slowly, "it's a doggie sweater for Bruiser." She cringed—actually cringed—after spitting the words out like bullets from a Gatling gun.

For a second, he remained silent, looking at the

pile of pink on top of her multicolored pajama bottoms and seeing it in a whole different light.

"God," he groaned, rubbing a hand over his face in disgust, "not another one."

"I know, I'm sorry," Grace apologized. "I didn't plan it, I swear."

Laying what she had done so far out on her lap, she smoothed her hands over the snugly woven stitches, careful to keep them from slipping off the needles. He could see the shape more clearly now and how the piece would eventually form a Bruiser-sized sweater.

"Charlotte gave me this skein of yarn a couple of months ago. I'd forgotten all about it, to be honest, but the other night at our meeting, she asked if I'd used it yet." She made a humorous, ashamed face. "Thank goodness I still had it tucked into my knitting tote, because it would have broken her heart if she'd thought I didn't appreciate her gift. So I was kind of stuck starting something with it right then and there, and this was the only pattern I could think of on the spot."

Surprisingly, he actually *wasn't* angry or upset. He supposed he wasn't *thrilled* she was adding Pink Sweater #42 to his Saint Bernard's already too-feminine wardrobe (God, a dog with a wardrobe—was there anything more ridiculous on the planet?), but in the scheme of things, what did it matter?

Instead, he found himself eyeing the simplicity of the pattern, imagining what it *could* look like, and how he'd do it if it were his project.

"You know," he murmured, reaching over to lift the half-sweater by where the yarn was connected to the long metal needles, "you could give that a lot more texture if you switched to a knit-purl or maybe even a checkerboard pattern."

For the space of a full minute, possibly going on two, the room was completely silent except for the background noise of the television, which she'd turned down to a low hum when he'd first come back from the bathroom.

When she didn't say anything for such a long time, he lifted his head to meet her eyes. She was staring at him like a zombie, gaze blank, mouth open wide enough to catch flies.

He realized his mistake almost immediately . . . but also sixty seconds too damn late. Licking his lips, he swallowed hard and dropped the sweater back to her lap, pulling away to his own side of the bed.

"Just a thought. Not that I know anything about knitting," he rushed to say, hoping it would be enough to cover up his idiotic comment, throw her off track, and appease any blatant curiosity she might have.

But why should anything start going right in his life at this point, when "freaking disaster" seemed to be working so well for him these days?

"Oh, no," she said, sending the mattress bouncing as she folded her legs and turned to face him more fully. "You're not getting out of this that easily."

"I don't know what you're talking about." *Keep your voice steady. Avoid eye contact. Hope she buys it.*

The mattress bounced again as she shifted around even more, moving closer. A grin that reminded him a bit too much of Jack Nicholson's the Joker in *Batman* or Pennywise the Clown in Stephen King's *IT* stretched across her face, sending a shiver of anxiety skating down his spine.

Up on her knees now, still springing a bit as she towered over him, she rapped him lightly on the chest with the back of her hand, right in the center of his plain white Hanes undershirt.

"Tell me how you know all that."

"All what?" When in doubt, play dumb.

She rapped him again.

"Ouch," he complained, rubbing the spot she kept smacking. Not that it really hurt. A tiny sting, maybe, but he was a six-foot-four Rockets goalie . . . If he couldn't take a little slapping from a blond-haired, blue-eyed, hundred-and-twenty-five pound girl, he didn't deserve to be back on the ice.

"Don't 'all what?', aw shucks, I'm-just-a-good-ol'-boy-without-a-brain-in-his-head me. You know exactly what I'm talking about. How do you know about knitting, purling, and checkerboard patterns?"

She sat back on her heels, crossing her arms over her chest. It was a nice pose. Except for the annoyed tilt of her head, it framed her breasts nicely and tugged the hem of her pajama top up to reveal a slim line of bare skin at her waist.

"And don't make me smack you again," she threatened with a scowl.

She would do it, too. Not just crack him in the chest again, but pummel him, if she needed to. Straddle him and put him in a frontal choke hold—which, come to think of it, might not be so bad. The straddling part, anyway; he was pretty sure he could take her on the choke-hold thing.

And he shouldn't forget that she had a pair of sharp metal knitting needles within reach.

Inhaling sharply, he made the difficult decision to come clean. "Okay, okay," he sighed. "But you have to promise not to laugh. And not to tell anyone else. *Ever.*"

"You're not messing with me, are you?"

He raised a brow. "Why would I mess with you?" he asked.

"Because you think you're funny. And sticking a bag of dog poop in a teammate's locker is your idea of adult hilarity."

He gave a snicker. She made a good point, he supposed. That *had* been pretty funny. So had the time he and a couple other guys from the team took a dump in Lubov's litter box. The Russian defenseman had come home from a weekend away, seen the gigantic turds, and rushed his poor cat to the vet, certain the tabby had some dread disease and needed immediate medical attention.

So his sense of humor was warped—sue him.

But what he said was, "I'm not yanking you."

She waited a beat longer, then said, "All right. As long as you aren't jerking me around, then I won't laugh or repeat to anyone what you're about to tell me. Deal?" She held out her hand to shake on it.

He took her hand, squeezing tight and holding on a fraction longer than was probably necessary. "Deal," he murmured softly.

Shrugging a shoulder and refusing to meet her gaze, he admitted in a low voice, "I taught myself to knit."

He said it quickly, matter-of-factly, like tearing off

a Band-Aid so it would hurt less. It would be better if she were suddenly struck deaf, but he figured he had about as much chance of getting lucky in that department as in buying a scratch-off lottery ticket and winning the million-dollar jackpot.

True to her word, she didn't laugh. Actually, she didn't react much at all.

He waited, still expecting something, because never in her life had Grace Fisher been left speechless for long.

Finally, she cocked her head in the opposite direction, and in a tone dripping with skepticism, said, "You did not."

Okay, that wasn't quite the reaction he'd envisioned. Bemusement, ridicule, the start of embarrassing rumors he might never live down, sure. But *disbelief*?

"I can't believe I bare my soul and admit something like that, and you think I'm lying."

Reaching behind her, she grabbed the sweater-in-progress and shoved it at him. "Prove it."

He caught it before the tips of the needles could jab him in the stomach and held it a few inches away from his body. "Excuse me?"

"Prove it," she repeated. "If you taught yourself to knit, then let's see how good you are. Show me what you learned."

He held her gaze a second longer, then lowered his attention to the knitting in his hands. He tugged the large skein of Charlotte's bright pink yarn closer, rearranged the needles in his fingers, and shifted around on the bed to find a more comfortable position.

Then, without missing a beat, he picked up where she'd left off, finishing her row and beginning one of his own. He did a couple more in a straight knit stitch, just to show her he did, indeed, know what he was doing.

He glanced up, pleased to find her once again looking like a deer caught in headlights—eyes wide, mouth open in shock. Ha! That would teach her to doubt him.

And now, to rub it in . . .

"This is nice," he said, "don't get me wrong. But I think it might add a touch of flair and uniqueness if you mixed it up a bit."

He started a simple checkerboard pattern, just as he'd suggested earlier. Knit five stitches, purl five stitches. Knit five stitches, purl five stitches. "Do this for five rows, then reverse and do the exact opposite, and when you're done, you'll have these cute little checks that stand out. You can even switch back to a plain knit stitch for the rest of the sweater, and the checked section will just be in the center like an extra special segment of the design."

When he lifted his head, he found Grace still staring as though he'd sprouted a second head or announced he wanted to leave the Rockets to join the Rockettes at Radio City Music Hall as soon as his knee was fully healed.

"What?" he asked.

Oh, he knew what had her gaping like a guppy, he just wasn't sure *exactly* what was going through that labyrinthine mind of hers.

She shook her head, and the movement seemed to ripple down her entire body. "I can't believe you know how to knit," she said, sounding truly astounded.

"When did you . . . ? How did you . . . ? Why did you . . . ?"

Her eyes widened in frustration and she waved a hand at him in a rolling, fill-in-the-blanks gesture.

"Who? What? Where? When? Why? Fill in the blanks," she ordered. "Right now. I want to know everything."

Finishing the row he was working on, he set the needles and yarn aside before meeting her gaze. "Truth?" he asked.

She nodded, forgoing a typical smart-ass retort.

"I missed you," he said simply. "You thought I was the Spawn of Satan, believed I'd done the unthinkable, and after you left"—his brow creased in remembrance—"wrecking my apartment, destroying my Hummer, and taking my dog with you, I needed something to take my mind off my misery."

His gaze skittered away for a moment, and he rolled a shoulder, slightly embarrassed by what he was about to admit. "And I thought maybe, after you'd calmed down some and realized there was a chance I *hadn't* cheated on you, that my knowing how to knit might impress you, since it's such a big part of your life."

The minutes ticked by while she absorbed his explanation, and he waited for her reaction, good or bad.

"You learned to knit for me," she said, her voice tinged with stark incredulity and something else. Surprise? Confusion? Awe?

He blinked and swallowed, his heart pounding in his chest—*pa-thump-pa-thump-pa-thump*—feeling more and more awkward the longer her gaze bored into him. "It seemed like a good idea at the time," he mumbled self-consciously.

Grace's lashes fluttered over the cerulean blue of her eyes. Her mouth loosened into a soft, open O the color of rose petals. And before he knew what was happening, before he could even register the movement, she'd thrown herself at him, wrapped her arms around his neck, and was kissing him like a soldier newly home from war.

Row 18

This time, Grace was kissing Zack, no doubt about it.

Whether she should or shouldn't . . . whether it was right or wrong . . . whether she would regret it in the morning or was giving him false hope . . . she just didn't care.

Hearing that he'd learned to knit, that he'd taught himself in secret to impress her and as a possible means of winning her back . . .

Oh, my gosh, had there ever been such a sweet, wonderful, amazing, thoughtful, or romantic man on the face of the planet?

She didn't want to think about what had driven her away from him to begin with. Didn't want to remember the pain and anguish of thinking he'd cheated on her.

What if he hadn't? What if his protestations of innocence were all true and her friends—and her friends' significant others—were right about him deserving another chance?

For once, she wanted to believe it. Really and truly believe it, not simply *wish* that were the case.

Just for a few hours.

Just for tonight.

So before she could talk herself out of it, before doubts and fears and old hurts could rear up and make her run for the hills, she let her instincts take over. She closed her eyes, opened her arms, and launched herself at him hard enough to knock them both back against the headboard.

He grunted as she hit him square in the chest, hands coming up to catch her by the waist. But he didn't resist, didn't falter for even a moment in accepting her weight, accepting her offer, and accepting her kiss.

She opened her mouth over his, tasting his lips and coaxing him to open with her tongue. And if there was one thing Zack had never needed when it came to intimacy, it was prodding.

He tugged her closer, until her breasts flattened against his hard chest and they were belly to belly. Oh, how she wished she weren't wearing pajamas so her skin could press flush to his. As it was, she could feel the heat of his bare skin radiating through the fabric of his undershirt and her top, slowly raising her temperature and causing a flush to wash over her from head to toe, as though she were trapped inside a tanning bed cranked to "extra crispy."

From the waist down, he was covered in cotton boxer shorts and three layers of hotel-provided covers—the sheet, a blanket, and the thick, quilted comforter. Not for long, though; not if she had anything to say about it.

Moving her hands to his face, she deepened the kiss, letting him know she was more than willing, and not calling a halt anytime soon. At the same time, she used her legs and feet to kick the blankets down, moving them slowly inch by inch until she hit Bruiser's immovable bulk.

The dog didn't budge an inch, didn't even act as though he noticed her piling the covers on top of him. If he hadn't been there, she'd have pushed them off the end of the bed entirely, but at least this gave her better access to Zack's remarkable body.

Almost belatedly, she remembered his knee—remembered their last kiss, and how one wrong move had stopped things cold.

Tearing her mouth away from his, she gulped in oxygen like a fish too long out of water. They were both panting, chests heaving, lips (and several other vital body parts) swollen and throbbing.

"How's your leg?" she asked, voice thick and ragged.

"Good. Fine. Don't worry about my leg," he replied, his own tone none too steady as his fingers tightened on her waist and he tried to tug her back against his chest.

"I don't want to hurt you," she told him, leaning forward, *wanting* to go back and return to that soul-stealing kiss.

"You won't. You can't," he said, sitting up to get closer, reaching for her mouth.

She kissed him because she simply couldn't resist any longer. A brief, fleeting brush of lips before drawing away again.

"Of course I can," she whispered. "It's happened before."

"Not this time. Nothing is going to stop us this time." He raised a hand to her face, brushing his wide palm across her cheek, past her temple, and into her hair to cup her skull. "Kiss me again, Grace," he . . . ordered? Begged?

"You have to let me be on top," she said, not giving in until he'd agreed to be careful.

He gave a low, strained chuckle. "And you expect me to argue? Backward, forward, upside down . . . I'll take you any way I can get you, sweetheart."

It had been so long since he'd called her that or used any endearments toward her—for good reason, she knew—that her heart thudded and her stomach took a tiny dip.

"You can't do anything that causes you pain or strains your knee," she insisted, wanting to be sure—really sure—he wasn't going to do something stupid or push himself past his endurance just to get laid. "Promise me."

"The sun and the moon and the stars," he murmured, nibbling along her chin and jaw and the lobe of her ear. "I'll promise you anything."

She moaned, fighting hard to keep her thoughts in her head until she was satisfied they wouldn't do anything to set him back in his recovery. But, oh, his hands and his mouth and his warm, solid body were tempting her with a million other forms of satisfaction with a capital *S*.

"Promise you won't let me hurt you, or do anything to hurt yourself," she made herself say. Or at least she *thought* those were the words that tumbled out of her open mouth; it could have just as easily been a long, heartfelt moan.

But she must have spoken, because he answered without missing a beat. "I promise. Now kiss me before I explode."

He wasn't the only one who felt like an over-inflated balloon. The blood was pounding through her veins like out-of-control floodwaters.

She did as he asked, meshing her lips with his and kissing him, letting him kiss her. It was like coming home, like being right where she'd always belonged, despite everything.

Her hands roamed his chest and shoulders and the flat, amazingly well-sculpted plane of his abdomen. His, in turn, pulled the scrunchie from her hair, running through the still slightly damp strands to spill them about her face, and stroked up and down her side, teasing the swell of one breast through the material of her top.

Beneath her shirt and bra, her nipples beaded. Beside her thigh, his erection pressed and strained.

But she didn't want him *next* to her, she wanted him *inside* her. So she straddled him, lifting her left leg and planting it on the other side of his hips.

Zack helped her, settling her into place and rubbing her just over the tip of his arousal, raising the front of his boxers. Then he went a step further, running his fingers under the hem of her top, running them up, up, up. The material bunched and climbed, and she lifted her arms, broke their kiss, just long enough to allow him to skim it off over her head. Then their lips were meshed again, tongues tangling, teeth gnashing.

His hands moved to the back of her bra, unhooking the clasp as though it were no more than a slipknot, invisible, even. But then, he'd had a lot of practice.

The lacy, barely there cups fell away, the straps trailing down her arms and leaving her open and naked.

Cool air wafted over her, raising goose bumps along her skin.

Not that they lasted long with Zack's constant attentions. He seemed to touch her everywhere at once, stroking, rubbing, warming her even as he caused chills to race up and down her spine.

Cupping her breasts, he tweaked the nipples. Already pebbled and hard, the tissue swelled even more, filling his palms, making her groan.

Without warning, he sat up, circled her waist with one arm, and twisted them both around. She landed on her back, bouncing gently against the mattress.

"Careful," she said, though he gave her barely enough time to get out even a single syllable between kisses. "Watch your knee."

"Screw my knee," he told her, taking tiny nips of her throat, across her collarbone, down to one breast, where he circled, licked, and occasionally sucked.

"Mmmm." She threw her head back, arching into his mouth, scraping her nails along his shoulders and biceps. "I'd rather screw you."

He chuckled, running the flat of his tongue around the peak of her breast. "And you will," he murmured wickedly.

Thrusting his fingers into the waistband of her pajama bottoms, he pushed them down, snagging her panties and shoving both all the way down her legs and off. They got tossed somewhere past the bed, the same as her top and bra.

She was blessedly naked, sprawled beneath him and enjoying everything he was doing to her. But he was still wearing his boxers, and that just wasn't fair.

Her goal was to strip him the same as he'd stripped

her, but that didn't mean she couldn't take pleasure in the chore. She let the pads of her fingers dance down his back like she was reading Braille. She counted his vertebrae, and kneaded the softer flesh on either side.

When she reached the elastic waist of his boxers, she didn't stop, but drove her hands straight underneath, over the curve of his buttocks. She scored him with her nails, gave him a squeeze, pulled him tighter into the cradle of her thighs . . . and grinned in delight when he groaned, gave her nipple a tiny love bite, and ground himself even harder against her.

She was ready to divest him of his shorts and roll him over so she could ride him already when a long, wet tongue slapped her cheek and licked her from chin to eyeball.

And it wasn't Zack's.

"Aaack!" she screamed in surprise, then started to giggle, squinting and turning her head against an overabundance of doggie slobber.

When she cracked open one eye, she found Bruiser poised over them. He was standing above them on her side of the bed, licking her, then Zack, and nudging them both with his big, cold nose and the occasional paw the size of a baseball mitt in an effort to get their attention.

Unfortunately, this wasn't the first time they'd experienced *caninus interruptus*.

Zack lifted his head, the corners of his lips twitching in amusement. "I think somebody wants to play."

"Yeah, *me,*" she growled, pretending to be annoyed. Pressing the flat of her hand to Bruiser's wide chest, she pushed. "Get off, you big horse. You weren't invited."

"Since when does he wait for an invitation to anything?" Zack asked, starting to pull away.

"Hey!" She grabbed him by the arms and held him in place. "Where do you think you're going?"

"Unless you're willing to make this a very peculiar threesome or like being watched, we're going to have to lock him in the bathroom."

"Aww, the bathroom?" she asked, patting the top of Bruiser's head. "But he'll be so lonely in there."

Zack snorted. "We'll give him his blanket and all of his toys and snacks, and we'll be really quick, but yeah—the bathroom."

He started to move away again, rolling to the far side of the bed.

"All right," Grace agreed, though she was already feeling guilty about it. "But I'll do it. You stay here."

She started to sit up and get out of bed herself, the task made more difficult by Bruiser's constant nudging and sloppy kisses.

"Why?" he asked.

She waggled her brows at him. "Because you're too slow, Hop-Along."

With that, she jumped out of bed, completely naked, but not the least self-conscious, and started zipping around the room, collecting Bruiser's things.

She was bent over, one arm filled with doggie bones and squeaky toys, the other busy gathering the Saint's thick, soft blanket from the floor, when she noticed that Zack hadn't moved a muscle. And while that was good—she had told him to stay put, after all—she also had a sneaking suspicion . . .

Turning her head forty-five degrees, she glanced

over her shoulder to find him staring at her. Or rather, staring at her derriere.

She straightened, holding the blanket in front of her, effectively blocking his view. "Stop staring at my bare ass, Hoolihan, and make yourself useful," she told him.

"Useful, how?" he asked without a hint of shame or apology for his ogling, and without bothering to shift his gaze so much as an inch. "You told me not to move."

Starting toward the bathroom, she gave a little whistle and patted her thigh so Bruiser would follow. "Well, unless you want things to end *really* quickly once I get back, I suggest you hunt up some condoms. Otherwise, you might just be spending the night locked in the bathroom with your dog."

Nothing got a man to hustle like the promise of sex . . . or the promise to withhold it if he didn't jump through a few well-placed hoops. One corner of her mouth curved up in a grin as she sauntered off . . . and Zack made a mad dash for his crutches to tear the room apart until he found the item she'd requested.

Walking into the nice-sized bathroom, she spread the doggie blanket on the floor in front of the tub and called Bruiser over.

"Come here, baby," she said, kneeling down and patting the spot where she wanted him to settle. Then she laid his toys and bones around so he would have something to occupy his time. Otherwise, there was a serious chance he'd eat the shower curtain, the toilet paper, the towels, and possibly even chew the knobs right off the sink and shower stall.

"We won't be long, I promise. And after, I'll take you out for a quick walkie before bed, okay?" She kissed his nose and ruffled his ear before darting out and closing the door firmly behind her.

Zack was back on the bed, leaning against the headboard, only instead of still being in his blue striped boxer shorts, he was now completely, gloriously naked.

She took a moment to stand there and admire him, not the least bit self-conscious of her own nudity. Not with him, anyway.

From the top of his sandy blond hair to his large, long-toed feet, and every magnificently muscled inch between, she admired him. And apparently, she had more in common with Bruiser than she might like to admit, because she thought she may even have drooled a little.

Cocking her head, her gaze strayed back to his lap and she arched a single brow. "I'd ask if you found some condoms, but all signs point to yes."

Grinning, he lifted an arm and dangled a strand of five or six plastic squares of protection. "Just call me Magic 8 Inches," he quipped.

"Only eight?" she challenged. "I thought you always claimed to be at least ten, fully erect."

His lips twitched. "This is the one and only time eight sounds better than ten. Of course, if you'd like to measure me to make sure . . ."

She put a hand on her hip and hitched it to the right. "No, thanks, I'll take your word for it. Besides, you know what they say: anything more than a mouthful . . ."

Even if he'd wanted to, Zack couldn't hide the involuntary jerk of his penis at her suggestive remark. Grace bit the inside of her lip to keep from smiling.

"Why don't you get your sweet ass over here and put that to the test," he all but growled.

She took a step in his direction, then another, taking her time and making sure he looked his fill. When she reached the end of the bed, she climbed on, one knee and then the other.

"We can't leave Bruiser in the bathroom for long," she reminded him, crawling slowly toward him, "so you have to choose. I can either make you happy . . ." She licked her lips as she reached his thighs and lifted a leg to straddle him. Then she took the string of condoms from his hand and dangled them in front of him. "Or we can make each other happy. Your choice."

His chest rose and fell with his rapid breathing, his stomach muscles going concave as she ran her fingers down the center of his torso and lower.

"Oh, I want us both to be happy," he said, voice grating. "We'll just have to save the other for later."

The corner of her mouth curved, and she chuckled. "Okay, but we'll have to be careful. We wouldn't want Bruiser to mistake this for one of his bones or chew toys."

Zack sucked in a sharp breath as her hand closed around his burgeoning cock. "Definitely not."

Sticking the corner of one of the plastic packets in her mouth, she bit down and tore the rest away along the perforation, tossing them aside. Then she tore open the single packet and removed the circle of latex.

"Do you want me to put it on?" she asked him.

"You have no idea how much," he replied, a huff of air bursting from his lungs.

As much as she would have liked to linger and play with him a while longer, she was also horny and eager and didn't want Bruiser getting any destructive ideas before they'd gotten to the really good stuff. So she wasted no time in fitting the condom over the head of his penis and rolling it down his thick, significant length.

Once it was securely in place, she leaned forward and took his mouth in a long, slow, luxurious kiss. His hands slipped to her waist, those wide palms spanning nearly from breast to hip.

After several long minutes, he pulled back, and she expected him to say, "Let's get to it," or pull her forward so that she was flush with his erection. But instead, he drove his fingers through the hair at her temple, caressing her and looking deep into her eyes.

There was something there, something serious and meaningful that caused her stomach to flutter. It wasn't just sex now. She didn't know what he was thinking, but she knew the mood of the room had shifted—imperceptibly, but significantly.

"What?" she asked softly, holding his gaze.

"I need to know . . ." He stopped, licked his lips, and started again. "Is this just blowing off a little steam, or is this . . . Do you believe me when I say I didn't cheat on you?"

Her heart seized inside her chest, a tight squeeze that stole her breath for a second. It was The Question. The Big One. A fork in the road. One of those superimportant, life-altering moments.

The problem was, she didn't have an answer for him. Not a definite one, at any rate.

She swallowed hard and gave him the only response her conscience would allow. "I don't know."

His lashes fluttered and a curtain dropped on the other side of his lapis-blue eyes, making her heart twist even more.

"I'm sorry, Zack," she apologized, and she meant it. "I *want* to believe you, really I do. I just . . . I know what I saw, and it's hard for me not to think the worst, but . . ."

Shaking her head slightly, she put her hands on either side of his face and held his gaze, trying to let him know without words that she *did* want to be here. Her emotions might be in turmoil, her mind might be racked by confusion and doubt, but the one thing she *wasn't* confused about was being with him at this very moment.

"Right now, this minute, though, I do believe you." Leaning in, she brushed her lips across his. "Please let me believe," she whispered against his mouth. "Just for tonight."

Row 19

Zack exhaled on a sigh.

Just for tonight.

It wasn't exactly an absolution of his supposed sins or even a declaration of undying love.

Just for tonight.

It didn't actually change anything for either of them. They might be naked and in bed together, about to take part in the most intimate act possible between a man and a woman, but when they awoke in the morning, they would be right back where they'd started.

Did he care?

Hell, yes.

Was he going to push her away, tell her they had to stop because she still thought—or at least believed there was a possibility—he'd been unfaithful?

Sigh. No.

A bigger man might say that pride was more important than getting laid—and it was. But being with Grace wasn't about pride *or* sex. And if it meant lying to himself, pretending she trusted him and that everything was okay . . . Well, then, he could do that.

Just for tonight.

Knowing there were no words for what they were

about to do or the million thoughts spinning through his head, he nodded.

Grace's shoulders, which she'd been holding military straight, slumped with relief, and the breath she'd been holding released in a *whoosh*. Her lips lifted in the gentlest of smiles.

Amazing how a woman straddled buck naked on his lap and promising all manner of naughty, dirty deeds to come could still look so freaking angelic. She was so beautiful, it was almost painful. His teeth ached just looking at her.

But other parts of him ached more.

Digging his fingers more firmly into her hair and along her scalp, he pulled her close and covered her mouth with his own. He kissed her to let her know this was all right with him, that everything was going to be all right, even in the morning, in the bright light of day when she might be faced with regrets for what they were doing now. And maybe, if he was lucky, in hopes of helping her to realize that he was worthy of her trust.

She kissed him back, her lips pressing against his, her tongue sucking and twining, driving him half out of his mind. His free hand splayed at the small of her back, bringing her close so that her breasts flattened to his chest and the tip of his cock nudged between her legs.

"I thought you said you were going to ride me," he murmured between nips of her lips, her chin, her throat. He wanted to kiss her everywhere at once, taste every inch of her skin, lick her from head to toe and back again.

"Mm-hm." Her eyes were closed, her platinum-blond hair dusting her shoulders seductively.

"Grace?" He spoke her name softly, amused by the blank expression on her face.

"Hmm?"

She was so caught up in the passion, in his kisses, in her own arousal, that he probably could have recited the Periodic Table of Elements or asked her to walk barefoot across flaming coals and she would have reacted the same way.

"And are you going to, or would you rather we keep doing this?" He trailed his mouth down her chest, leaving patches of wetness along her skin from the tiny love bites.

"Licking." He licked the swell of one breast.

"Nibbling." He moved to her areola, taking the softer, darker, more tender flesh between his lips, and giving it the gentlest of nips with his teeth.

"Sucking." He took the nipple into his mouth, doing just that.

"Yes," she groaned, pressing herself more fully into his ministrations. "God, yes."

He chuckled, more than happy to continue giving her pleasure. Something this delectable, he could do all night.

"Like that?" he asked, continuing to lave one breast for a few seconds longer before moving to the other and repeating the same slow, torturous treatment.

His gut clenched as she moaned in response, her fingers knotting through his hair. Lower, his dick twitched and his balls drew up.

God, he wanted to be inside her. More than his

next breath. He'd missed her so much. Dreamed about having her in his arms again for so many months.

He stroked her back, her hips, reveled in the feel of her buttocks pillowed on top of his thighs. She smelled of her favorite spicy-sweet perfume; something one of the high-end fragrance companies had sent her years ago that she'd fallen in love with and decided to make her signature scent. It was a heady mix of ginger and cala lily, and had always made him unaccountably hungry—for her.

Her nails scraped his scalp, sending shivers along his skin. Abandoning her breasts, he began to kiss a line down the center of her torso, leaning her back over his stretched-out legs, bent slightly at the knees.

She went willingly, bending like a Barbie doll so that he could reach her navel. He wanted to go lower, and had every intention of flipping her over onto the mattress in just one . . . more . . . minute.

Arching even more sharply toward his ankles, Grace put her weight on his knees. A flash of pain stabbed through the left one—not as bad as that day in the kitchen, but enough to make him suck in a breath.

She straightened immediately, the haze of desire gone from her eyes, replaced now by the clear shine of reality.

"I told you this was a bad idea," she said, her mouth tugging down in a concerned frown.

She started to pull away, to climb off his lap, but he was having none of that. Tightening his grip on her waist, he held her in place.

"Don't even think about it," he growled through gritted teeth.

"But I hurt you," she complained, still holding herself away from him, though no longer struggling to leave completely.

"No, you didn't. A puck, a net, twelve hockey players built like fucking steamrollers, and a shitload of bad luck hurt my knee. *You* make me feel better. *You* make me horny as hell. *You* aren't going anywhere until we're finished here."

"You promised—"

"And I'll keep that promise. I'm fine. My knee is fine. I just need you *closer*—" He yanked her forward, face to face, chest to chest, pelvis to pelvis. "And it won't be a problem. Trust me."

His words ended on a whisper as he held her gaze, his breath dusting her cheek.

"Do you trust me, Grace?"

Her tongue darted out to lick her lips and he saw the tendons of her throat contract and release as she swallowed. She gave a small nod, and the ball of tension in the pit of his stomach began to loosen.

It wasn't complete and total forgiveness, it didn't even apply to the big picture when it came to their relationship. But it was something, and he was desperate enough to take what he could get.

"Take me inside," he murmured, his voice ragged, his lips a hairsbreadth from hers.

She rose up an inch or two and he moved his hand down to her hip, helping to guide her as she centered herself over his throbbing erection. One hand folded over his shoulder, the other wrapping around his cock and positioning him at her entrance. And then she was sliding down, enveloping him, sending his temperature soaring.

He locked his jaw and ground his molars nearly to

dust in an effort not to groan, to scream, to beg. God, she was tight. And hot and wet and wonderful.

She felt like heaven. Paradise on plain white ten-thread-count cotton hotel sheets.

He wanted to pull her down, impale her fully on his aching rod, but he also wanted it to last. Slow was killing him . . . but what a way to go.

Her lips parted, and she started to take tiny panting breaths. He was right there with her, nostrils flaring as he fought to keep his heart from pounding out of his chest.

With a sigh, she sank down and covered him completely. The air huffed from his lungs, releasing some of the tension that had his muscles pulling cable-taut.

Grace grinned, just a tiny, contented lift of her lips. But it reached her eyes, glittering there with diamond-like satisfaction.

Her peaceful expression reached inside him, stroked him in places that hadn't been touched in a very long time. It warmed him and gave him hope for the future.

Sitting up, he wrapped his arms around her, hugging her close to his body. As close as possible without crawling into her skin.

"I love you, Grace." He hadn't planned to say that, hadn't planned to say anything. But the words were there, crowding his chest and burning a path up his throat. And when he opened his mouth, they spilled out like too many marbles crowded into a jar.

Her lashes fluttered, her pleasure fading slightly.

"I know that's not what you want to hear," he said. "I know you're not ready for that, or for anything more than right here and now. And that's okay—I don't expect more. I just need you to know how I feel."

Squeezing her even tighter, he brushed a hand over her hair, refusing to break eye contact, regardless of how uncomfortable he might be making her.

"I love you, Grace. I always have, from the moment I met you. And I suspect I always will, whether you believe me or not, whether you return those feelings or not."

He could see her bottom lip trembling, emotions swirling like a storm cloud across her face.

"And I will *never* do anything to hurt you. I never have, not intentionally." Running the pad of his thumb over that lip, he gave a sad half-smile. "I hope one day you can find it within yourself to trust the truth in that."

Her lips parted as though she were about to speak, but he didn't want to hear her arguments or denials, not even another apology for not believing in her soul that he hadn't—and would never—cheat on her. It was enough that he'd said his piece and made his feelings known.

"It's all right. You can relax, I'm finished now," he said, placing a single finger over her mouth to keep her from saying anything. He didn't want the evening thrown off track any more than it already was.

Although it took some doing, he forced himself to offer her a weak smile. "We can get back to the good stuff now."

For a minute, he thought she was going to bolt, thought he truly had ruined things for both of them. But then she took a shuddering breath and gave an even jerkier nod.

"Forgive me for getting all serious on you there for

a second?" he asked, rubbing his palms up and down her back, doing his best to soothe and comfort her.

She nodded, though he could tell her whole heart wasn't in it. And then she surprised him by saying, "This is more than just sex for me, too." Her voice was low, uncertain, the dark blue pools of her eyes reflecting the same. "I'm not sure how much more, but it is."

"Glad to hear it," he quipped, trying to add some much-needed brevity to the situation. "Of course, if we don't start wiggling around a little, I'm not sure we can really call this sex."

As he'd hoped, she laughed, and just that quickly the mood in the room lifted, lightened. Her arms looped around his neck, and she leaned in for a soft, slow, lingering kiss. When she broke away, they were both panting and the heat between their linked bodies had cranked up at least a dozen degrees.

"So are you going to fuck me, or do you want to spend more time talking about your feelings like some pansy-ass girl?" She cocked her head to the side, mouth curved in a mocking grin, eyes glittering with amusement.

"Oh, I'd much rather fuck you than talk," he said. No thought necessary. "Of course, since you're on top and you don't want me to strain my knee, maybe it would be better if you fucked me."

"Mmm, good idea."

Her inner muscles flexed around him—a deliberate (and debilitating) move on her part, no doubt— making him gasp. His head fell back against the headboard and his hands grasped her hips, holding her tight and close as she began to move on him.

She shifted back and forth, slowly at first, just enough to cause a slight friction. Although, as wound up as he was already, even those gentle motions were like touching the tip of a match to a pile of gas-soaked rags. And then she added a little up and down to the mix, and bursting into flames became a very distinct, very realistic possibility.

He groaned, biting the inside of his cheek to keep from cursing a blue streak. His cock ached. His balls throbbed. He wanted to come so badly, he was ready to beg.

But he wanted Grace with him. It was all or nothing tonight, no shortcuts and no one-sided finales.

He reached up, cupping her breasts, running his thumbs around and then over her nipples until she whimpered and pulled her lower lip between her teeth.

"Faster," she breathed, and then matched her actions to the desire. Her hips canted, picking up speed. Her thighs clamped around his.

His blood heated, running through his veins like molten lava. Leaving one hand on her breast, he slid the other down her belly, over the triangle of springy blond curls between her legs, and into her silken folds.

She groaned, licking her lips and letting her eyes slide closed, and he wasn't far behind. He felt himself moving within her . . . or rather, her moving around and atop him. It was sexy, erotic, irresistible. But it wasn't what would get the job done.

The pads of his index and middle fingers found her clitoris. Found and rubbed, using her own moisture to ease the way and build that slick back-and-forth slide.

He increased the pressure, which increased her

movements, making them both pant and huff and gasp for air. His chest squeezed like a vise, and every time she rippled around him, lifted off and drove back down, he could have sworn the top of his head shot off a good three inches. As close as he was to flying apart, he knew he wouldn't be able to hold back much longer.

"Come with me," he grated, giving the tiny nub between her legs a flick before circling, stroking, doing everything he could to push her over the edge. "Come with me."

She bit her bottom lip, so hard he worried she might draw blood. She came down on him harder and harder, and he raised his hips, meeting her thrust for thrust until his vision turned gray and hazy.

Her nails clawed at his shoulders while his hands clutched her hips and buttocks. She cried his name, stiffening above him, arching with pleasure, gripping him in the tightest, most exquisite iron fist.

It took no more than that for his own body to go taut, for the pressure that had been building in his cock and balls all night—hell, for months now—to reach a boiling point that was forced to find release or consume him from the inside out.

His fingers flexed against her soft flesh, brought her down on his still-rigid erection, and then he spilled. Wave after wave of uncontrollable ecstasy rolled through him, battering him against the shore, pulling him back, crashing over him once again. Her name passed his lips in a strangled whisper, almost like a prayer.

And when she collapsed on top of him, falling to his chest so that he could feel her ragged breathing, feel the warm flush of her cheek against his skin, he folded his arms across her back and held her there.

Right now, at this very moment, his life was perfect. Reality would intrude soon enough, he knew. But for just a while longer, he had the one thing he wanted more than life itself. He had Grace.

Row 20

Grace couldn't remember ever feeling so relaxed or content. She could lie here for a hundred years, she thought, and never want to move.

A scratching from the far side of the room, though, reminded her that that wasn't an option.

Zack groaned. "At least he waited until we were relatively finished."

She tried to chuckle, but it came out as more of a wheeze. Her head was on his shoulder, eyes closed, body limp and boneless with satisfied satiation.

One of the strong arms around her back tightened, and he rolled to his side—his right, her left. "My turn to deal with him," he said. "You stay here."

Like she was going to argue. She barely had the energy to draw oxygen into her lungs, let alone get up and do the doggie day-care thing.

He slipped out of her, slowly and carefully, leaving her feeling empty and bereft. He'd only been gone half a second—was still, in fact, occupying the king-size mattress right along with her—but already she wanted him back. Beside her, under her, inside her.

The mattress dipped as he moved to the edge and stood. She cracked open one eye, just a fraction, and watched as he hopped toward the bathroom on his good leg, keeping a hand to the wall for balance.

She heard a scrape and a creak as he turned the knob and opened the bathroom door. Bruiser gave a happy yelp, and she imagined Zack jumping out of the way to avoid getting run over as the giant Saint Bernard burst forward and loped into the bedroom. He gave another joyful bark and leaped onto the bed, sending her bouncing.

Grace knew exactly what was coming, but still she shrieked when paws the size of dinner plates pummeled her and Bruiser started licking her like a lollipop. Laughing and curling into a ball to protect herself from either massive bruising or melting from an excess of doggie saliva.

"I think he likes you," Zack quipped with a chuckle, leaning against the far wall.

"I think he hates not being the center of attention and is going to make us pay for locking him up for twenty minutes."

Zack glanced at the digital clock on the bedside table. "Forty-five, thank you very much."

One corner of her mouth lifted. "Sorry, forty-five." And then her brow creased. "He didn't destroy anything in there, did he?"

The curl of Zack's lips told her the big behemoth had, indeed, done some sort of damage.

"He kind of ate the shower curtain."

Her eyes widened. "The whole thing?"

"Most of it. But he left the rings."

"Oh, good," she replied, as though that made all the difference in the world.

Bruiser continued to use her and the bed as a trampoline, and she started to get the feeling he was more than just glad to be out of the bathroom.

"I think he needs to tinkle."

"I'll take him," Zack offered, pushing away from the wall and moving to find his pants.

"No," she told him, bending and squirming until she'd extricated herself from the hundred-and-fifty-pound ball of fur. "It will be quicker if I do it."

He didn't respond, but she felt his gaze following her as she dug a T-shirt and jeans out of her suitcase and shrugged them on. She slipped the room's key card into her back pocket, then found Bruiser's leash and snapped it to his collar.

"You know," she drawled, as Bruiser dragged her toward the door, "we do have a few condoms left over there." She tipped her head in the direction of the nightstand. "When I get back, maybe we can put them to use."

His expression didn't change, but his eyes glittered with heat and intense sexual interest. That same heat skittered through her veins as she skipped out of the room and sneaked Bruiser down a rear stairway for a quick potty call so she could rush back *up*stairs for a nice, leisurely booty call.

Thankfully, when she got back to the room with an empty-bladdered Bruiser, he settled right down on the blanket that Zack had retrieved from the bathroom and arranged on the floor at the foot of the bed and fell asleep. And a snoozing Saint—provided he wasn't snoozing smack-dab in the middle of the bed between them—allowed them to make love again. With any luck, more than once.

For the second time that night, Zack was naked and waiting for her—something that Grace decided she could easily get used to.

Stripping off her clothes, she let them fall where she stood, then slowly crawled her way across the mattress to join Zack beneath sheets warmed by his body heat. He wrapped his arms around her and drew her close for a long, leisurely kiss.

"Mmm," he murmured when he finally lifted his lips from hers, brushing the corner of her mouth with the pad of his thumb. "You were gone too long."

"Your dog has a bladder the size of the Goodyear blimp. Don't blame me if it takes him a while to empty it."

Zack chuckled. "Maybe we should stop giving him water until the end of our trip."

"That would be cruel."

"Well, then, maybe we should take advantage of every moment he *doesn't* have to take a leak."

At that, his hand smoothed down her arm, onto her bare hip, and along the outside of her thigh. She lifted the same leg, careful not to bump his injured knee as she draped herself over him. "I'm all for that."

She pressed herself close, loving the feel of his hard, only slightly hairy chest against her bare, beaded nipples and the eager press of his erection at the apex of her thighs. Reaching between them, she eagerly stroked his rigid length, only to find it . . . smoother than usual.

With a brow winging upward, she leaned back slightly to regard him. "Somebody was feeling rather sure of himself."

"Hey," Zack said, his face a study in seriousness,

"I'm a relatively hot guy, confined to a hotel room for the night with an equally hot babe who already let me into her pants once. I figured there was a fifty-fifty chance you'd come back raring for round two and thought I should be ready for action."

"You're a very arrogant man," she told him, still stroking his latex-covered penis.

"Was I wrong?" he asked, the words cocky even when grated through clenched teeth.

She shook her head. "Not wrong, just arrogant. Luckily, I'm a fan of the Boy Scout motto."

Slipping a hand between her legs, he found her curls damp and slid his fingers easily between her silken folds. "So am I."

With a moan, she arched her hips in an attempt to get closer to his erotic ministrations.

"I wish I were a hundred percent," Zack whispered near her ear while he nibbled her lobe and kissed a warm trail down the line of her throat. "If I didn't have to baby this damn knee, I'd have you pinned to the wall right now. I'd be taking you on the table, in the shower, up against the door . . ."

The erotic images he created seared themselves into her brain, leaving her gray matter singed and smoldering . . . and every other part of her sizzling like a live electrical wire.

"Here is fine. This way is fine. Just . . ." She shifted on his fingers, driving them even deeper inside. "Stop talking and take me already."

He started to chuckle, only to break off as she took his mouth, then released his cock and forcefully moved his hand so that she could drive herself down on his hard length. The bold action made them both groan, but it didn't slow them down. They were too turned on, too ready . . . and all too aware of what awaited them at the end of the blinking neon rainbow.

Ever cautious of his knee, they remained on their sides, using their lower bodies to create a rhythm, a steadily increasing cadence of up and down, thrust and retreat. Friction built. Tender, swollen tissue rubbed along slick, velvety steel.

Her nails dug into his shoulders and she wanted like crazy to cry out, but refused to relinquish his mouth. She needed him *everywhere*. Wanted to feel him, taste him, absorb him into her system until there was no Zack, no Grace, only a single entity intent on pleasure and fulfillment.

His hands moved along her bare skin, raising both gooseflesh and flames everywhere they went. He knew just how to touch her; he always had, from the first time passion had overtaken them. And she knew how to touch him—light here, more firmly there.

He groaned against her lips and she felt it down to her toes. Her legs tightened around his hips, her hands on his shoulders and biceps. His clutched her buttocks, pulling her harder, faster into his forceful pounding.

And then, without warning, she broke. Her heart stuttered in her chest, her inner muscles clasping, seizing, grasping at him like a swimmer drowning in a raging sea while wave after wave of perfect, intense pleasure broke over her head. But if she were to die, to drown in the complete ecstasy only Zack could give her . . . wow, what a way to go.

Zack followed her over only a split second later, biting her lower lip, yanking her to him in an almost painful grip while he stiffened. He growled his completion into the taut flesh of her throat where her pulse beat erratically, taking advantage of a store of oxygen she apparently didn't have access to. But she certainly shared the sentiment.

As he stilled beside her, her breathing slowed to a more normal pattern and she wrapped her arms around him, taking comfort in his nearness, his warm embrace.

She wished they could stay here forever. That they could stop the clock and lock themselves away in this cramped hotel room, forgetting about the rest of the world for a while.

Did she know where they were going from here? Other than to New York, no. She didn't know if she truly trusted Zack, didn't know if she could block out what she'd seen that day in Columbus and believe it hadn't been an act of infidelity. But, oh, how she wanted to try.

To that end, with his gentle snores filling the room and echoing in her ears, she forced her brain to turn off and *not* overthink what was going on between them right now.

In the wee hours of the night, with the lights turned low, that was simple. She let herself close her eyes and enjoy the feel of his skin caressing hers, of his chest rising and falling against her own. And when he woke her in the wee hours of the night with soft kisses and the stroke of his fingers on her breasts like butterfly wings, she made love with him again—happily, willingly, exuberantly.

But the hours ticked by too quickly, and when the alarm went off at eight A.M., neither of them wanted to move. The sharp, incessant buzz filled the room for a good three minutes before Zack reached over and smacked the snooze button. Nine minutes later, the buzz started again, and once again Zack did the ol' karate chop to make it stop.

Grace would have been happy to stay where she was, pressed like plastic wrap to Zack's side from shoulder to ankle, and repeat the process for the next twelve to twenty-four hours. But then Bruiser started to stir, to whine, to climb up on the bed and "massage" them awake.

"We'd better get up before Bruiser decides to flood the place," Zack said groggily.

Grace groaned and screwed her eyes shut even tighter. "Do we have to?" she asked, burying her face in the crook of his shoulder.

" 'Fraid so."

He stretched, reaching his long arms up over his head and his toes toward the end of the bed, dislodging her from her warm and cozy cocoon of drowsiness.

"We should probably get on the road, anyway. Those Insides Out folks will start to wonder if we drift into town a couple days later than expected."

She inhaled deeply, then exhaled on a sigh of resignation. "Fine, but don't blame me if I fall asleep at the wheel."

A large, warm palm spread across her left butt cheek and gave her a little morning goose. "Don't worry, I'll think of something to keep you awake."

She cracked open her eyes to find him grinning down at her. Her mouth opened on a witty retort, but then Bruiser's big, long-nailed paw goosed her on the other cheek and she gave a screech of shock instead.

Laughing, Zack climbed out of bed and began to dress. He took the bathroom first, giving her a few more precious moments of rest with a side order of panting, dancing dog.

When he returned, he collected his crutches, Bruiser's leash, and Bruiser himself.

"Are you going to be okay with him?" she asked, holding the white top sheet to her breasts as she pushed herself into a sitting position against the headboard.

"Sure. We'll take it slow and I'll let him lead."

"That's what I'm afraid of."

He shot her a smile before hobbling out of the room, a prancing, tail-wagging Bruiser preceding him into the hotel hallway.

Although she desperately wanted to hunker back down under the covers and grab a few more minutes of much-desired snooze time, she knew Zack was right about getting on the road. Dragging herself out of bed, she shuffled to the bathroom, and made quick work of washing her face and brushing her teeth.

Zack hadn't been kidding about the shower curtain. What was left of it hung from the hooks like the mast of a wrecked ship and looked as though a shark had gotten hold of it. Not that this was the first time she'd thought of Bruiser as a Great White of the canine world.

They would definitely have to pay for that when they checked out. The question was, how did they explain the curtain's condition?

A slip and near-fall while climbing out of the tub?
Really wild sex?

Multiple Personality Disorder, one of whom thought
he was Norman Bates?

Oy.

Drifting into the other room, she dressed in the
same jeans and mint-green Aéropostale tee she'd
thrown on to walk Bruiser last night. By the time
Zack returned with a much less wiggly pup in tow,
she had her suitcase and Bruiser's designer zebra-
print tote packed and sitting by the door.

While Zack collected his own things, she moved
about the room, cleaning up what little clutter they'd
made during their short stay. Housekeeping would
come in to *clean*-clean, she knew, but she'd always
had an ingrained need to straighten her own area and
not leave more of a mess than she absolutely had to
for someone else to take care of.

When Zack was ready, and they'd done the usual
under-the-bed-and-inside-the-drawers check to be sure
they hadn't left anything behind, she suggested he
take Bruiser down to the Hummer and leave the heavy
lifting to her. He grumbled about not being able to
pull his own weight, but she merely smiled, stretched
up on tiptoe to buss his cheek, and told him he could
make it up to her later.

It took two trips to get everything into the car, the
second time going through the lobby to check out and
turn in their key cards.

Once they were back on the road, the drive went
much the same as the day before. A bit of small talk;
the occasional argument over radio station choices;
warm, panting Saint Bernard breath tickling their

ears; and frequent stops for Zack to exercise his leg and Bruiser to water the local foliage.

The only difference was that today both their moods seemed lighter. Grace noticed the change immediately . . . as soon as they woke up, actually, but she was glad to see it carry over into their trip.

Zack's conversation was breezier, less tense and walking-on-eggshells than it had been the day before.

The day before? Who was she kidding? Since she'd moved into his apartment, and probably more accurately, since she'd raced away from that hotel room in Columbus and refused to look back.

Oh, there were times when they'd been civil to one another, and she thought they'd done an admirable job of getting along these past few weeks, but looking back now, she could definitely see that things between them had still been strained.

For good reason, she knew, and not particularly surprising.

But last night had changed that. Her fingers tightened around the steering wheel as snapshots of those hours together flashed through her mind.

How much they'd changed, she wasn't yet sure. The sex had been good—great, amazing, freaking fantastic—but she wasn't some bobble-headed stereotypical ditzy blonde. Zack could come bearing a vibrating, solid-gold dick that made her see the face of God, and she still wouldn't be willing to simply roll over and forget or forgive everything.

She had some thinking to do where that was concerned. More than thinking; some deep, dark, and intense soul-searching.

But what she did feel fairly certain of was her

willingness to *consider* starting over with him. Given that only a month or two ago she'd pretty much been wishing him into eternal damnation on an hourly basis, that was real progress.

For the first time in . . . forever, it seemed . . . she thought she might actually be willing to believe his claims that he hadn't slept with that woman in his hotel room. She *wanted* to believe it, anyway, and felt open-minded enough (for a change) to try to get to the bottom of what had really happened that day.

She didn't know how to go about that, exactly, but she would think of something. Some way to discover at least enough to put her mind at ease—she hoped.

Because even without being absolutely, positively certain he hadn't betrayed her, the truth was that she felt better around him than at any other time in her life. Happier, more relaxed and content.

So if there was a chance she'd overreacted and assumed the worst when he was actually innocent . . . Well, she would kick herself for all the months they'd lost, for sure. But she would also rejoice in being able to take him back, and then dedicate herself to making up for wasted time.

The radio station they were listening to went from a nice, upbeat Kelly Clarkson song to something much louder, with a lot more screeching guitar and migraine-inducing drum solos.

"Oh, no," she said, reaching for the button to find something else. "You can listen to that noise on your own time."

She expected him to start a friendly argument. To tell her to leave it, to dispute that it was a good song, and she would appreciate it if she just listened for a few minutes with an open mind. She knew for a fact it was one of his favorite bands, even if she couldn't stand them.

And given the rapport between them so far this morning, that should have been his lighthearted reaction.

But instead he remained silent. Not just listen-to-whatever-you-want-I-don't-care silence, but tense, distracted silence. He was staring out the passenger-side window, watching the scenery as it flew by.

"Zack?" she said softly. "Are you all right? Do you need to stop and stretch your leg or . . ."

He turned his head to meet her gaze, and she noticed immediately that his eyes were shadowed, shuttered. His mouth was a flat slash across his face, his jaw squared with tension.

"Think we could take a short detour?" he asked.

She blinked, startled by the request.

"Um . . ." She glanced at the dashboard clock. The Insides Out people expected them to get into town sometime Wednesday, but she hadn't been specific about their arrival. And except for a tentative meeting Thursday afternoon to discuss their plans for the photo shoots and such, they weren't scheduled for anything crucial until Friday and through the weekend.

"Yeah, sure, I guess that would be okay."

"Take the next exit," he told her in a low, unemotional voice.

Another mile and a half passed in utter quiet until they reached that exit, but inside her nerves were jumping. Her heart had adopted a slightly irregular beat, wondering what was going on.

Finally, she licked her lips and said, "Mind if I ask where we're going?"

For long, drawn-out seconds, he didn't respond. Then, in a low voice, he murmured, "My father lives about forty-five minutes from here. I thought I should stop in as long as I'm in the area."

Instead of putting his request into perspective, his explanation only confused and intrigued her more. Zack had never spoken of his family before, at least not in any great detail.

She knew the basics about them—that his father had left him and his mother when he was only a few years old, going on to remarry several more times; that those relationships had resulted in a handful of half siblings Zack had never met; and that Zack felt very strongly that his father's abandonment of them had forced his mother to work herself into an early grave just to keep food on the table and a roof over their heads.

Which was why his suggestion that they drop in and say hello caught her off guard. Of all the people she might have expected him to want to visit, his father would have been at the very bottom of the list.

"I didn't think you and your dad got along," she ventured to say. Tentatively, hinting that she was curious about their relationship, but leaving him room for privacy, if he preferred.

He shrugged a shoulder, returning his attention to the view out the side window. "We haven't talked in a while, but I know his health hasn't been great. I thought I should probably stop in and see how he's doing since I'm this close."

That was the last bit of conversation they shared—

other than Zack's roughly mumbled directions—until she brought the Hummer to a stop in front of a small, two-story brick house with white and black trim in a well-kept, middle-class neighborhood.

It was a nice-looking house. Neat without being ostentatious; in need of a little work without looking rundown. There were empty flower boxes lining the porch—which Grace assumed would be full of colorful blooms come spring—and the path leading to the front door had been shoveled free of snow.

Putting the Hummer in park, she shut off the engine and got out, moving around in time to help Zack. In the backseat, Bruiser danced around, excited about getting to explore another new patch of grass or meet new people.

But she didn't think Zack would appreciate having an overactive Saint Bernard tripping him up while he was reuniting with a parent for the first time in God knew how long. For that matter, he might not want her around, either.

Ignoring the stab of disappointment that came with that thought, she waited for him to get his crutches under him, then said, "Do you want me to wait here while you visit? I can take Bruiser around town for a little exercise until you're ready to go."

It took a minute for him to answer, but when he did, it was with a shake of his head. "No, you can come in."

That was it. No "Don't be silly" or "I want you to meet my family," just "You can come in." But it was enough of an invitation for her.

Leaving Bruiser to soak the seats and paint the windows with pupsmears, she followed him up to the front door. He knocked and they waited, and seconds later the door opened to reveal a tall, gawky teenage boy with a mop of brown hair and spattering of adolescent acne dotting his long face.

As soon as he spotted Zack, his eyes went wide and his mouth fell open. "Holy shit!" he exclaimed. And then he was gone, taking off back into the house yelling, "Mom, Dad, it's Hot Legs! Hot Legs is actually here, in my house. Holy shit!"

Grace chuckled. "Your reputation precedes you," she told him.

"Yeah," Zack muttered. Rather than being flattered, though, he looked slightly embarrassed and more than a little uncomfortable.

A few seconds later, a woman appeared, brows drawn together in a mix of curiosity and confusion. Her too-black hair (from a bottle; definitely, definitely not natural) was teased and sprayed in a style reminiscent of the 1980s . . . or perhaps modern-day New Jersey. She wore too much makeup and too-tight clothes, and put Grace in mind of the Peggy Bundy character from *Married . . . With Children*. She was even wearing a pair of high-heeled slides. Indoors. In the middle of winter.

"Can I help you?" she asked, taking hold of the door and closing it a few inches in a gesture that clearly said she wasn't sure yet if they were welcome or not.

"I'm Zack. I'm here to see my father." Straight to the point, not even offering his last name. Assuming, Grace supposed, that this woman should already know who he was.

Grace, however, was still clueless. Was the Peggy Bundy wannabe Zack's stepmother, his father's most recent wife? She looked awfully young for that, if Grace's math was right. But then, if Zack's dad had gone from woman to woman, wasn't it likely that he'd gone for younger models each time he'd traded in a previous wife?

And wasn't it strange that she didn't recognize Zack, either from a prior meeting or because he was practically a national celebrity?

Grace had more questions than answers, and had to bite her tongue to keep from asking every single one.

If anything, the woman's expression soured even more at Zack's lackluster introduction, but she didn't try to shut them out. Stepping back, she said, "He's in the other room. I'll show you the way."

Grace followed Zack inside, closing the door behind her. Without being obvious, she studied her surroundings.

Like the outside of the house, it was tidy; if there was a speck of dust on anything, she didn't see it. But unlike the exterior, the interior carried an air of hauteur.

The furniture looked expensive . . . or maybe was *supposed* to look more expensive than it really was . . . and was made up of modern versions of old-fashioned designs. Victorian or Edwardian or Louis the XVIII knockoffs. Grace might not be up on her time periods, but she knew fakes when she saw them.

Zack's crutches made *clop-clop* sounds on the hardwood floor, following behind the *click-click-click* of the other woman's heels. The farther into the house they went, the less comfortable Grace became.

She knew Zack didn't exactly hold warm and fuzzy feelings toward his father, and if they hadn't seen each other in a while . . . well, they deserved a private reunion.

Laying her hand gently on his arm, she whispered, "You go ahead, I'll wait here."

Without missing a step, he nodded, though he didn't seem overly happy about the prospect of going off alone.

Grace remained where she was, and a moment later, the ebony-haired woman returned. Her mouth was set in a lemon-sucking moue.

Since they didn't call her "Amazing" for nothing, Grace pasted on her dealing-with-pissy-people smile and held out her hand.

"We haven't been properly introduced," she said in an upbeat tone. "I'm Grace Fisher."

The woman eyed her as though she were about to steal the jewelry from around her neck, but lifted her own hand to shake briefly.

"Patsy," she said.

Ha! Patsy, Peggy . . . she hadn't been too far off, had she? Grace wondered if her maiden name had been anything close to Bundy.

"Grace Fisher," Patsy repeated warily. "Are you that woman from the talk show?"

The corners of Grace's mouth lifted into Dealing with Awed Fan Smile #3. Not the most sincere of her Dealing with Awed Fan smiles, but it was up there. "Yes, I am."

"And you used to be engaged to Zackary." A statement, not a question.

The grin slipped a fraction. "Yes."

Patsy narrowed her gaze. "I thought you broke up. So what are you doing together again?"

Rude, much? Nosy, much, you frigid bitch? Grace thought, wishing she could curl her lip and show her disdain.

But then, this was Zack's stepmother, and even if he didn't love her, didn't even like her or know her the least little bit and didn't have a very good relationship with his father, she should at least try to be civil while she was a guest in their home.

"We've been seeing each other again," Grace told her, enjoying the surprise her words brought to the other woman's eyes.

Besides, it was moderately true. They had been *seeing* each other again, since they'd both been blessed with perfect twenty-twenty vision. And even seeing each other naked, so it totally counted.

"Come on into the living room," Patsy said, more order than invitation, turning on her heel to lead the way. "I'll get us something to drink."

She didn't ask what Grace would like or even offer a selection of choices, so Grace supposed she would have to take what she could get. She just hoped that whatever it was wasn't laced with poison.

Taking a seat on the pristine sofa—which was so squeaky clean, the cushions so firm, it looked as though it bore a plastic cover five days out of the week—Grace waited for Patsy's return by taking in even more of the room's decorations. Her hostess apparently collected crystal figurines of every shape and size, and those miniature souvenir spoons. Both fell under the Dust Collector/What's the Point? column in Grace's book, but to each her own.

Patsy returned a few minutes later with a tray—an honest-to-God silver tray—holding a floral-pattern china tea set. She filled two dainty cups that looked infinitely breakable, and Grace added a touch of milk and sliver of lemon to her own, waiting for it to cool enough to drink.

"So what are you two doing here?" Patsy asked in what Grace was coming to believe was her typical straightforward (bordering on downright impolite) manner.

"We're on our way to New York for a photo and commercial shoot," Grace told her, and then went on to explain a bit about the endorsement deal with I.O.U., and that they were driving rather than flying because of Zack's injury.

Patsy's dark brows rose in what Grace could only categorize as keen interest. "An endorsement deal," the woman all but crooned. "That sounds . . . lucrative."

A trickle of dread snaked down Grace's spine.

Uh-oh, had she said the wrong thing? Obviously, she had; or at the very least she'd said too much. Given the woman the wrong impression.

Then again, what business was it of hers how much she and Zack were receiving from Insides Out? Or how much they earned from their regular jobs, for that matter? She certainly hadn't waltzed into Patsy's house and started asking how much she'd paid for all of her museum-quality furniture.

Grace opened her mouth to respond, even though she didn't have a clue what she should say, when noises from the back of the house caught their attention. She heard the staccato clop of Zack's crutches, along with at least one other set of footsteps, and above that, an eager, rapid-fire voice.

A second later, the teen boy who had opened the front door to them appeared, walking into the living room backward. He was gesturing wildly, and when Grace caught a glimpse of his face, she noticed that it was cheerful and animated with excitement.

"Oh, man, that was awesome," he was saying. "And then that time you blocked a shot from Sellers just as the clock ran down. Sweet!"

Zack smiled, and Grace could tell he was genuinely enjoying his half brother's enthusiasm. His expression was no longer strained, his shoulders no longer stiff with trepidation.

"Mom," the boy said, spinning on one foot to face Patsy. "Did you meet Zack? He's the *star goalie* for the Cleveland Rockets. And he's my brother! I can't believe he's my brother!"

The boy positively vibrated with pleasure, and Grace wondered if he'd just discovered his relation to Zack. Did Zack's father not talk about his oldest son—or his other children from other marriages, for that matter? Or had the young man known that *technically* they were related, but never met Zack, and therefore never believed there was true familial potential between them?

"He's going to send me a jersey signed by the whole team," he continued. "How rockin' is that?"

Grace chuckled, meeting Zack's gaze over the boy's shoulder.

"Grace," Zack said, still grinning, "this is Ian. Ian, Grace."

"Hey!" the young man greeted her, chest still heaving from his breathless monologue.

"Hi, Ian, it's nice to meet you."

An older man with thinning, light blond hair going to gray came around both Zack and Ian, taking a seat in the armchair opposite his wife. He wore a pair of charcoal Sansabelt slacks and a navy blue sweater over a plaid button-down shirt.

"And this is my father, Frank," Zack added, his smile slipping a fraction, his voice taking on a less happy note. "Dad, this is Grace."

She shook the man's hand, offering a polite hello. He didn't seem overtly ill, even though Zack had mentioned he'd been sick. But when Grace looked closely, she did notice a slight pallor to his skin, and that his clothes hung a bit loosely from his tall but thin frame, as though he'd recently lost weight. She would have to ask Zack later what was wrong with him.

"Frank," Patsy said, ignoring her son's desire to continue raving about Zack's accomplishments on the ice. "Did Zackary tell you that he's on his way to New York to shoot an ad campaign for Insides Out Underwear? They're paying him a mint, I'm sure, and you know how I've been wanting to move into a bigger house in a much better neighborhood."

Row 21

From there, the visit went downhill fast. Or, as Zack would have said, it went to hell in a handbasket down a very slippery slope.

Grace had been right about saying too much to Patsy about their reason for going to New York. In the space of only five minutes or so, it became crystal clear to Grace that the woman was a consummate and shameless gold digger.

She went on and on about all the things Zack could do and buy for them, and Grace could have sworn her brown eyes turned green, the pupils reshaping themselves into dollar signs. It was both eerie and sickening.

The longer Patsy blathered on, truly believing Zack would just open his wallet and shower her with cash, the more regretful Grace became that she'd ever said anything about the endorsement deal, and the more stoic and quiet Zack became.

She understood now why he didn't visit more often. Whatever his relationship with his father, she wouldn't have wanted to deal with the money-hungry barracuda just to get to him, either.

Because she could feel the tension rolling off Zack in waves, Grace quickly stood and suggested they get going. Bruiser was waiting in the car, after all, and they really should get back on the road.

Zack heartily agreed, and clomped to the door faster than she'd ever seen him move on those crutches, and she was only too happy to follow him out. They said their good-byes and made their way to the Hummer, climbing in and driving off as quickly as possible.

Bruiser pranced back and forth on the backseat, but neither of them wanted to stick around long enough to let him out. God knew how much longer Patsy's windfall wish list would grow in the span of time it took for the dog to tinkle on her lawn.

Reaching behind her, she patted the Saint's furry head. "It's okay, baby, we'll stop in a few minutes so you can go potty."

She returned her hand to the steering wheel, taking a deep breath and then letting it out. "I'm sorry, Zack. I had no idea your stepmother was going to be like that. I should have kept my mouth shut."

He lifted one broad shoulder, staring straight ahead as she maneuvered them through town and back toward the highway.

"I didn't know she was like that, either. I'd never met her before."

It wasn't exactly a free pass, but the fact that he hadn't known she was a gold digger either was some small consolation.

"How long has it been since you last saw your dad?"

"Years," he said. "Patsy and Ian weren't home at the time. Before that, he was married to a different woman with a different set of kids, and lived in a different part of the state."

She gave a snort of ironic laughter. "You know, we make quite the pair."

"Why?" he asked, turning a dark blue gaze in her direction.

"Because we both come from completely fucked-up families. My mother let everyone around her run her life, thinking they were going to make her a star, but ended up drinking and drugging herself to death. I never knew my father—I'm not sure my mother actually knew who my father *was*—and ended up being raised by my grandmother. And you," she went on, "had a great mom, but a deadbeat dad who went and got himself bitten by the Bride of Dracula."

It was Zack's turn to chuckle, the corners of his mouth creasing for the first time since they'd pulled up in front of his father's house.

"All in all, I'd say we could be the poster children for Dysfunction Junction," she told him, pulling off to the side of the road in front of a park on the outskirts of town.

A small, square plot of land, it boasted a few benches, picnic tables, and flower beds, along with a sliding board, a set of three swings, monkey bars, and a couple of those cute animal-shaped seats on giant metal springs—in this case, a duck and a dolphin—for kids to play. Two of the swings were occupied by girls who looked to be about nine years old.

Grace smiled at them as she hopped out of the Hummer and moved around the hood to open the door for Bruiser. He jumped and bounced, eager to get out and run around, but making it difficult for her to get the leash snapped onto his collar. Once that was done, though, she let him out and gave him a long lead to run ahead and sniff everything in sight.

Zack got out, too, collecting his own crutches and following along at a slower pace while Bruiser dragged her to and fro all around the playground. Zack made his way to one of the picnic tables and climbed up to sit on the top set of wooden planks, his feet and the crutches propped on the seat.

When Bruiser brought Grace around to the swings, the two girls wanted to know if they could pet him. And big attention hog that he was, he nearly knocked them over trying to get more and more full-body pats. Grace almost offered to let them ride Bruiser around for a while, but then reminded herself that he only *looked*—and ate—like a horse.

Finally, the girls grew bored and Bruiser's energy level tapered off a bit, so she wandered over to where Zack was sitting.

"Hey," she said, taking a seat beside him. Bruiser continued to sniff and explore, pacing to the end of his leash and back again. "You about ready to go?"

"In a minute," he said, staring off across the park.

"What are you thinking?" she asked quietly, knowing it must be something serious to put such dark shadows behind his eyes.

He shook his head, and for a second she didn't think he was going to answer.

"I promised I wasn't going to bring this up again," he said in a frustrated tone.

Whether frustrated with himself or whatever situation he'd vowed not to broach again, she wasn't sure, but she simply waited, knowing that he would open up when and if he was ready, and not a moment before.

"My dad," he began slowly several minutes later, head bowed as he studied his clasped hands balanced between his spread knees. "You wouldn't know it by looking at him now, but he used to be quite the ladies' man. He cheated on my mother multiple times before taking off, cheated on all of his other wives, and most likely cheated on every woman he's ever had any sort of relationship with. I hated him for that as much as for the fact that he abandoned us."

Zack straightened, flattening his palms on his knees and rubbing roughly along the faded denim. "I know you don't want to hear this—or maybe you just aren't ready to yet—but that's the number-one reason I would never be unfaithful to you. I watched my father go through women like they were toilet tissue. I saw the trail of devastation his infidelity left behind. And I swore long ago—long before I met you—that I would never be *that kind* of man."

He turned then to meet her gaze, his blue eyes Arctic clear and brimming with sincerity. It reached in to cut off her oxygen and grip her soul. God, how she wanted to believe him.

"I may pretend to be a player. I may grin and wag my tongue at the female fans. I may even have gone home with a different woman each night before I met you. But I never once lied to them or let them think there was more to it than a simple one-night stand. And when I date a woman, I date *that woman,* and that woman alone. No stepping out on her, no having a girl in every port—or every game city, as the case may be. And if my eye did start to wander, that's how I knew it was time to break things off and move on. Which I did, *before* I started anything with anyone else."

He lifted both shoulders in a careless shrug and clapped his hands together. "That's it, Grace, that's all I've got. The ball's in your court now, I guess. You're going to have to decide for yourself what kind of man you think I am. And if you think I'm someone who would lie to you, betray you, cat around on you . . ." Another shrug, only one shoulder this time. "Then you're right to kick me to the curb and walk away. No woman should put up with an asshole like that."

His lips twisted in a sad, defeated grimace before he slid down from the picnic table, retrieved his crutches, and fit them under his arms. "I wish to hell my mother hadn't."

He murmured the last in a low, resigned voice, then turned and hobbled back toward the Hummer, leaving her both speechless and moved . . . and so confused, she felt as though she were being torn in a million directions at once.

Zack sat at the round table at the front of The Penalty Box where he and his friends normally gathered on Wednesday nights. The same Wednesday nights the girls had their Knit Wits knitting meetings.

Grace would be there, he was sure. And sooner or later, Dylan and Gage would wander into the bar to join him, although he had every intention of getting the hell out of Dodge before the girls showed up for their after-meeting drinks.

For now, though, he was early and he was alone— just the way he'd planned.

He'd done all he could where Grace was concerned. Bared his soul and laid it all on the line.

Fat lot of good it had done him. She'd hardly said three words to him since.

She'd put Bruiser in the car and pulled away from the tiny park near his father's house, driving them the rest of the way into Manhattan almost like a chauffeur—silent and ghostly, there to get him where he was going, but not much else.

They'd even skipped their second planned stop and driven straight through, checking into the Manhattan hotel early, then sat around waiting for the I.O.U. reps to get in touch and set up the numerous hoops they were expected to jump through.

Needless to say, any chance of having her let down her guard enough for them to heat up the sheets again was out of the question.

There were meetings with Insides Out representatives, with Quentin North in attendance. Then a photo session for the print ads that would appear in magazines and on billboards across the country, and a shoot for the commercials that would run on some of the more popular television networks. Both of which involved the two of them stripped down to their I.O.Us, and in various versions of hockey gear, striking any number of sensual, suggestive poses.

If Zack hadn't been so worried that he'd fucked things up royally with her, and blown any chance he'd ever had of getting her back, he thought he probably would have even enjoyed the weekend.

They stayed in New York through Tuesday before heading back to Ohio. And, oh, what a great trip that had been. Right up there with a root canal, sleeping on a bed of nails, or having a colonoscopy without anesthesia. Not because they'd been fighting, but because they'd barely talked at all.

As soon as they'd gotten home, she'd helped him get settled, then packed up the remainder of her things and moved back to her own apartment. She hadn't seemed angry or upset when she'd left; if anything, her demeanor had been calm and accepting. But she hadn't taken Bruiser with her, leaving the dog to keep Zack company instead.

That's when he'd realized she was gone and she wasn't coming back. She was cutting ties with him, leaving him and everything that reminded her of him behind.

One would think that after being dumped by her once before and spending so many months certain that he would never see her again, this wouldn't come as such a shock to his system.

But then she'd come back into his life. Moved back into his apartment, helped him get back on his feet, and let him back into her bed.

Idiot that he was, he'd thought it meant something.

Or maybe *hoped* was a better word. He'd *hoped* it meant something. *Hoped* they were building up to renewing and reviving their relationship.

Now that he knew differently, though, it was time to move on. No more moping, no more trying to convince her of something she obviously wasn't going to believe no matter how many times he repeated himself, how loud he shouted, or how hard he banged his head against the wall.

Nope, that was over and done with, and as soon as the alcohol content of the beer in front of him hit his bloodstream, he thought he might even start to feel okay about that.

The door behind him opened, letting in a blast of cold air. The temperatures had been warmer when they'd first returned from New York, but in the past couple of weeks had dropped again, bringing a few new inches of snow and ice to the city.

Gage and Dylan tromped in, stomping snow from their shoes and heading directly to the table where he was sitting. They took one look at the empty Coors bottles already littering the flat surface, and brows went up.

"Guess you've been here a while, huh?" Gage asked, shrugging out of his black leather jacket and draping it over the back of his chair before taking a seat.

Not as long as he might suspect, Zack thought, but didn't say so. He didn't say anything at all.

Dylan followed Gage's lead, removing his coat and taking the last empty chair at the table. Raising a hand, he signaled Turk, the bartender, to send over fresh drinks.

"I take it you haven't heard from her, then," he said.

This was the first time they'd met up in person since Zack's return from New York, but they'd talked a couple times. They knew how the trip had gone, and that for a brief, flickering moment, he and Grace hadn't been at each other's throats . . . at least not in the usual "Die, demon, die!" way.

"Not unless she's sending up smoke signals and I'm not seeing them," Zack replied dryly, bringing the beer he'd been nursing for the past twenty minutes to his lips and taking another long swig.

A waitress came with bottles of beer for Dylan and Gage, disappearing again without a word.

Gage twisted the cap off his Coors and took a drink before returning it to the table with a soft clink. "I suppose this means you won't be needing the polygraph test I went to so much trouble to set up," he said, his annoyance at being put out for no good reason clear in his tone and the wrinkling of his brow.

"'Spose not," Zack responded, unable to find it in him to feel guilty when he was busy feeling so many other, more important things.

"Shit," Gage bit out. "Do you know how hard it was to schedule the equipment and get the guy to agree to administer the test off the books? Do you know how bad a whipping I'm going to take if anybody at the precinct finds out about it?" He shook his head and took another swig of beer. "This is why I said no in the first place. This is why I didn't want to get involved."

"Jesus," Zack cursed, though there was no real inflection to the word. "Stop your bitching, Mrs. Marshall. I'll take the damn test, if it'll make you happy. Maybe I'll get a parakeet to keep Bruiser company while I'm on the road, and I can use the results to line the bottom of its cage."

Gage harrumphed, and turned his head to take another sip of his drink. Zack drank, too, still waiting for the booze to take effect.

"You don't think it will make a difference, even if it shows you've been telling the truth the entire time?" Dylan asked, reaching for the bowl of peanuts in the center of the table and tossing a handful one at a time into his wide-open mouth.

"I don't think it would make a difference if I had a

time machine and took her back to *show* her I didn't fuck that woman. She's made up her mind. And I'm moving on," he added decisively. "Life's too short to spend it mooning over one woman."

One beautiful woman. A perfect woman. The only woman he'd ever opened himself up enough to love, asked to marry him, or planned to do the whole "till death do us part" thing with.

But, hey, it was only his heart, crushed and broken and skewered beneath her size-seven stilettos. No big deal, right?

"I'm going back to work next week," he said, changing the subject and hoping it would stick. "The doctors have cleared me for some light scrimmages, and I'm going to travel with the team to practice games in the spring."

A beat passed before his friends responded, and then it was with less enthusiasm than he'd expected.

"Great."

"Good for you."

"Yeah. It'll be good to get my head back in the game. To move on," he added more softly, his gaze shifting away from his friends so he wouldn't have to see the pity in their eyes and on their faces.

And while he was on the road, he was going to bang every puck bunny who batted her overly mascaraed lashes in his direction. Tall or short; big tits or little; blonde, brunette, or redhead . . . He didn't even care if they were particularly attractive, not at this point. After all, as the saying went, you didn't look at the mantel while poking the fire.

And it wasn't like he had anyone to be faithful to. Not anymore.

Row 22

Grace shouldered her way into her apartment early Friday evening, hands and arms full with items for French Night. Ronnie and Jenna would be here any minute, so she left the door unlocked, kicking it closed with her foot before heading for the kitchen to portion the quiche Lorraine she'd just picked up at a local eatery. She also needed to find her fondue set, and start cubing and melting the brie she'd bought earlier in the week.

Setting the warm bakery box on the counter, she yanked off her coat and boots, and dumped her bags from work on a nearby chair. It would have been easier to make a couple of trips to get everything in, but who wanted to run back and forth out into the cold, especially since she hadn't even eaten any rich French food yet? She would worry about burning off extra calories *after* she'd enjoyed copious amounts of cheese and wine.

Moving around the kitchen, she quickly dealt with plating the quiche, starting the cheese to melt, and moving everything to the living room, where they would spend the rest of the night watching sappy and

pretentious French films and speaking with truly de-
plorable, but hilarious, French accents.

After collecting wine glasses and getting everything pretty much set, she took a breath and wandered
back to where she'd left the rest of her stuff, digging
through for the day's mail. Before she had a chance to
study it, however, a knock sounded on the door, and
her friends poked their heads in.

"Allo, allo," Ronnie called, letting herself into the
apartment, Jenna close on her heels. She held up two
sagging fabric totes and waggled her brows. "We
come bearing wine and bread crusty enough to break
a tooth."

"Not after we soak it in cholesterol-tripling brie,"
Grace laughed, taking one of the bags of wine from her
friend and leading them into the kitchen.

"We also have *Chocolat* and *chocolat,"* Jenna
added, holding up the movie DVD in one hand and a
nice-sized bag of dark chunk candy in the other.

"Bien."

Grace grabbed a cutting board and bread knife,
and the three of them moved into the other room after
shedding their heavy winter outerwear. Crowding
around the low coffee table, they started the movie
and dug in to the bevy of food spread out before them.

An hour or so later, they sat back, stuffed to the
gills.

"Okay, this skirt was a really bad idea," Ronnie
groaned, rubbing her stomach. "Remind me to wear
only stretchy materials with elastic waistbands for
Girls' Night from now on."

It wasn't the first time one of them had said such a

thing . . . or forgotten what pigs they made of themselves on Friday nights.

"I've got sweatpants, if you want to borrow a pair," Grace offered.

"Nah, I'll just pretend I'm a man and undo a couple buttons," she said. Then she tipped her head in the direction of the television screen and whispered, "Just don't tell Johnny."

Grace and Jenna both chuckled as she did exactly that before stabbing her fondue fork into another chunk of bread and going right back to enjoying her meal.

"Uh-oh, looks like we're out of chardonnay," Grace said, topping off Ronnie's glass with what was left of the single bottle they'd brought in with them. She hopped to her feet and headed toward the kitchen, the empty bottle and a few dirty dishes in tow. "No worries, I'll get some more."

On the way back, this time with a nice cabernet sauvignon, she grabbed her mail and glanced through, just to see if there was anything of interest in the pile. Unlikely, but worth a look-see.

Bill, bill, one-time offer for better cable (of which she'd gotten six such one-time offers already), letter from a long-distance friend, catalog, catalog, manila envelope, magazine.

The only thing that caught her attention was the manila envelope, mostly because it contained no return address. Tearing open the flap, she slid out the contents and read the note scribbled on a plain yellow Post-it stuck to the top of a sheaf of papers.

Thought you should see this, was all it said. And it was signed simply, *G.*

"Correct me if I'm wrong," she muttered, peeling off the note and holding it out to Jenna without taking her gaze from the documents in her hands. "But isn't this your husband's handwriting?"

Jenna took the Post-it and looked it over, frowning in confusion. "Yeah. I mean, I think so."

"Why is Gage mailing you something?" Ronnie asked, putting voice to the question running through all of their minds.

"I have no clue. I don't even know what it is."

She turned the pages one way, then the other, but saw nothing more than a bunch of spiky lines, all in different colors. They looked like something a child would create with one of those Spirograph games, only going up and down instead of round and round.

She pulled those pages away—or rather one very long piece of paper folded accordion style—and passed it along for the others to study while she began to read the typed lines on the pages beneath.

The more she read, the harder her heart began to beat. Her breaths came faster, as though trying to keep up with her eyes as they scanned the paper.

"Oh, my God," she murmured.

It was a report of sorts, written in question-and-answer form, dated three days before.

Is your name Zackary Hoolihan? Yes.

Were you born March 22, 1972? Yes.

Are you a goalie for the Pittsburgh Penguins? No.

It went on and on like that for the first two pages, questions with simple yes or no answers meant to establish a baseline. And beneath each, in bright red ink, was a statement declaring the testee's response as being either truthful or deceptive.

So far, every one of Zack's responses was one hundred percent truthful, according to the polygraph operator. And those guys had to be trained and certified, right?

She swallowed past the lump forming in her throat and skimmed ahead.

Did you invite a woman other than your fiancée, Grace Fisher, to your hotel room in Columbus, Ohio, while you were on the road with the Rockets last summer? No.

Truthful.

Did you have sexual relations of any sort with the woman in your hotel room in Columbus? No.

Truthful.

Have you ever had sexual relations with any woman other than your fiancée, Grace Fisher, since becoming engaged? No.

Truthful.

Have you ever had sexual relations with any woman other than your fiancée, Grace Fisher, since the two of you started dating? No.

Truthful.

"Oh, my God," she said again, tears pricking behind her eyes.

"What?" Ronnie wanted to know, leaning forward in an effort to get a glimpse of what she was reading. "What is it?"

"It's a lie detector test," Grace whispered, voice thick with emotion. "Zack took a polygraph test to prove he didn't cheat on me."

"I thought you said he'd already told you he didn't cheat on you, on the way to New York, and you believed him." Jenna's brows drew together. "And he took a lie detector test to prove it, but why would Gage send you the results instead of Zack showing them to you himself?"

Grace didn't know, and she wasn't sure she cared. Her chest heaved as she tried to catch her breath, regain her equilibrium. Her vision clouded, there was a dull ringing in her ears, and the pages were actually trembling in her shaking hands.

"I don't know," she replied softly, lifting her head to meet her friend's questioning gaze. "Why don't you call that husband of yours and find out."

Licking her lips, Jenna nodded, then climbed to her feet to retrieve her purse and cell phone. She dialed, waited while it rang, and began to speak as soon as Gage picked up on the other end. Explaining the situation as quickly as she could, she came straight to the point, asking why he'd sent the polygraph results to Grace instead of Zack.

Grace watched intently as Jenna inclined her head, occasionally uttering a soft, "Uh-huh. Uh-huh." Then, "I don't know yet. I'll call before I leave. Okay, love you, too."

She hung up, and Grace was on her feet, arms crossed beneath her breasts, waiting, even before her friend had shifted to face her. "Tell me," she demanded.

"He says Zack asked him to set up the test before you two went to New York. When you got back, he didn't want to go through with it anymore, but did because Gage had gone to so much trouble."

"And the results?" she pressed. "Why didn't Zack give them to me himself?"

Cocking her head to the side, she glanced at Grace, a sad sympathy darkening her eyes. "Zack told him it wouldn't make any difference and to throw them away. That he'd told you the truth, and you'd either believe him or not, on your own. He also, um . . ." Jenna bit her lip, looking reluctant to share the rest.

"Go ahead," Grace said, bracing herself. "I want to know."

It took a second for her friend to work up the courage to relay whatever else she had to say, but finally she added, "Gage said Zack seems resigned to the fact that you're gone, and is moving on with his life."

A pain unlike anything Grace had ever felt before stabbed through her heart, through her soul. It nearly doubled her over, ricocheting inside her like a runaway bullet.

For a minute, she couldn't think, couldn't seem to get enough oxygen into her lungs to keep her brain cells functioning. And then, suddenly, she did.

Her chest swelled as she inhaled deeply. Her tongue darted out to wet her dry lips. And her brain was not only working, it was *shrieking*.

"The hell he is," she muttered.

She darted around the apartment, climbing into her boots, yanking on her coat, hat, gloves, grabbing her purse and the polygraph results, which she shoved back into the manila envelope.

"Where are you going?"

Ronnie was on her feet now, too, both of them watching her warily, matching expressions of concern etched on their faces.

"Over to Zack's," she replied without slowing down. "He doesn't get to write me off just because I needed a little time to think. Just because I wanted to be sure."

She jerked open the front door and started to rush out.

"Wait!"

Ronnie and Jenna were behind her, hurrying into their own coats and shoes.

"He's not home," Ronnie told her, words ragged in her rush to gather her things and catch up. "There's a game tonight. He's at the arena. Dylan said he's not back on the ice yet, but he's still attending games until they give him the okay to play again."

Grace exhaled a huff of frustration. That would certainly make things less convenient.

"Fine, then I'm going to the arena." She spun on her heel and marched down the hall.

"Wait!" her friends called again. "Wait for us!"

They slammed her apartment door shut, joining her as she pressed the button for the elevator.

"We'll go with you," Jenna said, her pale cheeks rosy with anticipation.

"What are you going to do?" she wanted to know. "What are you going to say to him?"

The elevator doors slid open and Grace stepped inside, her best friends in the whole world flanking her on either side like military backup.

"I don't know yet," she murmured quietly, "but whatever I come up with, I'm pretty sure I should have said and done it weeks ago."

The noise in the Quicken Loans Arena was deafening. The Rockets were ahead by six points, and fans were going crazy with every new shot of the puck.

Grace couldn't have cared less about any of that;

her only interest was in finding Zack, and since he wasn't on the ice, she wasn't entirely sure where to look.

Her gaze scanned the crowd nearest the glass and bench on the Rockets' side of the ice, since she highly doubted he'd be anywhere near the visitors' side.

"There he is," Ronnie said close to her ear.

Grace followed the line of her pointed finger, her stomach jumping like Mexican beans when she spotted Zack.

His blond hair was ruffled, longer and slightly scruffier around the edges than when she'd last seen him. He was wearing a team jersey, even though he wasn't playing tonight, and when he shot to his feet to cheer his team on, she saw that he was using a cane now rather than crutches.

Her mind raced for a way to talk to him, to get him alone for what she needed to say to him.

Yeah, like that was going to happen any time soon.

But she didn't want to wait for the game to end, for the crowd to file out, for him to come back out of the locker room and head for the parking lot.

She glanced around, frantically trying to decide what to do. *Think, think, think,* as Winnie-the-Pooh would say.

And then it came to her, in one of those lightbulb moments. A smile spread across her face, and she turned in the direction she needed to go.

"You guys go ahead and find seats, I'll be back in a bit."

Her friends opened their mouths to ask where she was headed, she was sure, but she simply didn't have time to share her plan. She had a lot of work to do, and a short amount of time to do it.

The clock buzzed, and the crowd jumped to its collective feet to cheer and hoot the Rockets' win. Win, hell, they'd pummeled their opponents into the ground.

Zack grinned at the trouncing his teammates had given the visiting players, even as he wished he'd been out there, doing his part to kick ass and take names.

Maybe next time. Well, not next time, but soon. His knee was getting better by the day, and the doctors said he'd be ready to get out there again in a matter of months, maybe weeks.

Even if the season was over by then, he'd be happy just to be able to participate again and be a part of the team . . . and be out there next season, ready to hit the ice running and lead them straight to the playoffs.

People were starting to mill around in the stands, not yet ready to leave the arena, but not having a lot to hold their attention any longer, either.

His teammates were skating off the ice, and he took great pleasure in being one of the people just behind the bench, high-fiving every one of them as they passed.

Overhead, the announcer's voice came back on the intercom. Odd for this portion of the game, when there was no more play-by-play and no more color commentary needed.

Then he heard his name, and his brow creased.

Whoa, say that again, he thought, straining to hear.

". . . turn your attention to the big screen," the announcer said.

Zack craned his neck, staring at the scoreboard. For a minute, he didn't see anything but the usual— the game scores and some colorful, animated graphics congratulating the Rockets on their win. A second later, though, the text changed, and his heart skipped a beat.

Hey, Hot Legs, it said, scrolling slowly, *will you marry me?*

His jaw dropped in shock, and there was a buzzing in his ears that had nothing to do with the high-decibel hum of voices inside the arena. He felt his face flame as hundreds of heads swiveled and hundreds of sets of eyes locked on him.

What kind of dumb-ass joke was this? he wondered, waiting for the punch line.

"So . . ." a soft voice murmured from just behind his left ear. "What's your answer going to be, Hot Legs?"

If his heart had skipped a beat at the question flashing larger than life on the big screen, it screeched to a smoking halt now. He turned slowly to face Grace, who stood one step above him, looking like an angel in her long, white coat and with the overhead fluorescents casting a halo effect around her pale face and curly blond hair.

While he watched, she stepped down and moved directly in front of him. He lowered his chin, but never took his gaze from hers.

"What are you doing here, Grace?" he asked, surprised he was capable of speech at all, but not that the words came out graveled and rough.

She raised a brow, one corner of her mouth lifting with amusement. "The whole big, giant, very public gesture didn't clue you in?" she tossed back, laughter dancing in her eyes.

"I don't get it."

Was he missing something here? Was he being *Punk'd*? Had he fallen into some bizarre parallel universe where black was white, green meant stop, and red meant go? It certainly felt that way to him.

"Then let me clear things up for you," she said.

Something hit him in the solar plexus and he grunted, raising a hand to take whatever she'd just thrust at him. Glancing down, he found a plain yellow mailer. Not thick, not heavy, which meant she'd backed the envelope with a hearty, well-placed, very intentional punch.

God, he loved this woman, even if she didn't love him back. Not anymore.

"I didn't need this," she told him. "I needed time, I needed a little space, I needed to be sure I could trust myself as much as you before I threw myself back into our relationship. But I didn't need a lie detector test to tell me you didn't cheat on me."

So that's what was in the envelope. No doubt Gage had taken it upon himself to give the results to Grace after he'd told his friend to toss them.

Zack hadn't needed to see them, since he *knew* the truth. And he hadn't seen much sense in making sure Grace saw them, since he'd been fairly certain that ship had already sailed off into the sunset.

Now, though, he couldn't quite gauge Grace's reaction, so he didn't know whether he owed his friend a swift kick in the ass or a grateful handshake.

His gut lurched. The blood drained from his brain, leaving him light-headed and slightly confused.

"I believe you, Zack," Grace continued in a near-whisper. "I believed you the minute you looked me in the eye and told me you never wanted to be the kind of man your father was. That you would never hurt the woman you loved the way your father had hurt your mother."

Something warm and pleasurable blossomed in his chest. He thought it might be . . . hope.

"I should have told you then," she said. "I realize that now. But I'd behaved so badly, treated you so terribly . . . I needed to put everything into perspective and figure out how to apologize, how to mend things between us . . . and how to swallow my pride and ask *you* for forgiveness."

Her mouth curled in distaste, and he smiled. Oh, no, the eating of crow and groveling for absolution was not his Grace's style.

He swallowed hard, appalled when his throat closed and his eyes began to sting.

Shit, he couldn't get weepy here, in front of all these people. They'd send him home with his chestnuts in Grace's purse and never let him live it down.

"You're forgiven," he said, without a qualm, without even having to think about it.

Her lips curved in a shaky grin, her own eyes growing damp. "I really do love you, you know. So much, it hurts. Otherwise, the thought of you betraying me with another woman never would have sent me so off the deep end."

He returned her crooked grin. "Yeah, I got that. But at least you brought my dog back. Eventually."

She let out a watery chuckle. "The name Muffin never really suited him," she admitted.

"Just enough to drive me crazy, right?"

"Right."

Lifting a hand, she wiped at her running nose as a single tear slid down her cheek. A happy tear, he knew, because no way was this discussion leading to anything but the best—of everything.

He caught the moisture with the side of his thumb and brushed it away.

"This is where you proposed to me, but I messed that up, so now it's my turn. What's your answer, Hoolihan?" she demanded, cocking her head toward the message still flashing across the scoreboard, and studying him with those sapphire eyes, bright and filled with anticipation. "Will you marry me?"

He leaned in, pressing his forehead to hers, letting their noses touch. His fingers ran over her soft, smooth cheeks before delving into her even softer hair.

Holding her face in his wide palms, he tipped her head back and brushed her lips with his. "Just try to stop me."

Bind Off

It had been only a week and a half since all the pieces fell into place and *everyone* had been blessed with their own happy ending.

Charlotte just wished she could have been there to see it, up close and personal.

But the role of a fairy godmother/secret matchmaker, she supposed, didn't allow her that privilege. She would have to content herself with secondhand knowledge and basking in the glow of the young lovers she'd played a part in getting together.

Unable to control her glee, she stopped right in the middle of the main aisle of The Yarn Barn on her way to join her knitting group at the rear of the store, and did a little jig.

The magic spinning wheel that had been passed down from generation to generation in her family was three for three. There was no question now, no way that anyone could doubt it had very special true-love powers.

After all, it had brought true love to six individuals in only a little over a year.

Deep, abiding love, Charlotte was sure. All three of the young couples she'd slyly gifted with skeins of enchanted yarn had gone through too much not to appreciate their mates and what they had together.

And *she* had orchestrated their relationships from behind the scenes, without any of them ever being the wiser.

She let out a happy, private chuckle as she approached the circle of chairs where the other Knit Wits were waiting.

"Charlotte!" they greeted her, almost in unison, sending a satisfied warmth spreading through her body.

She loved this group, and every single woman in it. Although, yes, if someone held a match to her highly sprayed and shellacked hive of hair, she supposed she would have to admit that she had a few favorites— namely her niece, Jenna, and her two friends, Ronnie and Grace.

Was it any wonder, then, that she'd chosen those three girls for her magic yarn and spinning wheel experiment? They also happened to be the only three in the group who'd really *needed* a bit of supernatural help in the romance department, but that was neither here nor there.

Taking an empty seat, she dug out the supplies for her latest project. Even nearing the big seven-oh, Charlotte was a hopeless romantic, and had decided that if the ancient spinning wheel had woven strands of yarn that could bring young people together— especially those who had been so dead set against each other in the beginning—then it might just work for her, too.

After getting the grand news that Grace had reconciled with her hockey player beau, Zackary, she had stayed up all night watching the repeated coverage of their surprise engagement—which had been taped from several angles because it had taken place in the middle of a crowded hockey arena—on one of the sports stations, and using her magic wheel to spin a thick, wonderful yarn just for herself.

Well, for herself and the special man she hoped the yarn would work to tie her to forever. She was making it into a big, comfortable blanket, wide enough for two—or at least two vertically challenged individuals like herself—to cuddle beneath. If she was lucky.

The first ten minutes of the knitting meeting were spent in idle chitchat, mostly about the weather and everyone's week at work. The conversations were punctuated by both laughter and the muted, uneven *clickety-clack* of metal, plastic, and wooden needles as each of them worked on their respective items.

"Grace, dear," Charlotte said, meeting the other woman's gaze without missing a stitch, "I see you've decided to try your hand at that homemade wedding gown again."

Grace laughed, lifting the teeny-tiny needles and thread-thin yarn she was using to make merely one small piece of the many, many panels she would need to complete the entire dress.

"Yeah. I'm feeling kind of stupid now for unraveling what I already had done. I wouldn't be so far behind now if I hadn't."

"So you and your man have really patched things up, hmm?" Charlotte asked, though she knew very well the answer.

"Oh, yeah," the perky blonde murmured, cheeks flushing a becoming shade of pink. "Over and over and over again."

Tittering giggles rippled around the circle, and Charlotte joined in, happy that Grace and her young man were once again able to find love and happiness, despite the rocky road they'd traveled to get there.

"And what about you, Ronnie?" she wanted to know. "Are you and that Dylan fellow still getting on well?"

The stylishly dressed brunette blushed more than Charlotte would have expected and ducked her chin. "Actually . . ." she murmured in a low voice, letting the word trail off for several long seconds.

Then she raised her head, took a deep breath, and said, "I've been waiting to tell you, and just can't stand it anymore, so . . ." Another deep breath before she thrust her left hand out in front of her, squeezed her eyes closed, and blurted, "He proposed, and I said yes!"

Knitting forgotten, shrieks and screams and whoops went around the circle, and every single woman in the group jumped up both to get a closer look at the rock on Ronnie's finger and to hug her in hearty congratulations.

They all wanted to know when and how, and a glowing Ronnie explained that after witnessing Grace's very public proposal to Zack and their re-engagement, Dylan had decided it was high time they tied the knot, as well. He'd apparently thought about doing something equally public and spectacular, like putting an ad in her paper, the *Cleveland Sentinel,* or finding a way to turn his proposal into one of their notorious challenges.

But in the end, he'd opted to simply take her out to dinner at her favorite restaurant and slip the ring onto her dessert plate. She admitted to not even noticing the piece of jewelry at first—or rather, not realizing what it was. It had sparkled in the candlelight, but she'd thought it was just another frilly decoration the restaurant used to fancy up their meal presentations.

When it had dawned on her that it was a diamond ring, and that it was real, she'd squealed and hopped up to hug him, doing the whole *yes, yes, yes* chant to make sure he knew that she did, indeed, accept his offer.

Quite the switch from the days when she'd thought Dylan was scum and had taken great pleasure in calling him every name in the book—plus a few that she'd coined herself. And though Charlotte had been thrilled when the two of them hooked up and started dating, it surprised her as much as anyone else to hear that Ronnie was willingly headed for the altar. She would have expected a lot more kicking and screaming from a woman who seemed to thrive on disagreements, and had prided herself on not needing a man. Any man.

This was wonderful, though. Even more definitive proof that the spinning wheel and yarn worked exactly as it was supposed to.

After they'd all settled down and finished admiring Ronnie's gorgeous, one-and-a-half-carat diamond and white gold engagement ring, Charlotte turned her attention to her niece.

"And how are you, Jenna? Feeling all right these days?"

Jenna nodded, still beaming in delight over both her friend's good news and her own pregnancy. "Except for the daily bouts of morning sickness, I feel

terrific. I know it's early yet, but Gage and I are trying
to decide how to decorate the nursery. We don't want
to know the baby's gender ahead of time, so we'll
probably end up going with something neutral like
yellow or green, but he wants teddy bears and I want
zoo animals."

"As long as you don't go for a carnival theme,"
Grace put in. "Those scary-ass clowns will scar the
kid for life."

Everybody laughed, most of them in agreement on
the scary-ass clown thing.

"I did clouds and angels for my first, and *Sesame
Street* for my second," Melanie said, barely looking
up from the purple hat-and-mitten set she was making. "I much preferred the *Sesame Street* characters.
They were more fun, and after a while, those chubby-
cheeked angels just started to look demonic. Especially at four in the morning when I had to go in for
the five hundredth feeding and changing of the night."

Ronnie elbowed Jenna good-naturedly. "See all the
great stuff you have to look forward to."

"Hey," Jenna returned, "I've been wanting a baby
for so long, I'll go without sleep for a year after this
one is born, if that's what it takes. But I've already let
Gage know that he *will* be carrying his fair share of
baby weight . . . figuratively speaking, unfortunately."
Her lips curled wryly. "Otherwise, this child is des-
tined to be an only child, because he won't be getting
close enough to knock me up again any time soon."

"You tell 'im, girlfriend!" Melanie chimed in, and
the others joined her show of support for layin' down
the law.

"Well, I'm just so happy for all of you," Charlotte said, unable to hold back the wide grin stretching across her face. "Everything's really coming together for the three of you, isn't it?"

They nodded happily in agreement.

A second later, though, Grace slowly said her name. Slowly and softly—so softly that Charlotte raised her head from her knitting.

"Yes, dear?"

"You didn't . . . do anything, did you?"

A skitter of panic rolled down her spine. Oh, she shouldn't have said anything, should have bitten back her smile and enthusiasm so they wouldn't become suspicious. But she was just *sooooo* pleased that her machinations and the powers of the enchanted spinning wheel had worked exactly the way she'd intended. Better, even, than she ever could have hoped.

"Do what, dear?" she asked, lowering her gaze and doing her best to play innocent.

"I don't know."

Grace had stopped knitting, and Charlotte could feel her steely stare burning through the triple-stacked curls of her Lucille Ball 'do and all the layers of hairspray surrounding it.

"You just seem a little too . . . chipper tonight. A little too . . . pleased on our behalfs."

"Oh, you know me," she responded with an airy chuckle. "I don't have much of a life of my own these days, so I like to live vicariously through you younger girls who are out there having fun, enjoying yourselves, and falling in love."

From the doubtful glint in Grace's eyes, Charlotte

didn't think the young woman believed a word of it. But thankfully, when Charlotte glanced at the wall clock, she discovered that the meeting hour was up.

Normally, she would be sorry about that, but tonight she was grateful for the fast passage of time if it meant escaping Grace's too-keen inquisition.

"Oops, looks like we're done for tonight," she said, quickly stuffing her yarn and needles into her bag and hopping up to grab her coat.

"What's the hurry, Aunt Charlotte?" Jenna asked, and now even she sounded suspicious.

This, at least, she could be honest about. "I, my dears, have got a hot date."

Several sets of eyebrows shot up, and she enjoyed a brief moment of gratification at catching them all off guard.

"But you just said you don't have a life," Ronnie pointed out.

"Well, I don't," Charlotte admitted as she zipped and then buttoned the double layers of her big, over-stuffed lime-green coat. The other ladies were starting to rise, putting away their knitting projects and collecting their coats, but Charlotte was already goose-stepping her way to the edge of the circle of chairs. "But I'm certainly not giving up on finding one."

With any luck, her very own skein of enchanted yarn would work its magic and help her find her own happily ever after. She was optimistic that Willy, her date for this evening, would turn out to be her true love. But if not, she'd keep right on looking . . . and spinning and knitting.

"Toodles, darlings. I'll see you next week."

She tossed a quick finger wave over her shoulder before toddling toward the front of the store.

Behind her, Grace, Ronnie, Jenna, and a few of the other women from the group exchanged glances. All on the same page, and all thinking identical thoughts, they grabbed their belongings without a word and rushed after her.

"I didn't know Aunt Charlotte was seeing anyone," Jenna said in a harsh whisper, a dozen sets of shoes, boots, and heels clattering away on the hard parquet flooring as they marched down the center aisle.

"I think your aunt is up to something," Grace said. Her tone wasn't accusatory, merely quizzical.

They reached the double glass front doors just as a large, rumbling black motorcycle pulled up to the curb. An older, slightly overweight man with long, gray hair braided into a single thick rope down his back straddled the seat.

As soon as she saw him, Charlotte started forward, rounding the bike and climbing into a matching black sidecar. She tucked her knitting tote inside, between her feet, then pulled on a pair of giant, World War II–style goggles and fit an equally old-fashioned helmet over the Eiffel Tower of her bright orange hair.

Glancing up, she flashed the elderly biker dude a wide, eager smile, which he returned with a gap-toothed grin of his own. He revved the engine, and a second later they were off, disappearing into the dark night and crowd of strip mall traffic.

Silently, Ronnie and Grace pushed open The Yarn Barn doors, and they all stepped out onto the raised sidewalk.

Grace swallowed, blinked. "Anybody want to go to The Penalty Box for a drink? I think I could use one."

"Yeah," Ronnie murmured in a stunned tone. "Me, too."

"Uh-huh. I really wish I could *drink*-drink, because it's going to take something a lot stronger than 7-Up and cranberry juice to help me make sense of this," Jenna muttered.

They all nodded in agreement, but instead of making a move toward their cars, they all simply stood there, frozen in place, gazes locked on the taillights of the motorcycle and sidecar as it zipped out of sight, taking dear, sweet—*innocent?*—Charlotte with them.

GRACE'S DOG SWEATER PATTERN

*(as knit by Grace, despised by Zack, and tolerated
by Muffin...er, Bruiser...er, Muffin...)*

For dogs with a 28-inch chest

Materials:

Size 7 knitting needles
Size 8 knitting needles
Size 8 circular needle
3 5-ounce skeins of yarn

Instructions for Neck & Body:

With size 7 needles and one skein of yarn, cast on 88
stitches. K1, P1 for 2 inches.
Change to size 8 needles.

Row 1: Knit across.

Row 2: Purl across.

Row 3: Increase in first stitch; knit across to last
      stitch; increase in last stitch.

Rows 4–10: Continue to increase in first and last
      stitch of **every** row for the next 7 rows.
      Increase in first and last stitch of **every
      other** row until 124 stitches are on
      needle, ending with a knit row.

Preparation for Leg Openings:

Row 1: With those 124 stitches on needle, P8, K16,
      P76, K16, P8.

Row 2: Increase in first stitch; knit across to last
      stitch; increase in last stitch.

Row 3: P9, K16, P76, K16, P9.
Row 4: Repeat Row 2.
Row 5: P10, K16, P76, K16, P10.

Instructions for Leg Openings:

Row 1: K13, bind off next 10 stitches, K81, bind off next 10 stitches, K12.

(Note: Two other skeins of yarn need to be attached at this point because all three sections are worked at the same time, using separate yarn for each one.)

Row 2: P10, K3. With second skein of yarn, K3, P76, K3. With third skein of yarn, K3, P10.

Row 3: With first skein of yarn, K across. With second skein of yarn, K across. With third skein of yarn, K across.

Rows 4–12: Repeat Rows 2 and 3 nine more times.

Row 13: P10, K3, turn. Add on 10 stitches, turn. With same yarn, K3, P76, K3, turn. Add on 10 stitches, turn. With same yarn, K3, P across to end. (Should have 128 stitches on needle.)

Instructions for Lower Leg Band:

Row 1: K across.

Row 2: P10, K16, P76, K16, P10.

Rows 3–6: Repeat Rows 1 and 2 two times. Continue in stockinette stitch pattern (knit one row, purl the other) until piece measures 13 inches from very beginning, ending with **purl** row.

Shaping Instructions:

Row 1: Bind off 14 stitches at beginning of row, K across to end.

Row 2: Bind off 14 stitches at beginning of row, P across to end.

Row 3: Slip 1 stitch, K1, pass slipped stitch over knit stitch (PSSO), K across to last 2 stitches, K those 2 stitches together as one (K2tog).

Row 4: P across (98 stitches).

Rows 5–18: Repeat Rows 3 and 4 fourteen times (70 stitches remaining after last row). Piece should measure 25 inches from beginning to end. Leave remaining stitches on needle. With right sides facing each other, sew up seam. Pick up those remaining 70 stitches, with right sides still facing each other, onto circular needle. Work in ribbing pattern (K1, P1) for one inch. Bind off.

Optional A: Weave elastic thread through first row of neck ribbing.

Optional B: Decorate with sports emblems or patches of your choice.